To the praise of the glory of his grace.

EPHESIANS 1:6

DATE DUE

ROBERT FARRAR CAPON

Between Noon and Three

• •

Romance, Law,
and the Outrage of Grace

WILLIAM B. EERDMANS PUBLISHING COMPANY
GRAND RAPIDS, MICHIGAN / CAMBRIDGE, U.K.

© 1997 Wm. B. Eerdmans Publishing Co.

255 Jefferson Ave. S.E., Grand Rapids, Michigan 49503 /

P.O. Box 163, Cambridge CB3 9PU U.K.

Printed in the United States of America

01 00 99 98 97   7 6 5 4 3 2 1

Library of Congress Cataloging-in-Publication Data

Capon, Robert Farrar.

Between noon and three: romance, law, and the outrage of grace /
Robert Farrar Capon.

p.   cm.

ISBN 0-8028-4222-4 (paper: alk. paper)

1. Grace (Theology)   2. Law and gospel.   3. Ethics.
4. Sexual ethics   5. Eschatology.   I. Title.

BT761.2.C33   1997

234 — dc20   96-35871

CIP

Contents

CONTENTS

PART II
COFFEE HOUR

PART III
THE YOUNGEST DAY

Contents

INTRODUCTION

Back at the Beginning

The volume you now hold in your hand is, for all practical purposes, the first edition of *Between Noon and Three.* Although the book was written in 1975 and published by Harper & Row in 1982 and 1983 as two separate volumes, no one outside my immediate circle of friends has ever seen the original version. I'm delighted that Eerdmans has seen fit to publish it in its entirety, and thus bring it back to the beginning it never enjoyed.

Let me give you the briefest possible sketch of the book's shape. As you can see from the table of contents, it consists of three parts. The first, called *Parable,* is a novella of sorts about an illicit but totally successful love affair between an English professor and a graduate student — an affair in which the intolerable requirements of the lover's romanticism become a stand-in for the unmeetable demands of the law of God, while the beloved's unconditional love becomes a sacrament of the grace that raises the dead. In the second part, called *Coffee Hour,* I introduce a group of critics (designed to represent you as the reader) who are outraged by my use of an adulterous liaison to portray grace, and who keep us occupied with their problems through the entire middle of the book. Finally, in *The Youngest Day,* I give you a short story about a Mafia execution to provide myself with a corpse on which to do the eschatology of grace. The remainder of the book is the working out of that project: a top-to-bottom rethinking of death, judgment, hell, and heaven in the light of a forgiveness so sovereign and so unconditional that it reconciles everything and everybody, bar none.

When Harper & Row decided to publish the book in 1982, they did to it what Solomon only threatened to do to the child that was brought to him: they cut it in two, and took away its life. It wasn't that either of the volumes they brought out was a bad book; both, in fact, were quite decent. It was just that, even if they were read one right after the other, they simply were not the work that had first engrossed and moved me. The 1982 volume (which was entitled *Between Noon and Three*) contained most but not all of *Parable,* plus about half of *Coffee Hour;* but it omitted *The Youngest Day* entirely. I recast that last section completely as a piece of nature writing (by tying the four seasons to the "four last things": Winter was death; Spring, judgment; Summer, hell; and Autumn, heaven) — and it was published the next year as *The Youngest Day.* The damage was done, though. Neither book had ever been meant to stand on its own; published separately, they languished until they died the literary death of going out of print.

But back to the brainchild that Eerdmans has so kindly put back together. *Between Noon and Three* was uncategorizable from the start, and it remains so to this day. Those who hope to enjoy it as a novel are doomed to disappointment: at every turn, the story line entangles itself in the ropework of theological commentary. On the other hand, those who prefer their theology straight up — no ice, no olives, no *twists* — are equally doomed. They will recoil at the plethora of oddments I serve with it, and they will balk at my penchant for mixing purple prose with low comedy — not to mention my habit of working both sides of the street at once, running from store to store and picking up what strikes my fancy. Veteran shoppers seem to like this trait; but buyers who can't linger over things that are not on their list are driven mad by it. But if you can stand the switching back and forth, it makes for a diverting experience. A friend once told me that my books had minds of their own. No matter what shelf he chose for one of them after he first read it, when he consulted the book a second time, it would want to go elsewhere. Scripture studies would wander off to the *Theology* section, novels drifted to *Pastoralia,* and cookbooks left the kitchen for *terra incognita.* Prepare yourself, therefore, to be led in a number of directions at once.

But enough, perhaps, of background. Suffice it to say that all three parts of the original book, with all their twists and turns, have been fully restored in this edition. Except for some minor editing, nothing has been changed: not the book's setting in the nineteen-seventies (however out of fashion that may seem now); not its outrageousness (which I think we need now even more than we did then); and certainly not the small army of ringers I brought in from time to time to punt for me on fourth downs. They're all still here in force: Paul the Apostle, Augustine the Teacher, Abelard the Lover, Luther the Reformer, and Donne the Preacher; Newton the Hymnodist, Eliot and Auden the Poets, Golding the Novelist, and last but not least, Norman, another English Professor who, while he is a fictional character, is the only person I ever lost an argument to in print — and who, in the earlier editions, was dispatched before he had a chance to nail me to the wall.

I hope that *Between Noon and Three* will be for you what it has always been for me: a watershed experience. Quite simply, I consider it the most important piece of writing I have ever done. No work of mine before it ever moved me as far or as fast toward astonishment at grace as this book did — and everything I've written since has been an expanding commentary on it. I'm indebted to Mary Hietbrink, my editor at Eerdmans, for her corrections of the text, and especially for her suggestion that I supply chapter titles — which I think are an improvement on the original. Above all, though, I'm indebted to my wife, Valerie, who has lived with this book for as long as we've been married. Over the years, she's typed the manuscript (beginning on an old Royal portable and continuing through a succession of word-processing programs) more times than any human being should have been asked to — and she's read it aloud in proofreading sessions even more often than that. She's a tough critic; yet "she openeth her mouth with wisdom, and in her tongue is the law of kindness." No matter how glad I may be to see this book finally brought to birth as it was conceived, she has to be gladder still; twenty years is a long labor. But now at last, "her children rise up and call her blessed; her husband also, and he praiseth her."

So with nothing more than the obligatory disclaimer, we commend *Between Noon and Three* to you for the first time. All the characters in these cautionary tales are fictitious; any resemblance to persons living or dead is coincidental and unintended — but hardly surprising.

ROBERT FARRAR CAPON
Shelter Island, New York

PART ONE

PARABLE

1

Law, Grace, and the Free Drink

By and by, I want to tell you a story. It will be about a man and a woman who actually succeed in getting away with something. I think I shall make him a university professor and her a suburban housewife finishing some long-interrupted work on a master's in English. Paul, perhaps, will do for his name: forty, tall, dark, handsome. And for hers? Linda? No, Linda is a waitress with a sad, uncomprehended history of failed romances. Laura? Yes, Laura: thirty-five, intelligent, chestnut-haired, and beautiful. I insist on proper romantic types. I want nothing unconventional here except the success of the affair.

That is a promise. I shall allow not a single development that might in any way take the edge off their triumph. No divorces, no car accidents, no erotic failures, no natural disasters. I shall make them immune to headache, pique, curdled moods, and the common cold. I shall even make them religious but leave them happily unburdened by scruples. You will be spared those tiresome scenes in which lovers fill the pauses of their passion with lugubrious wonderings about whether they are failing their spouses, their children, or God. Better yet, you will not even have to endure the tension of wondering whether they will fail each

3

other. They will not. I shall make the affair his last and her first: chastened experience will meet devoted innocence and, like giant smiling at giant, bring off the improbable with style. Best of all, they will not be discovered, ever.

They, of course, will not know that. But you and I do, and that is all that counts. For this story is about grace. I will have no tensions here except the tension of grace itself, no other scandal than the divine foolishness by which the human race is assured, in full and in advance, that there is nothing it isn't going to get away with — except disbelief in that assurance.

Do you find that odd? I hope so. But I also hope you find it odd for the right reason. Such a story as I propose is bound to be unsatisfactory if either you or I look to it for a novelistic enrichment of our fantasy life. It will simply be — well, let's be honest — too dull. The true romantic novel requires conflict, comedy, danger, and ultimately tragedy. In the end, the protagonists must be made to bear the disdain of a universe whose final reaction to the *O Altitudo* of romantic love is the snubbing stare it reserves for unimportantly disreputable performances, like breaking wind at a banquet.

For in our fantasies, immorality can never be allowed simply to succeed; cosmic disapproval must be given the last word. The assignation is accomplished, but the lover's water pump breaks down on the way home, necessitating a call to his wife to pick him up thirty miles off course. The beloved gives herself entirely, but her husband's firm moves him to Dallas, and out of the very givingness for which she is loved, she packs up dolls and dishes and goes sadly into the sunset. Or she loses a child in a fire that starts while she is in the motel with her lover. Or her lover loses his nerve. Or they marry at terrible cost and both lose their interest. Whatever happens, the books are always balanced, the notes due called in, the mortgages foreclosed.

No, much as you and I prefer that sort of thing, I shall not give it to you. First, because it is a strange preference, no matter how universal it is. You would think, given the routinely low level of our performances at the higher reaches of our being, that we would, in our fantasies at least, welcome a respite from these inexorable audits — that we would imagine for ourselves romances in which the celestial bookkeeping department was given a long and well-deserved vacation. But no, we put it on overtime instead: however much we hate the *law,* we are more afraid of *grace.*

Oh, I know. You will say that the broken water pump or the child burned in the fire are simply elements of conflict or suspense introduced for the sake of proper dramatic development. I let that pass. Perhaps they are. My point here is that, novelistic development to one side, they are in one respect totally unnecessary and, in another, necessary for a reason we have yet to face.

They are unnecessary because if we are the least bit interested in holding up our imaginings as a mirror to real life, mishap and mischance are simply not going to appear in our glass with anything like the frequency you imply. We do in fact get away with almost everything. The last time my water pump broke, I was on business and still arrived at my meeting one minute early. I have yet to be in my first fire or to have anyone close to me in hers. And so, perhaps, have you — with minor allowances for difference of circumstance. *Eppur si muove.* While it works at all, the contraption of the real world works very well indeed and with practically no regard for moral necessities. The sun shines on the just and the unjust. A successful exercise in shacking up need not necessarily be any more improbable than a successful vichyssoise. A rarer treat, perhaps; but not the impossibility we so morbidly expect.

Therefore, the inevitability with which, in our fantasies, the heroine makes infallible soup but tragic love derives from some other exigency than the pressure of events. It stems not from the universe but from our view of it. We are uneasy with the grace of a simply successful love affair not because it is unrealistically dull but because it is all too obviously dangerous. It threatens to blow apart the imagined framework by which we hold ourselves, however inconveniently, in one piece. As long as the law is upon us, we feel safe. Its bitching, score-evening presence assures us that something out there has our number. Whether it approves or disapproves of us is almost a matter of indifference; the main thing is that, having our number, it absolves us from the burden of learning our name. The law of retribution reigns supreme in our fantasies precisely to keep us off the main question of our lives: *What would you do with freedom if you had it?*

Our romantic imaginings are designed specifically to frustrate our principal exploration. With a perversity we would never permit in a discussion of cookery, we resolutely disallow the success of the romantic omelette and concentrate upon — no, it must be stronger — we revel in, we preoccupy ourselves with the imagined necessities by which the stove must go cold, the pan crack, the eggs corrupt, the butter go rancid. For all its trappings of reality, however, the lion we thus see in the way of our self-discovery is philosophical, not real. As long as we give it credence, we give it power; but one straight look and it is gone.

And that is the second, and the important reason why I propose to give you the story of a triumphantly, even boringly successful adultery. Grace cannot prevail until law is dead; there is no way of seeing clearly the freedom to which we are being driven until morality has been bound, gagged, and stuffed unceremoniously in the trunk. That is the fundamental oddity of our condition; and while there is no way of tempering its oddness, there are at least precedents to keep us from expecting it to go away. The classic parables of grace always involve the flaunting of some immorality, some inequity, some gratuitously offensive detail. The Father's free acceptance of the Prodigal is not fully portrayed until he orders the slaying of the fatted calf and the Elder Brother rightly observes that all his years of goodness never got him even a goat. The gracious beneficence of the Owner of the Vineyard is not driven home until those who worked but one hour are paid not only equally with the rest but ahead of them as well. The Good Samaritan is simply an insult: to Jesus' Jewish audience, there were no good Samaritans; to make a hero of one was to stand truth on its head.

Let me refine that a little. I said grace cannot prevail until law is dead, until moralizing is out of the game. The precise phrase should be, until our fatal love affair with the law is over — until, finally and for good, our lifelong certainty that someone is keeping score has run out of steam and collapsed. As long as we leave, in our dramatizations of grace, one single hope of a moral reckoning, one possible recourse to salvation by bookkeeping, our freedom-dreading hearts will clutch it to themselves. And even if we leave none at all, we will grub for ethics that are not there rather than face the liberty to which grace calls us. Give us the parable of the Prodigal Son, for example, and we will promptly lose its point by preaching ourselves sermons on Worthy and Unworthy Confession, or on The Sin of the Elder Brother. Give us the Workers in the Vineyard, and we will concoct spurious lessons on The Duty of Contentment or The Moral Aspects of Labor Relations.

Restore to us, Preacher, the comfort of merit and demerit. Prove for us that there is at least something we can do, that we are still, at whatever dim recess of our nature, the masters of our relationships. Tell us, Prophet, that in spite of all our nights of losing, there will yet be one redeeming card of our very own to fill the inside straight we have so long and so earnestly tried to draw to. But do not preach us grace. It will not do to split the pot evenly at four A.M. and break out the Chivas Regal. We insist on being reckoned with. Give us something, anything; but spare us the indignity of this indiscriminate acceptance.

Lord, let your servants depart in the peace of their proper responsibility. If it is not too much to ask, send us to bed with some few shreds of self-respect to congratulate ourselves upon. But if that is too hard, leave us at least the consolation of our self-loathing. Only do not force us free. What have we ever done but try as best we could? How have we so hurt you, even by failing, that you should now turn on us and say that none of it makes any difference, not even our sacred guilt? We have played this game of yours, and it has cost us.

Where do you get off suggesting a drink at a time like this?

2

The Tyranny of Angels

I know. I have overstated things slightly. But only slightly. In any case, enough of that for the time being.

• •

It was just before noon on the first warm day of April. Paul swung his '74 Nova into the left lane of Route 343, just south of Stony Brook on Long Island. He waited out the light, and turned into the restaurant parking lot. Laura was standing in front of some junipers by the main door. He pulled the car into a space at the side and walked around to meet her. "I hope you haven't been waiting long," he said. "Are you always this early?"

"Only when I want to be. The official line on me is that I'm a scatterbrain. I'm supposed not to be able to find places or tell time. Don't blow my cover."

"I wouldn't think of it. Especially not on the first date." He guided her into the restaurant with his hand on the small of her back. Seats. Waitress. Conference on drinks: two Cinzano Red, twist, no ice, please. Sorry, Sir, no Cinzano. All right, two Martini & Rossi, same. Have to ask the bartender. Wait. Sorry, no Martini

& Rossi; how about Duval? No, thank you. Two Dubonnet. Nobody doesn't have Dubonnet.

She sat watching, elbows on the table, chin resting on clasped hands, her eyes moving between him and the waitress. "You're a flirt, you know," she said after the girl left.

He put on a chastened look. "Damn! Found out, even before lunch."

"Oh, it's all right. It's just your style. You act as if you and the person you're talking to have the same inside joke in the back of your minds. It's . . . flattering."

"Usually I'm told I don't really pay attention to people."

"That's probably true, too. You have lots of styles. I was just telling you about a nice one."

When the waitress came with the drinks, he lifted his glass. "Well! To me for finally having asked you out; to you for saying yes — and to your master's program for having suggested it in the first place."

She clinked her glass against his. "I'll be glad when that part's over. I'm tired of fighting with Irving Schiffman. He's having an absolute fit, you know, over my insistence that Reilly, Alex, and Julia in *The Cocktail Party* are actually angels. If I do any more Eliot, I want to stay clear of him."

"Irv has his blind spots, but he's a damned good judge of what is and isn't poetry. He's mostly right about Eliot's later stuff. *The Elder Statesman,* for instance. Except for the one speech that makes the main point, it's pretty thin."

"The Quartets aren't."

"Agreed. Just don't write Irv off. In any case, though, what are you going to do after you get the degree?"

"I don't know. Auden, maybe; though I'm not sure where I want to go with him. I just don't want to have to apologize to Schiffman all the time for trying to do something with what's really there."

10

"You thinking of a doctorate?"

She sipped her Dubonnet and made a little ritual of centering the glass and the cocktail napkin between the flatware. "Not yet. If I can, I want to go back to teaching full-time in the fall. For now I'd just like to work to the point at which I had a master's plus thirty. If a good idea for a thesis turns up, so much the better."

He put down his glass, reached for the breadbasket, hesitated, then settled for arranging it at right angles to her knife. "Funny," he said. "Breadbasket to Knife 4. Black's classic response to the Centered Glass opening. Did you ever read that piece in the *New Yorker* about the middle-aged man who was having lunch with his father? The actual conversation just pooped along, but they kept outmaneuvering each other with the objects on the table: ashtrays, saltshakers, glasses. Their real relationship came across in the analogy to chess. Clever."

"I didn't see it, but that's true. It's the moves that count." She smiled, picked up her knife, and put it on her bread-and-butter plate pointing toward him. "There. What does black do now?"

"Easy. I offer a course on Auden in . . . September."

She repeated the word "September" in exactly his tone of voice.

"Wouldn't you be interested?" he asked, thrown off by her response.

"Of course."

"Then why did you hesitate?"

"I didn't hesitate; you did. This is April."

"Hmm," he said; "I seem to be in check. Well, let me ask you something. Where does your husband . . . fit in?"

"He loves me without liking me, I guess. That happens. We deal with each other mostly on the level of house and children. It's a kind of civil standoff."

"How long has it been like that?"

"From the beginning. Although when you're first married, you don't pay attention to it. I didn't admit it to myself for about three years, but eventually I realized it had been like that all along. The trouble is, he doesn't realize it even now. He simply doesn't know what's happening. He resents my interests, but he can't admit it because he has none of his own to fall back on. And there's no use my becoming a zero just to keep him company." She took a drink, then looked up. "That's not pride or stubbornness. It's just a fact. He wouldn't want it if I did. The trouble is, he doesn't really want anything. What he needs is a mistress."

"That's not usually the woman's solution."

"Maybe it isn't, but it's true. I have my own center, and most of the time I can draw into it when I need to. That's just luck, I guess. Some people have it, and some people don't. But if someone hasn't got it, and some other interest isn't supplied from the outside, he has a hard time."

"Still, a mistress? That's something a wife isn't supposed to be able even to say, let alone live with."

"I didn't say it would be easy to live with. Only that it would work. As a matter of fact, I know what my biggest problem would be. If he did have one, I'd have to fight the temptation to become friends with her, to take her over — to disarm him that way too. The hard thing would be for me to leave him free, to keep my hands, my mind, my will completely off the subject. But I could do it. I'm not really castrative, to use that stupid word. If he just once got past having to compare himself to me, he'd find that out. It would work."

"It's tricky, though. American men aren't very good at saving their marriages by means of affairs. The minute they get involved in the quagmire of romance, they assume it's time to bolt out of the first marriage into a second. The most likely prospect is that you'd get left."

"It would still be better for him, even if it came to that. He's under a curse of inaction."

"You know something? You have a knack for saying things that sound totally dubious. But when I try to argue them down, they turn out to be unassailable. Not welcome, or pleasant, or even wise. Just unassailable. I can only say 'You're probably right' and then think, 'God help us all.' We really are trapped in our characters."

"I guess so."

"Let's have another round of drinks and order. At least make the trap pleasant."

The waitress came. Small debate over what to have. Choice narrowed to fish, then to grilled sole or striped bass, Greek style — then decided by a lifting of the waitress's eyebrow at the mention of the striped bass. He smiled, bowed a silent thank you to her, and ordered sole. When she left, he toasted Laura again. "Saved by the kindness of the help from a fish worse than death. It must be pretty grim if onions, tomatoes, oregano, and ouzo can't arm-wrestle it into submission."

"See? Your unconscious style pays off. You've made a conspirator of her. It's very physical, you know. You don't do it just with your eyes, like most people. It's your hands, your head, the way you lean back to one side. And I've decided it's not all that unconscious. Second nature is more like it. You don't think about it, but you're aware of it."

"No comment. If I opened my mouth, you'd probably X-ray my teeth for good measure. Change the subject."

She thought for a moment, then smiled. "All right. Romance."

He drew himself up and tilted his head slightly. "Romance?"

"Yes. Romance. Why is it a quagmire?"

"Who said that?"

"You did. Not five minutes ago. You sounded . . . well, cynical. Is that too strong?"

"A little, I think. The right phrase is probably 'Sadder, Budweiser.' You know the limerick?"

13

"Yes. Just tell me about the quagmire."

"You really want to listen to theories?"

"It's better than waiting till September."

"O.K. But don't say I didn't warn you." He picked up a breadstick and held it like a piece of chalk. "The first thing you have to understand is that Romantic Love is not human. It's angelic. Human beings may think it up, but once it gets thought, it acquires a life of its own. It becomes a kind of purely spiritual Power — an Angel — that's fundamentally unsympathetic to flesh and blood. We sit around down here in our warm, furry bodies with all kinds of reasonably manageable urges like sexual desire, infatuation, affection, even love; but somehow we're never content. We insist on asking in this Principality, this Dominion, this Power called Romance. It's gorgeous, of course — as are all the other angels we've invented: the State, Marriage, Family, Justice, Art. But they're all aliens. They play by rules we can't live up to in the long run.

"And therefore, if you live long enough, you find out two things. The first is that the likes of us can't make any peace with the likes of them. We love to have them around, but they steadfastly refuse to become either pets or friends. They get invited in on nights of wisteria and moonlight, but their demands smell like fire and iron in the end. They damn you no matter what. If you leave your wife for your love, you offend the Angel of Marriage. If you try to have your love without leaving your wife, you welsh on the Angel of Romance. Either way, they win and you lose.

"But the second thing you learn is that in spite of it all, we never seriously think of giving up on them. Cynicism is just a temporary shelter. It lasts only as long as you have enough pain to keep your unbelief going. And the pain lasts only until somebody comes along who can make you forget it. Then it's angel time all over again. We're just sitting ducks, waiting for the vision to return."

The waitress brought the food. Laura ate a mouthful of fish and put down her fork. "You really think nobody lives up to them? Not even for a while?"

"That's the catch. You can say we live up to them for a while. But they don't deal in whiles. Their demands are eternal. Even claptrap love poetry gets that much straight. In their terms, eventual failure is utter failure, in spite of all the glory of the temporary success. The romantic commitment is forever. The marriage vow is till death. Anybody who tries to monkey with that doesn't know what he's dealing with. The hell of it all is simply that there can never be any accommodation between their eternity and our temporality. To recreate them in the image of our failure is to destroy the beauty we love. To leave them in their beauty is to guarantee that, sooner or later, we will never do anything but fail."

"You sound as if you've been through something grim."

"No grimmer than most, I guess. It really is a universal trap. The beauty of it calls to you, but you can't do it justice. And that's where the worst part comes in. In the end, Romance just can't deal with failure. We sleep, we forget, we overlook, we forgive. We even help. A drink. The loan of a car. A hug. We can fail each other and still not insist on failure as the last word. But nobody gets away with letting the angels down. They have no mercy. They never offer you a whiskey. The one who fails must never be hugged again while the world lasts. The Principalities and Powers we live by can't forgive, and we can't live without forgiveness. Catch-22. Q.E.D."

They ate for a while without talking. Finally she spoke. "There is such a thing as the tyranny of the angels, you know."

"How do you mean?"

"They refuse to be our pets. But we can also refuse to be theirs. Everything you say is true, except you've got it put together wrong. Or you just haven't got it put together. You have to start where you are."

"Where's that?"

"At the warm, furry body. That's what we are. Human, not angelic. Do you know the poem by Auden?

> "Lay your sleeping head, my love,
> Human on my faithless arm;
> . . . in my arms till break of day
> Let the living creature lie,
> Mortal, guilty, but to me
> The entirely beautiful."

She looked straight at him. "I don't care how beautiful the Principalities are. They're not us. We have our own beauty, and they mustn't be allowed to trample it. Not in the name of anything. Not even God."

"How do you stop them?"

"Well, if you find yourself living by something that can't forgive . . ." She sat silent. Finally she reached out, drew his hand toward her, flashed a smile, and said, very rapidly, ". . . then you die to it and look around for something that can."

He held her hand and said nothing.

There is an exigency of time in these matters. Five seconds of holding hands at such a point leaves all the options open: a grateful pat, a resumption of the discussion, a change of subject, an evasion of the issue. Ten seconds introduces a note of doubt: something must be done; but what? Fifteen, and nothing seems possible but continued silence. Twenty, the first hint that whatever must be done is already in the works. Thirty, that it is several sizes larger than anything we had in mind; and somewhere between thirty and forty, the inevitable ratification of it all by the oldest device known to the human race: the naming of names.

"Paul . . . ?"

"Laura . . . ?"

She let another silence go by. "Forget the pain. It's dead."

He turned his wrist to see his watch. "Just like that? Between noon and . . . one?"

"Just like that . . . between noon and one." She smiled again. "Say 'Us.'"

"Us?"

"Say it without the question mark."

"Us."

"Good. I love you, Paul."

"Laura . . . God! I never thought . . ."

"Then don't think. Just listen:

> "Beauty, midnight, vision dies;
> Let the winds of dawn that blow
> Softly round your dreaming head
> Such a day of sweetness show
> Eye and knocking heart may bless,
> Find the mortal world enough;
> Noons of dryness see you fed
> By the involuntary powers,
> Nights of insult let you pass
> Watched by every human love."

He smiled, shook his head, and after a long while, drew her hand to him and kissed it. "I'll be damned. This has got to be the East Coast record for quiet devastation. What happens now?"

"Just dessert, I guess. I have my period."

●　●

(By the way. If you laughed, or smiled, or even felt the least twinge of satisfaction at Laura's last remark, you and I have further to go before we understand each other. You should distrust your smirk

17

of appreciation at such a contretemps. It suggests, quite falsely, that the universe can be expected to resolve the dilemma of our freedom by interfering like a mother-in-law in our plans for the season — that the cosmos has an interest in our choices which will protect us from the dangers of choosing our interests. I meant nothing of the kind. Any interest that cannot brook four or five days' dull delay is of no interest at all. Laura just had her period. It's no excuse for you to have an attack of the metaphysical gloats.)

3

'Twas Grace that Taught My Heart . . .

When the waitress came back with the change at the end of the meal, Paul set aside the tip, picked up the two remaining dollar bills, stuffed one into his tobacco pouch, and handed Laura the other. "A souvenir."

"That's nice." She picked up her cigarettes and started to throw them into her shoulder bag. He held up an admonitory forefinger, reached over, took the pack from her hand, and extracted the matches from under the cellophane. She looked at him. "What are you doing? I always take restaurant matchbooks."

"Not anymore, you don't. Stick to the supermarket jobs. Tomato paste ads keep things quieter on the home front."

She took back the cigarettes, shook her head smilingly, and plopped them into the bag. "There . . . clean."

"Good. Now. Where's your car?"

"Out in back. But I have to make a stop first."

"Easily done. It's on the way out. C'mon, I'll show you."

He followed her, guiding her from behind with his hand. When they reached the hall, he came alongside, put his arm around her waist, and drew her to him while they walked. She

19

pressed her leg against his without breaking stride and turned her face up to him. He kissed her lightly, on unparted lips.

Chasteness is always the biggest surprise. We are so inured to the conventions of torrid lovemaking that we forget how many light years love can travel on physical understatement. The ham-handed explicitness of the sexual behavior generally held up for our edification seems to be little more than a frantic checking out of the equipment to see if it's still in working order, a conjuring act to keep away fear of failure. Our years of sheep-like imitation of it, in marriage or out, leave us unprepared for the day on which the need for conjuring never arises and the thought of failure is impossible. Sex, as we have been taught to think of it, is probably the stupidest of all the twentieth century's contributions to the demise of humanity. To have isolated, as a tricky and problematical study in itself, that which is only the reflux, the refulgence of something so grandly certain as to bring tears of laughter . . . Oh, well.

Paul used the men's room while he waited for her. It is a lesser but no less real surprise to be alone for the first time after a declaration of love. Necessarily, in a case like his, the first note struck is always something like, "What the hell have I done now?" But that is only a last, reflex stab at Putting It All Together, the final gasp of an integrative habit left over from the days when he had no company in his solitude and could spend his quiet times thinking about himself. Now, however, midway between urinal and washstand, he finds his solitude so full of her as to absolve him from further efforts to make things jibe. He observes, no doubt, that according to the received wisdom of the race, nothing is supposed to be capable of doing that. The observation, however, is of such a perfect detachment that it is meaningless. This is now a sovereign solitude. Not one into which he retreats in order to balance his books or hide from his creditors; one, rather, to which he goes gladly, simply because she has taken up residence in it. The lover, when he drives alone, drives with the radio off; washrooms, waiting rooms, solitary walks — all the classical locuses of mindless boredom or fretful reckoning — become for him places of assignation instead. The beloved's name is called to leopard-print walls and black Spanish-tile floors. In a perfectly normal conversational voice, Paul said, "Laura. I love you." He dried his hands, smiled at himself in the mirror, and said, still aloud, but more slowly, "And that . . . said John . . . is that."

He waited for her in the deserted back foyer of the restaurant. When she came out, he took her in his arms and they kissed — once again, gently, chastely. He held her face in his hands. "You smell good."

"That's Charlie."

"That's only one layer. The second is cigarettes and Drambuie. And the third is the base of your nose: oysters; the wind across a salt marsh."

"All that?"

"More. Your hair is something else. A closed bedroom in an old frame house on a warm afternoon."

"You're making that up."

"Not really. I have a nose with a long memory, and you are a symposium, a convivium of redolences. The only thing I find missing is liver and onions. The single flaw. The baseline from which the greatness of the achievement can be measured."

"I love you."

"Seriously, I love your smell. People can think they're in love, but if they can't stand to breathe each other in, they'll never bring it off."

"I like that. It proves I was right about your being physical. Another validation."

"Of course."

"Of course."

They walked out the rear entrance and over to her yellow Volvo sedan. She unlocked the door and he drew her to him

again, his hands dropping from her waist to the ungirdled round-
ness of her. "Nice."

"Nice."

He looked at his watch and patted her on the backside.

"Don't do that."

"Do what?"

"Look at your watch and pat me. That says 'Toddle off.' Pat
all you like, but don't do it to telegraph your good-byes. It isn't
that easy to leave you."

"All right. Never again. To hear is to obey. I am your liege
man of life and limb. Am I forgiven?"

"You're forgiven."

"Hey, you know what's going through my head? Something
else by Auden — from the *Horae Canonicae:*

> Nothing is with me now but a sound,
> A heart's rhythm, a sense of stars
> Leisurely walking around, and both
> Talk a language of motion
> I can measure but not read. . . .

"I can't remember what comes next, but eventually he gets
to a line where he says that the constellations 'sing of some hilarity
beyond all liking and happening.' I don't know — it just seems
to fit. I'll look it up for you. Another souvenir."

"Good."

"Seriously, though, I have to get back."

She said "All right," kissed him, and slid behind the wheel
of her car. "You leave first. I want to watch you walk."

At the corner of the restaurant, he turned and waved. By the
time he got his car started, the Volvo was already out on the
highway, headed east.

22

• •

Back at his office, Paul found a folded note tucked between the door and the jamb. He went inside, opened the blinds, and read it standing in front of the window.

"Paul. I waited till 3:00. Sorry (?) I missed you. This makes twice — J."

He looked at his watch: three-thirty. "Damn!"

Downstairs and outside once again. Fast walk to the class-room where the graduate poetry seminar was held at four. Irving Schiffman was already there, talking to a couple of students.

"Irv. How're you doing?"

"With a two-hour seminar on a Monday afternoon? Bloody but unbowed is the best I can tell you. What can I do for you?"

"Has Janet Grigson been by here yet? There's something I'm supposed to give her."

One of the students spoke up. "She was here just a minute ago. Said she'd be right back. That's her stuff on the table."

Paul headed for the door. "Thanks. I'll catch her outside. See you, Irv. Sorry to interrupt."

"If you're really sorry, take this seminar for me."

"No way. See you."

He went out into the corridor, walked slowly toward the women's washroom, passed by it to the far end of the hall, and leaned against the window. Four minutes.

She came out of the lavatory and headed for the seminar room. Designer jeans. Heels. Turtleneck top.

"Janet."

Quick turn of the head, but no break in stride.

"Wait. Please."

He caught up with her and cut her off. "Listen. I'm sorry about missing you, but I really did think we said Tuesday. I just got back from lunch. When I got your note, I figured I'd have time to catch you before four, so I came over."

She kept her eyes down. Flushed cheeks. Hair tied back severely. "Look, Paul. This is no time to talk. Frankly, I'm angry."

"I know. And I really am sorry about it. Last week and this. You free tomorrow?"

"It isn't just two missed dates, Paul. I've been getting funny signals from you for months."

"Don't be like that, love. I'm still around. Nothing's changed."

She looked up at him. "Don't *you* be like that. That's the whole trouble. You're just around. And not even that, sometimes. Who was the lunch with — male or female?"

"That's got nothing to do with it. It's no skin off your nose."

"Your wife?"

"No, Sarah's in New York today."

"Paul, I don't know how to figure you. You're a great guy, and you're very sweet, and you're marvelous in bed. But I can't take your disappearing act anymore. You've got a head full of little compartments, and you keep the people in your life locked in them. Maybe your wife is happy with the visitation schedule you've worked out for her cell, but I'm not happy with mine. You just vanish too often. And I don't mean only broken dates. I mean *you* vanish."

"Look. I'm sorry. I really did think we said Tuesday."

"You said that already. The trouble with you is, you just don't understand what I'm saying. I don't know if it's that you won't or that you can't. All I know is that I can't take it anymore. If it makes you feel better, it's not that I don't love you; it's just that I can't cope with you. Maybe your marriage really is great. If it is, that's nice for you. But mine isn't, and I can't handle any more destructiveness than I already have. Let me go now. I have to get to class."

"Let me call you tomorrow."

"Oh, Paul, Paul."

"Janet. Come on."

"Paul, I had a friend who used to say that when a conversation got to the point at which two people were simply saying each other's names, either they were busy making love, or they had sunk so deep in misunderstanding that there was no use going on. This is the second."

He reached out his hand and touched her cheek. "Is it really that bad?"

"I don't want to talk anymore. Really. Please. Let me go. We're not talking now, anyway."

He tried to meet her eyes, but she looked down.

"All right, love. I'll see you soon."

She turned, strode down the corridor, and walked into the classroom without looking back.

•   •

In fairness — if there is any such thing as fairness in these matters — it should be said that women found it easy to fall in love with Paul. If it was true that his behavior toward them could be described by the unsympathetic as predatory, it was also true that for as long as their sympathy held up, they made little effort to avoid him. Especially the ones who, like him, were emphatic and volatile sexual presences. Such people simply recognize each other and close in; sour questions about who did what to whom occur only later on, when the sad, bitchy days start coming. For as long as the volatility is in charge, no one is to blame. By the same token, however, no one is particularly responsible, either. The timing of romances thus gladly and mutually provoked is seldom convenient. They obtrude themselves not only on marriages but also on other and previous romances — sometimes before any time has elapsed to allow them to become decently previous. In Paul's life, his relationships with women tended to overlap rather than succeed each other. Love as a many-layered thing. The romantic hero as juggler: one in the bed and two in the air — all night, all month, all year.

Physically, he was simply good-looking: trim, six-foot-two, black, curly hair conservatively cut, olive skin. Forehead a little too short for handsomeness, but the face clean shaven, with a cleft chin, full lips, and deep-set dark brown eyes. Bedroom eyes. The hack phrase is precise: if he had a single obviously sexual physical characteristic, it was the lights thrown off by them even behind the glasses he wore for reading — and the way the fine lines at their corners gave the impression of a collusive smile even when his mouth was in repose.

His overall sexual charm, however, sprang from a self-deprecating, sometimes self-mocking manner — and from a tenderness, a gentleness which, in spite of his general air of competence and strength, gave off hints of some hidden vulnerability waiting to be hunted out. Janet's "you're very sweet" caught it accurately, if grudgingly; but her exasperation at his "vanishing" just as accurately caught the catch in it. The vulnerability, so tantalizingly attractive, was hidden better than anyone suspected at first. Paul was easy to get to, but almost impossible to get at. The gentle manner that provoked the instinct of the huntress was itself the lair in which he avoided discovery. He hid behind his sweetness, gaining from it a privacy most other men achieve only by feistiness or withdrawal. Women frequently lost patience with him; and some, though by no means all, actually broke with him. He, however, never did the breaking: he felt himself capable, in sweet gentleness, of going on with anything he started. The fear of having begun something he could not sustain was alien to him; as he saw it, the defalcations came from other hands than his. Only once, and that only in the last year, did a woman ever learn enough about him — penetrate sufficiently the devices of his hiding — to enable her anger to attack the sweetness itself as dishonest and manipulative, and to leave him flat because of it. That was Catharine; and sadly enough, but not so oddly, she had mattered most of all. The painful invitation to self-knowledge had been delivered in the one Dear John letter he had been least able to bear.

Most of the rest of his lovers, however, simply became confused by the impenetrability. If they broke with him at all, it was not because they understood what they were up against, but only because, like Janet, they finally decided they just couldn't cope with it. Such breaks, though, had a way of turning out to be impermanent: the ability to cope was eventually refreshed; the angry resolve to stay away from him, unnourished by any clear perception of injustice, withered; and the volatilities simply hung around waiting for another chance — which they often enough got, and used, with their customary disregard for the proprieties of timing. The overlapping got worse instead of better. He juggled more but enjoyed it less, and for the first time in his life, he wondered seriously whether he had the strength to keep it up. On good days — and there were many of them — he was his old self; but on the grim ones, he was a man playing out a bad hand at bridge. He had losers he couldn't slough, and he had thrown away his lead to the winning suit. It was just a matter of time till they bled him dry.

It is tempting, of course, to become clinical about these things — to jump to the possibly correct conclusion that he really didn't like women after all, and that the qualities by which he attracted them were, subconsciously, the weapons of a vendetta. Unless you are a disinterested psychologist, however, or a patient with five years' worth of money and a clutch of lovers so long-suffering as to hold off foreclosure while you pay your way to wholeness, thinking about a clinical cure for misogyny is like standing on a wind-whipped cornice at the twentieth floor and wondering whether you should see a psychiatrist about your acrophobia. There just isn't time. The facts are simply contrary to the conditions of the cure.

And it is just as idle to moralize. Morality helps most when it has the least to object to. If it is a guide at all, it is a guide to the perfecting of one's virtues, not to the reform of one's vices. It keeps non-gamblers from being foolish at the racetrack. It does not keep child abusers from beating children, compulsive liars from lying, or lechers from leching. For those in the front trenches of their faults, it is just a lovely, cruel vision of a home they cannot get to. Life, at their extremity, is luck or lumps. The law only makes sin exceeding sinful; it never saved anybody who really needed help.

There is, of course, grace. But grace, besides being unclinical and non-moral, is also, for someone in Paul's position, unimaginable beforehand and terrifying when offered. It is also, to be sure, curative. But that is the most unimaginable and terrifying thing of all:

> 'Twas grace that taught my heart to fear,
> And grace my fears relieved . . .

Always, unfortunately, in that order.

But while the subject was now ready for him, he was not — so far at least — ready for the subject. As he saw it, all he was doing was dropping cards on other people's tricks: the lesson being taught was not grace; it was a graduate course in what it feels like to have all the leads in somebody else's hand: *Inexorability 321.*

● ●

He walked back to his office, put his feet up on the desk, and stared at the ceiling.

28

The texture of his newfound solitude, so silken not an hour ago, was coarser than he expected, Laura's sovereignty over it sharper, more steely. He was still her liege man, and gladly; but for the first time he took note of the possible jeopardy of life and limb. Not that he immediately noted it in depth. At the start, only his body really took it in: the skin at the back of his neck tingled slightly; he almost, but not quite, shivered. His mind was busy weighing plausibilities. If Janet wanted out, let her out. The attractiveness of at least that much simplification of his life struck him with all the more force because, for once, he found himself contemplating it as a possibility he wanted to encourage rather than as an eventuality that would probably dally forever in coming.

Even intellectually, however, the contemplation flushed some distressing propositions. First: he knew himself well enough to know that if Janet — alas, not *per impossible* — ever decided she wanted back in, he would most likely just say yes and drop into the old pattern again. Second: a simplification that consisted of reducing the number of concurrent liaisons from five and a half to four and a half while at the same time starting a roaring love affair with Laura was a distinctly bush-league simplification. Third: the number of people who would be happy with it, himself included, was probably zero. Fourth: it was practically certain not to simplify anything, but to complicate everything. He played with the words for a while. Simplicate and complify. Why not? But either way, no simplexity. Only complicity.

Fifth and finally, though: he knew he was trapped by Laura no matter what. In less than a minute, he had come skipping back across the supposedly unbridgeable gulf which the disastrous end of the affair with Catharine had put between him and Romance. The self-protective armor of his luncheon discourse on the impossibility of living with the Dominions, Principalities, and Powers had gone whistling down the wind like so many feathers.

He was not even a sitting duck; he was a plucked one. The speech might as well have been delivered by another man in another century. The Law of the Exclusivity of the Romantic Attachment, so recently and so clearly seen as the murderous infeasibility it was, had been blithely reinvoked as the Law of Life it could never be for the likes of him. He knew he had to give himself only to Laura; and he knew he couldn't do it. The avenging Angel had been invited in for tea.

There is a reek of death that hangs around the Law of Life; and Paul sensed it all the more clearly because there had been a time when he didn't smell it at all. He was alive without the Law once. For the ten years of the affair with Catharine, he had been simply and happily beyond its jurisdiction. In the first years, because his only sin then against the Angel of Romance consisted in his continuing to make love to his wife. But there were so many good reasons for that — kindness, fairness, responsibility — that they effectively exempted him from compliance with the Law, even though he had, in principle, invoked it.

But as the affair went on, other offenses against the Angel began to accumulate. He made love not simply to the wife of his youth and the lady of his heart, but to an impressive number of the English Department's brightest and best. However, since good reasons for these infractions did not come as easily to hand, he was forced to deal with them by constructing the compartments to which Janet referred. He made them Law-tight and hid in them safely: either what he did with the others was not what he did with Catharine; or if it was, it did not mean the same thing; or if it became obvious that the others thought it did, he still knew in his heart of hearts that it simply could not. In any case, he managed on all counts not only to put himself beyond the Law in practice but, even better, to make himself metaphysically immune to its demands. He had only one love. He really believed that. And it was true. He really did.

The trouble with such casuistry, however, is that it cannot successfully be explained to anyone else. Because while we can all convince ourselves of its validity on the rough-and-ready level of our furtive bodies and scrawling, misspelt minds — while we can indeed believe we love only one and yet go on having affairs with any number we find convenient and/or possible (it is done day in and night out, probably not too many doors from where you are now so comfortably and domestically seated) — we also know that the race has tacitly agreed that it's not supposed to be that way once you've invited in the Angel.

Therefore (to give Paul short and merciful shrift): when, in the last years of his grand passion for Catharine, the fragments shored against his ruin began one by one to wash out — when the day came on which there were no words left that had been spoken only to Catharine, no remaining venereal acts that had not been essayed with at least one other Venus — he began to wonder just what, if anything, he still believed in his heart of hearts.

The upshot of it, of course, was that in his effort to regain his faith in himself — in his panic to render credible once again the largeness of the love that was his life — he did the one thing that was simply and absolutely undoable: he told Catharine the truth. Having offended the Angel, he proved his worthiness as a Knight of Romance by conceding the Law's dominion over him and confessing his offenses against it. To which the Angel, as anyone with his wits about him would have known, replied, "That is one hell of a note," and slammed the door in his face. Catharine cut him off. Completely. He had invoked the Law, which was holy, just, and, good; and quite properly, he got the only sentence possible: sin revived, and he died. And that also is true. He really did. First, tears. Then, terror. Then the coldness of the grave.

But now. Oh, damn, damn, damn! To begin to try to live again. To raise the dead only to the certainty of a second death.

31

To submit once again to the inexorability of Romance and thus revive the exceeding sinfulness of his inevitable faithlessness. To turn into unpardonable offenses against a new sovereign Lady those unendable liaisons which, since Catharine left, had at least seemed more like penances than vice. To put himself so irrevocably on the path to some bed, some day, where, with Laura, he would slip and say, "Oh, Cath!" To know all that, and to be able to do nothing but wait in the cold light of that knowledge for the axe to fall. Stupid, stupid.

But of course it was all irrevocable. Finished, done, too late, no way back. Best, perhaps, not even to think of it. Play out the hand. Hope that the compartments can somehow be made to hold. Is that irresponsible? Who's to say? If you're going to gyp everybody in the end, what's the rush to go running around insisting on gypping them sooner rather than later? Impossible promises, badly kept, are still promises kept as best you can. Maybe, with luck . . .

He put his feet down, locked up the office, and drove aimlessly for ten minutes. Then he headed for the highway, drove to the restaurant, circled once through the parking lot, and went on toward home. "Laura. Laura. Laura."

4

Interlude with Augustine

At this point, it may be useful to put Paul's problem in its proper, larger context. Romance being simply a special case of the generality called Law, perhaps we can best understand the shipwreck of his love life and the prospects of the salvage operation so diffidently just begun by looking at one of the classic texts on Law and Grace: Proposition XIII of Augustine's *Expositio Quarumdam Propositionum ex Epistola ad Romanos* (Migne, *Patrologiae Cursus Completus, Tomus XXXV: Sancti Aurelii Augustini Hipponensis Episcopi Omnia Opera*, p. 2065). Let me quote it for you in the original:

> Quod autem dicit, Quia non justificabitur in lege omnis caro coram illo: per legem enim cognitio peccati, et cetera similia, quae quidam putant in contumeliam legis objicienda, sollicite satis legenda sunt, ut neque lex ab Apostolo improbata videatur, neque homini arbitrium liberum sit ablatum. Itaque quatuor istos gradus hominis distinguamus; ante legem, sub lege, sub gratia, in pace. Ante legem, sequimur concupiscentiam carnis; sub lege, trahimur ab ea; sub gratia, nec sequimur eam, nec trahimur ab ea; in pace, nulla est concupiscentia carnis. Ante

legem ergo non pugnamus; quia non solum concupiscimus et peccamus, sed etiam approbamus peccata; sub lege pugnamus sed vincimur. . . .

I shall gloss the passage for you in the old manner, taking perhaps a liberty or two in the translation but leaving the original Latin untouched so that you may be the judge of my responsibility or the lack of it. As I see it, my only significant departure from the customary rules will be my insistence on Englishing the word *Law (lex, legis)* as *Romance*. Aside from that, I consider my reading to be thoroughly consonant with the letter of Augustine, as well as distinctly redolent of the spirit of Luther — and therefore irreproachably both Catholic and Reformed. But judge for yourself. Here it is.

●　　　●

In his exposition of Romans 3:20 — "Therefore no flesh is justified before him by Romance, for by romance comes the knowledge of sin" (*Quia non justificabitur in lege omnis caro coram illo: per legem enim cognitio peccati*) — Augustine points out that there will always be certain dummies (*quidam*) floating around who will interpret such remarks as a crack at Romance (*in contumeliam legis*). He adds, however, that if such boneheads would only learn to read carefully enough (*sollicite satis*), they would see that neither does the Apostle take a dim view of Romance (*neque lex ab Apostolo improbata videatur*), nor is the free will of human beings taken from them and hauled off to the cosmic garbage heap (*neque homini arbitrium liberum sit ablatum*). The general mess we find ourselves in, Augustine feels, will not yield to such lame-brained attempts to tidy it up.

He suggests, accordingly, that we distinguish carefully the four necessary steps or stages (*quatuor istos gradus hominis*) by which we pass from our fallen state to the fully human condition. He lists them as follows:

> before Romance (*ante legem*),
> under Romance (*sub lege*),
> under grace (*sub gratia*), and
> in peace (*in pace*);

and he construes them as follows:

Ante legem (before Romance), he says, we go racing around, tearing back the lid of the sardine can of life and acting, in general, as if we had a metaphysical right to the full fruition of every luscious desire that occurs to us (*sequimur concupiscentiam carnis*). *Sub lege* (under Romance), however, the condition is reversed: we are dragged about, willy-nilly and without ceremony, by our commitment to what now seems like nothing but a bevy of well-muscled beauties who no longer care a fig for our discomfort and who stop their ears at anything that pleads, however sweetly, for our undistress (*trahimur ab ea*). *Sub gratia* (under grace), though, things are better: we neither pursue the riot of desires nor are bullied about by it (*nec sequimur eam, nec trahimur ab ea*). And *in pace* (in peace), finally and securely under the Mercy, the riot simply stops: the wolf and his lambs (Laura, Sarah, Catharine, Janet, *et aliae*) dwell together in gardens and gallant walks, the leopard lies down on an eschatological bed of green with all the kids he has ever pursued, the sucking child plays on the hole of the asp, and they neither hurt nor destroy in all my holy mountain, saith the Lord (*in pace, nulla est concupiscentia carnis*).

Augustine then continues: *Ante legem ergo non pugnamus; quia non solum concupiscimus et peccamus, sed etiam approbamus peccata: sub lege pugnamus, sed vincimur . . .*

Before Romance (*ante legem*), he says, it's all tea and cakes (*non pugnamus*): we not only desire incompatibilities and gobble indigestibilities (*non solum concupiscimus et peccamus*) but we actually get away with it all, our hearts unhaunted by any fear of judgment and our minds sustained by an unshakeable conviction that it's the greatest thing since the pop-up toaster (*sed etiam approbamus peccata*).

Once under the dominion of Romance, however — once we have, by the tough luck of our better nature, acknowledged ourselves to be *sub lege* and taken the lovely, deadly vow to put our nose between the Angel's teeth and hang on tight — we have a fight on our hands (*pugnamus*). But then, alas, far from finding it a fair fight, let alone one from which we might hope to go forth conquering and to conquer, we find to our deep pain and abiding sadness that we are consistently and without interruption — and at every hour of the day and night, with no time off for good behavior — having the living shit kicked out of us (*sed vincimur*). . . .

Which, if it is not a happy place to leave off this exposition of Augustine, is still a suitable one. We are at least reassured: we have arrived, by a consideration of Scripture and the Fathers, at the very point to which Paul (*non Apostolus*) got by staring at the ceiling. We all, of course, have considerably farther to go; *pro tanto,* however, it is a comfort to have struck a trial balance.

5

The Rising Tide

Paul himself, however, did not remain long at the balance point. The ten minutes of aimless driving, plus the nostalgic swing through the restaurant parking lot, obliterated the boding negativism of his office meditation and switched him onto automatic pilot for the conduct of an affair. It was, of course, a device with which he was familiar; and if you have the least knowledge of how it works, you know perfectly well what happened next. He passed a pay phone, checked his watch (four-fifty-five), stopped at the next booth he came to, looked up Laura's number, and dialed it. (He also memorized it — deliberately, but passing no particular judgment in the process. No matter that he had already learned a whole catechism of numbers by heart; it was simply convenient that he now learn this one — merely unavoidable that the romantic ratchet should thus move him another inch forward and the pragmatic pawl drop into place behind him.)

The phone rang. Laura and a child picked up the two extensions simultaneously. Paul hesitated. "Laura?"

"It's all right, Jimmy," she said. "It's for me. Hang up."

Paul waited for the click. "Can you talk for a minute?"

"Hold on." She set down the phone, closed the door, and

came back. "Now I can. I'm upstairs in the bedroom. I was just thinking of you."

"Likewise. Obviously. I love you."

"I would have died if you hadn't called."

By another reflex action of his mind, he noted one more pull of the ratchet, one more click of the pawl. "So would I. Listen. Is there any chance I can see you tomorrow? I'm tied up with classes and conferences till about one, and I have to drive up to the Catskills for a dumb conference that starts with supper; but I can get free for a while in the early afternoon. Can I meet you somewhere? Even if it's only for a few minutes. I just want to see you again."

"So do I. But a conference? You didn't say anything about that. When will you be back?"

"Thursday afternoon late."

"Paul! That's forever."

"I know. That's my second reason for calling. Can you meet me for lunch on Friday?"

"Of course. Give me a minute to think about tomorrow, though."

She was silent for a while. "I have to be at Jimmy's school at three, but before then is all right."

"Good. I really should be on my way by two-thirty anyhow."

"Where should I meet you?"

He hesitated only a second. "You know the Hill's Shopping Plaza about a mile past the restaurant?"

"Yes."

"Well, suppose I meet you there at the far end of the parking lot at one-thirty?"

"You mean the west end?"

"Hey! You really are amazing. You're not only punctual; you actually know east from west."

"I'm just a born Girl Scout."

38

"You're a lot more than that. But you can come then? I mean, it's not going to be too much of a hassle?"

"If I'm not there, it won't be my fault."

"Good. One-thirty. Hill's Plaza. West end. Right now, though, I have to run and liberate the babysitter before she pauperizes me. Sarah won't be back till after supper. I love you."

"I love you."

They wound down over the next minute in an alternation of endearments and a series of hesitations over who should hang up first. I spare you those. Pillow talk, even on real pillows, makes dull reading. Transcribed from phone conversations, it is a sovereign soporific.

●   ●

You may wonder, however, why I have said so little about Laura's and Paul's relationships with their respective spouses. There are two reasons. The first is that it is not to my purpose to do so. I am not developing here either a full-fledged cast of characters or a convoluted plot. My intention is simply to isolate a single moment in the relationship of two lovers; I shall give you only as much of its wider context as is necessary to that end. I am convinced, as I said at the outset, that to introduce any more than a little of the tissue of their lives would cause your mind to cast such a moral pall over the narrative that it would distract you from the vision of grace.

The second reason, however, is that in an affair of this sort, where people are not playing conventional matrimonial guilt games (where they are not perpetually canvassing each other on the subject of fidelity in order to expiate whatever it is they think they have left undone at home), there is a tacit agreement that the names of the spouses involved should come up only in a moderate and neutral way — that they should be neither completely suppressed nor extensively discussed. I state this simply as a fact: it just happens that some people do make such a decision. I pass no particularly favorable — or unfavorable — judgment upon it.

In the case at hand, Paul and Laura arrived at the decision by similar routes, but for slightly different reasons. They were both convinced their partners were not about to bolt: Paul, because he thought his wife was genuinely pleased with the tenor of their life; Laura, because she felt that while her husband was frequently displeased with their marriage, he was not about to be sufficiently interested in anything else to make a break. Needless to say, they were both right and both wrong. They had the insights, and the blind spots, of strong characters — of the kind of people who cause rather than experience jealousy.

They were right about discounting any strong possibility of action against them: Paul, because he was as graciously private from his wife as from anyone else and so gave her anger no provable inequities to feed on; Laura, because her husband had been jealous without cause for so many years that he simply had no faculty left for satisfying himself about the difference between a real wolf and an imagined one. They were wrong, though, in that they underestimated the potential vehemence of the objections they themselves so easily dismissed. The infirm, imperfect jealousies they aroused seemed to them a kind of vindication; in reality, however, their spouses were frequently more upset at their own inability to justify their envy than they were at the objects of it. Those who are stymied have, in the very fact of their being boxed, a taproot to their anger that is almost always overlooked by those who box them. People who stymie others are never as safe as they think they are.

In any case, however, it is all irrelevant. In spite of the dangers, nothing happened. Nor was there any reason to expect that it should have. Affairs, while they are commonly thought of as being conducted in the interstices of lives, are not the inevitable problem the imagery suggests. There is more room in the cracks of our existence than anywhere else. Lives, like atoms, are in fact mostly interstices. Even the densest of them, the ones so filled with projects and associations as to present a facade of seamless busyness, are full of gaping, interstellar distances. The brief, mindless times of the stirring of the breakfast coffee, of the fastening of the seat belt, of the moment alone in the washroom — all open out into vast, silent halls for which no heart's leap or mind's journey will ever be too great. Romance does not, except in the hands of fools, necessarily attack what already exists in a life, any more than the tide has to uproot the marsh grasses in order to rise. Love and water flow around obstacles, and in flood are just as likely to nourish roots as tear them out. That is not a wish. It is simply the way things are, given half a chance. The lover sings in the shower, pats his dog, and is generally a pleasure to be around. The beloved's complexion improves. You need bold souls to bring it off, of course. It can't be accomplished by a pair of enamored fussbudgets continually trimming their sails to every mean-spirited wind they meet; but it can be done, and it has been done, and that is that. Don't let the false notion that the cosmic vice squad is on twenty-four-hour duty lead you into the even falser expectation that everyone who breaks the received rules will be hauled in and fined. Until you see that we get something both far better and far worse than that, you won't see grace at all.

So for now, accept Paul's and Laura's luck and wish them well. If it comforts you, your sacred conviction that there is no such thing as a free lunch is still true — and in a more terrible and wonderful sense than you have yet understood. Grace is neither indulgence nor permission. The divine comeuppance is still there — literally, and with a capital "C."

In the immediate instance, though, Paul and Laura proceeded without a hitch to their respective kinds of meal and evening. He, having once turned his mind to the subject of domesticity, did not take the sitter home after all; instead he fed the children, picked up Sarah at the station on the 7:54, and took her to a seafood house for dinner. Laura, after Paul hung up, called a couple to whom she knew her husband was not averse, invited them for drinks around nine, and spent the meantime with her husband, her children, and Keats, respectively, in the approximate proportions of one part to five parts to two. Paul got to bed at eleven; Laura at one. Both their evenings were successes. Neither of them — and for the same reason — made love.

6

Greater Trumps

L aura got to the shopping plaza at one-thirty-five. She pulled
up next to his car and said, "My place or yours?"

"Mine," he said, leaning over to open the door. "The shift is
on the steering column."

When she got inside, there were no words; just a sudden,
long kiss in the twisted, half-trapped position dictated even by
bench front seats. After a while, Paul reached down and slid the
seat back. "This is ridiculous. Turn around, put your feet up, and
lie across my lap."

"Here? In the parking lot?"

"Sure, here. The best hiding place is where nobody expects
to find anything hidden. 'The Purloined Letter.' He put his left
hand on the steering wheel, and she laid her head in the crook
of his arm. "That better?"

"Much."

They kissed again. He touched her face with his fingers,
outlining her lips, her eyebrows, the line of her jaw. Finally she
spoke. "I read the tarot last night. Yours, mine, and ours."

"Was it good?"

"Very. Another validation. It's all safe."

43

"You're serious about that, aren't you? I mean about the tarot. I've never paid any attention to it except as a literary device. Too much residual scientism in my head, I guess."

Her eyes widened, and she lifted her head animatedly. "But that doesn't have to stop you. I figured out the answer to at least a part of that long ago. It's really just a way of letting your mind . . ."

He waited for her to finish, but she didn't. "Of letting your mind what?"

". . . of letting your mind meditate on certain images. At least, that's one way you can think of it, even if you don't go any further."

"That's still just inside your own head, though. How do you get from there to the conclusion that you and I are safe?"

She fell silent again, then half sat up and looked straight at him. "Well, for one thing, the images — the cards themselves — are facts. They're not just inside your own head. They're out there on the table, being whatever they are. And of course, if you believe there's anything behind them . . ."

"How do you mean?"

"Like in Charles Williams. *The Greater Trumps.*"

He puzzled for a minute. "You mean the cards represent forces that actually reach you through the reading?"

"I guess so."

She didn't say anything more, so he tried explaining it himself. "Well, I can see one way it might work. The cards are representations of actual elements in the experience of the race: the Fool, the Hanged Man, and so on. Those things definitely have power; so if the cards, as images of them, manage to turn them loose in your mind. . . . Hey, listen. You've not only got me arguing your case; you've got me leaving off the ends of sentences just like you."

"You work too hard to be clear."

"My curse, I guess."

"It's not a curse. But it's not everything, either. You have to be more open, that's all. Then it just comes. You interrelate . . ."

He ran his fingers over her forehead. "You know what? I've figured out how you got tagged as a scatterbrain. Your mind isn't scattered; it's elliptical. It leaves out steps because it sees where it's going and figures everyone else does too. But your speech is also elliptical, especially at the ends of sentences. Aposiopetic. The trouble is, it takes more getting used to than most people are prepared for."

"Apo- what?"

"Aposiopetic. Aposiopesis: the trick of trailing off into silence for rhetorical effect. Example: 'But for anyone to have thought the Democrats were a genuine threat in 1972 . . .' Your silences aren't that rhetorical, but they have their effect."

"I never thought about it. And I especially never thought about apo-whatever-it-is."

Something bumped the back of the car. She made a sudden move to sit up, but he kissed her before she could. "It's nothing," he said. "Just a couple loading groceries into the back of a wagon. Their shopping cart rolled into us."

"How'd you know that?"

"The rearview mirror. I spotted them a minute ago when they walked up. Panic not."

"I like that. Your coolness, I mean."

"What else is there to do? If they don't know you, they will quite intelligently assume you're two lovers having a tryst at a shopping plaza; and since that's one of the main uses of such places, they'll think no more of it than that cigar-smoking old party over there who's been watching ever since you got here. On the other hand, if they do know you, there's always the hope that in their preoccupation with their own lives, they still won't notice you. However, when a woman, not previously visible, sits up suddenly in a front seat, straightens her skirt, and arranges her hair . . . Aposiopesis again."

She threw her arms around him and held herself close to him. "I love you, I love you, I love you."

They talked for a while about the conference he was going to at Grossinger's: an ad hoc affair, pulled together for one measure of serious discussion about the miserable estate of English among freshman classes, three measures of eating and drinking, and, depending on individual tastes, an optional number of measures of fun and games on the golf course, in the pool, up and down the corridors, or in the skin bars around Monticello. Apropos of the last, Paul said he wondered whether tractor salesmen in such places pretended to be English teachers, because in his experience, most English teachers certainly made a point of acting as if they were tractor salesmen.

Laura turned her head toward his chest and buried her face. "I wish I could go."

"So do I. Maybe someday — who knows?" He made a point of not looking at his own watch. "What time do you have?"

"You look. I don't want to."

He turned her left wrist so he could see her watch. "I really should go."

"I don't want you to."

"But I still have to."

She buried her face again.

"Laura?"

"I'm being a brat." She held herself against him for a few seconds more and then sat up, turned herself around on the seat, and smiled. "You have to come and sit in my car for one minute. I can't walk away from you, you know."

●　　●

After they parted, he drove up to the Catskills in high spirits, spending the whole stretch of Route 17 on the prospect of being naked with her. At Grossinger's his behavior was part that of a veteran conference-goer and part that of a man in love. He skipped sessions that didn't interest him, called her every day, wished she were at the poolside or in the Pink Elephant Lounge, got roped into an expedition to Monticello with a party of top-less-bar connoisseurs, and lay down, happily discontent, in a lonely bed.

He called her again just before he left on Thursday afternoon but got no answer. He tried later, still without success, at several pay phones on the way down. By the time he got though the traffic jam near the City, it was suppertime, and too late.

7

Catharine

Paul woke at six on Friday morning in an unexpected state of morbid agitation. He had gone to bed early the evening before to catch up on the sleep lost at the conference, and he slept heavily until three A.M. After that, however, the night deteriorated into a series of dream-ridden naps, the worst of which took him into one of his recurrent nightmares about Catharine.

Their principal theme was estrangement, harped on till his nerves gave out. Sometimes she would be next to him on the fringes of a party, obviously upset at being seen with him and constantly trying to get away; at others, he would run into her downtown only to find that she had a train to catch. In any case, he was always an inconvenience. She either refused flatly to speak to him or, if she condescended, launched into a monologue about the enormity of his deception. When he pleaded, as he always did, that he had at least eventually told her the truth, she dismissed the argument out of hand: it was too little, too late, and for too much. Besides, why was he wasting his time with her? He still had plenty of other places to peddle his papers.

He would cry, of course, and swear he loved her, and ask why she refused to understand; and she would marvel at his

48

denseness, daring him to tell any of the others what he had told her and see what would happen. Then his frustration would boil over into rage, and he would call her a vengeful bitch and swear at her until remorse stopped him with the thought that he had finally gone too far. And then there would be fear, and sadness, and one more desperate attempt to plead his love before she left.

But none of it made any difference. She was pure ice. She would not hold him or touch him. If the dream lasted long enough, she simply turned her back and left him for dead. Once or twice during the past year, the scenario had been different: not a nightmare, but a dream of reconciliation, or of the way it was. But if anything, that was worse. The bad dreams simply confirmed the death of hope; waking from a good one, he had to go through the dying all over again.

He got up, dressed, and went for a walk. About a mile out of the village, he found a spot under some trees at the edge of a field and stretched out on the grass.

Usually he found that watching clouds through the branches disengaged his mind and cut it back to an idle. This time, however, it didn't work. He was locked into seeing Laura at twelve-thirty for lunch. The clutch was jammed; his mind simply sputtered and backfired its way along.

He first went through a series of revisionist considerations about his new love. Perhaps, like a fool, he had simply gone in over his head in the hope of a revival of what he had had with Catharine. What, after all, did he really know about Laura? Well, for one thing, that she had the kind of intellect he normally gave the widest possible berth: diffuse, mystical, elliptical as hell. How do you prove to the gallery of watchers you carry inside your head that you haven't just bought yourself one more romance with a price tag you can't afford? Answer: you don't. Inside your head or out, your enemies won't believe you, and your friends — including, especially, yourself — are too confused by the facts to make up their minds. There's no point in evaluating what you've done. The only point is, it's done. If you've made a mistake about her, you've made it; there's no way out without still more mistakes. Just hold onto your cold feet and shiver quietly.

And anyway, maybe Laura wasn't just a rerun of Catharine. He repented of his revisionism. She was herself, and that was enough. Maybe he would be better off with somebody who could say her husband needed a mistress and really mean it; somebody who, finally and thank God, knew east from west, and who seemed to do what she damn well pleased with no problems except about practicalities. Maybe she really was great, with her "of courses," and her stacked tarot deck, and the easy openness of her moods.

But then he repented of that, too, because it was just a cheap shot at Catharine. Sure, she had backed and filled and bucked and reared the whole time of their affair; but she really had been his life, and he had borne it all gladly as a small enough price to pay. It was hypocritical to make comparisons now that he wouldn't have allowed then. He was wrong no matter what he did. There was no way of feeling good about anything. He watched the clouds and tried not to think.

His tongue, however, had found the loose tooth. In spite of the pain of having lost Catharine — and in spite of the ease with which he could still become furious with her for having killed, in ten minutes, what they had nursed together for ten years — he was finally able, after a year now, to see it from her point of view. On two levels. The first was the level of the woman scorned. He saw at last that the intentions of the scorner didn't matter a damn compared with the feelings of the scornee. Every one of us has to live with the gallery of watchers we carry inside our own head. It makes no difference that real watchers, outside the injured mind, would no doubt be more lenient in their judgments as to who had been made a fool of, and more accurate in their assessment of just who was the real fool. The fact of the matter was that when the gallery inside cries "fool," the owner of the head has no choice but to take it personally.

But he also saw her point on a second, more devastating level. The real trouble was him. His compartmentalized life. His trick of being apparently open but actually closed. His buying of peace with silence, of other people's happiness at the price of integrity.

He railed for a while at the thought of integrity. Bullshit! To take the likes of us, with our half-assed commitments and our two-bit gifts, and to insist on principle that we run around informing every love, however happy, that she is not the only being in the world whom we have, in a burst of enthusiasm, told she was the greatest thing since the electric pencil sharpener — to ask us to spell out in words of one syllable the fact that our oblation of life and limb, so grandiloquently and so personally offered has, alas, a string or two attached, and that at times she will never note on her watch, and in places she will never visit, and in ways which we know can never compromise the fullness of our gift, she is being somehow shortchanged — to require, in fine, that her lover print a surgeon general's warning on his forehead stating that he is not exactly Jesus Christ himself . . . well, what the hell did she expect? Not even Origen could pass a test like that.

And yet. And yet. You can say "bullshit" all you like. You can appeal from the inapplicability of the Law until your breath runs out. But Harry, Harry, Harry! You can't abrogate the stupidity by which you first filed this suit you would now so dearly like to drop. Who appealed to Caesar to begin with? You, Paul. Whose idea was it to take a stand on his citizenship in the City of Romance once again? Who rewrapped the two-bit gift and handed it to Laura on the sterling platter? You, you dummy. You!

The railing stopped. What was the use? The dare still stood:

tell somebody — anybody — *everything,* and see how long you last. He had enough Christianity left to believe that somehow, after all, there was Grace. But in the last year, he had hedged his bets and said there was no grace except Grace itself — that everything else was Law, and therefore death. Maybe God could deal with honesty; unfortunately, no one else could. People asked you, in all sincerity, to tell them the truth. What they didn't understand was that when they got it, they would have to blow your head off.

And yet. Always, and yet. What was he to do with Laura? How be literally naked with her, and still hide? How make her all, and then have to treat her as one more part to be kept in ignorance of the other parts? In plain English, how bed her in the grand romantic tradition and still go on making time and place for all the other bedding down that was still, except for Janet (maybe), unavoidable? Answer? No way.

No way except the dare — which was no way. It was only a trick to get you to stick your head up over the parapet again. He thought back to Laura at the restaurant: "If you find yourself living by something that can't forgive . . ." Hope sprang up in the aposiopesis. The rhetorical axe was laid to the root of the unacceptable tree, but then suddenly, dazzlingly, sheathed: ". . . then die to it and look around for something that can."

But was that even believable? Forgiveness is for bad boys who finally see light at the end of the tunnel: ". . . for these, and for all my other sins which I cannot now remember, I am very sorry and firmly purpose amendment. . . ." What about the poor slobs who couldn't say that if they wanted to, for whom the future will be only a repetition of the unrelieved darkness of the past? What are they supposed to do? Walk in and say, "Darling, forgive me for what I am about to do? I don't really want permission, but I'm afraid that if you and I are going to do business, you'd better sign this hall monitor's pass just in case?" Just try it and see how far you get. There really was no grace except Grace, if indeed there was that. The only true filling in of the ellipsis was ". . . then die." The rest was pious pap.

And so it had been over all along. It was not a matter of waiting for a slip of the tongue to kill him; he had been dead from the beginning. The illusion of life had served only to trick him into telling the truth that was untellable, into walking once more into the confessional where the priest waited with a pistol. It was only sad that, in six hours, the corpse would have to be propped up and shot again.

8

Death

Paul dropped off to sleep.

There are people (perhaps you are among them; there was a time when even Paul himself was) who think that the kind of internal debate he was going through is simply a large fuss over not much — that all he really needed was a swift kick to get him off the dime of fooling around and onto the dollar of commitment. But they are wrong. They are deceived by the imagery of the salutary jolt, the earnest but almost playful nudge administered by an attentive friend to one whose mind has momentarily wandered from its purpose. The swift kick, as actually bestowed, is never like that. When it is given by someone who has paid careful attention to the friend for whom it is intended, it is not only swift but fatal. Think back to Paul's experience with Catharine: she cut him off and let him bleed to death.

On the other hand, when it is administered by the universe — by the passage of time, or by the changes and chances of this mortal life — it is seldom swift and almost never attentive. The universe is just as deadly, of course, but it kills us the way a cat kills a cockroach. It stalks us with a distracted implacability, piercing us now with a claw, then chasing its own tail, coming

54

back by and by to crunch us once with its teeth and spit us out in disgust, going off in pursuit of dust kittens, and returning to us only as long as we are alive enough to interest it. It doesn't want our death, really; it is simply that in its mindless amusement with our life, it never leaves until it has finished us off.

But the final reason why the supposedly therapeutic boot never works lies deeper. No refinement of the way it is applied — no gentling of it in the hands of our lovers, no more systematic direction of it in the advances of the cosmic cat — can overcome the intractability of what it aims to reform. Our mind has not momentarily wandered from its purpose. It is a dead horse. Neither love taps nor systematic violence work when you have a corpse on your hands.

Perhaps, however, you think that all this talk of death and corpses is a bit overwrought — that Saint Paul, when he cries out, "O wretched man that I am! Who will rescue me from this body that is taking me to death?" (Rom. 7:24), is being more rhetorical than factual. After all, you say, no one in such a state is all dead. Give him time; there's life in the old boy yet. He'll be back on his feet in a week.

To which I can only say that you haven't paid attention to what death is. I insist that you sit through a short excursus on the subject.

Death is the separation of body and soul. You do not believe in souls? That is quite all right; neither, I think, do I. At least, I have nothing to say about them except in this context. If you like, think "life" when I say "soul" (in Greek, the same word does for both); we are simply casting about here for some concept that will fix in our minds the difference between a body and a corpse.

The point is crucial. A body is capable of nourishment, growth, recuperation, locomotion. There is no use feeding corpses or putting Unguentine on their burns. Death, whatever it is, puts an end to the practicability of all that. But note precisely what is involved. Distinguish carefully between dying and death. Dying happens; death slowly catches up with it. One minute after I have died, my corpse will still be teeming with lives. My kidneys, perhaps, or my heart, if otherwise sound, will be quite capable of being transplanted into someone else. Indeed, if you care to be whimsical and endow my heart with an intellect of its own for a moment, you can imagine it frantically phoning the local paper and running a Situation Wanted ad:

Sound heart, low mileage, never driven by anything but beautiful women, desires new life in which to resume unfortunately interrupted projects. Prefer poet or guitarist, but will settle for bassoon player.

Do you see the point? My heart's problem is not that it has died, but that it is still alive in the midst of death. It is trapped in a corpse instead of flourishing in a body. Something — indeed, the one and only necessary thing — has walked out on it. That is why *soul,* or some other word which will do the same work, is inevitable. The difference between life and death is the presence or absence of something like an interambient fluid by which the parts of a body communicate with each other, by which they are enabled to coinhere in the whole. Catharine, you see, really was Paul's life, his soul; she was what the beloved always is, an *aqua vitae* filling him, a vivifying cordial that warmed and unified the parcels of his existence. Everybody knows that: the lover sings in the shower and pats his dog . . . ; and everybody knows what happens when, by death or desertion, the beloved leaves: shower stall, soap, bath mat, towel, mind, body, furry paws, and floppy ears are all still in place, still functioning. But now, not in life but in death. He who was alive and whole has been reduced to the mere sum of his parts. It isn't just that he feels dead; it's that he has entered deadness itself.

Which is why, when you think about it, Saint Paul is quite

accurate in his choice of words. He has, in Romans, been trying to pinpoint the essence of our fallen romantic condition, and he has arrived at the concept of Sin with a capital "S." Not sins, not infractions, not intermittent derelictions, not vices; quite sensibly, he sees that they are not the problem: a living lover can have many things wrong with him and still love magnificently. No, he is looking for the heart of the matter — for a word to describe a condition in which even virtue and truth and beauty and intelligence and kindness, and love itself, somehow can't manage to bring off what they know perfectly well how to do.

So, having settled on the concept of Sin, he then proceeds to illuminate his insight by equating it with three other words: with *concupiscence;* with *the flesh;* and with *death.* Notice that all three notions have one thing in common: they describe a condition in which the parts are somehow condemned to act in the absence of the whole — in which the most they can do is masquerade as the whole, and in which they frequently do a good deal less than that.

Concupiscence, or desire (misleadingly, at least for our times, translated as "lust"), refers not to desire properly so-called, but to the free-for-all of conflicting desires we commonly experience. Not one life-giving love, unifying and edifying, but a wearing, tearing riot of separately gorgeous affections that leads us, six ways for Sunday, by the nose: Laura, Sarah, Janet, Catharine . . .

The flesh does the same conceptual work. It refers not to the body as a body, but to the body as mere meat. And meat always comes from a corpse: loin, rib, rump, or shoulder, it is all nothing but parts going their own way because the unifying life has departed from them. They have a certain acceptability only because they are not yet corrupt; but the soul that animated them is gone; by and by, corruption will have its perfect work.

And *death* . . . ? Well, I have done that one way; let me change the approach slightly.

Imagine with me a scene of utter tranquillity: a tidal marsh in the morning sun. No houses, no people; a place ages ago returned to nature — its only record of human occupation, the vestiges of a long-abandoned wharf. Think of it at high tide: fish swim among the ancient pilings; mussels in great black clumps open and close at leisure, taking nourishment from the seawater; currents flow among the grasses at the bottom, and the wind textures the surface with a thousand hammerstrokes. The place is a *symbioticum,* an ecological whole; a *convivium,* a living thing, a body.

Postulate next, however, a maximum depth at high tide of two feet, and a difference between high and low water of three feet. Then imagine the place six hours later: the pilings stand exposed, the mussels are shut tight, and the grasses lie in clumps on the sand. No fish swim; no currents eddy. The water — the interambient, circumambient medium that made the parts a whole — is gone. None of the individual elements is any different than it was before; the lives that were there in the morning are still lives now. But the place itself, the *convivium* that it was, is in death and not in life. Catharine, if you will, has simply drained herself out of it and, unlike the tide, has sworn she won't be back.

Worse yet, some idiot — namely, this sleeping Paul himself — has come along and so bulldozed and damned the channel that no water will ever reach him again. The tides will rise and fall everywhere as before, and down to the last dying of the last part of his life, he will sense them and long for them. But for all that, he will never know them. Catharine gone, Laura precluded, he is a drained marsh. His death is accomplished; his history as a living thing is over. For the rest of his existence he will simply be the annalist of his own corruption.

• • •

Paul woke, got up from the grass, and walked home, mulling over his options. They were, as he saw them, three.

The first was the boldest and the most elegant: stand her up. Just don't go to the restaurant at all. For once in your life, do something brave for a change. Stop palming tenth-rate love off on people; when she asks you why and pleads her love, say nothing. Be the bastard you are. Don't apologize, don't explain; just say "It's over" and make it stick. That was cruel, of course, but it was the least unkind thing in the long run.

It was also, however, impossible. No one does anything of that magnitude for once in his life. We are all, at the core of our self-regard, nice bastards; in the clutches, we don't change — we revert to form. He could no more violate his self-image of the gentle, loving man than he could shed his skin. Nor, finally, could he deny either his love for Laura or his longing for the escape from death she so poignantly — if so impossibly — held out to him. He went only thirty paces before her last words at the shopping plaza caught up with him — "I can't walk away from you, you know" — and his heart dissolved in an insanity of desire and compassion. His quite praiseworthy wish to see only the briefest, most surgical pain inflicted by his hand went the way of all concupiscent desires: it was just another lovely part of his nature, and it was mugged by all the other parts in the grand, eye-gouging, knee-in-the-groin war in his members — in one of the endemic rumbles between rival street gangs that was the only action left in the ghetto of his being.

The second option was to show up, go on with the affair, and just hope she never found out about his inevitable welshing on her. But that possibility went whistling even faster than the first. It had, in fact, been closed out long ago by his invocation of the Law of Romance: he really did believe that the impossible commitment was holy, just, and good; and after Catharine, he knew he could never even try to serve it again without being honest. It was the old double bind: by your very delight in the Law in your heart of hearts, you are brought into captivity to the

59

law in your members. The faker who has finally come to a noble loathing of his fakery has no choice but to expose himself as a fake.

Which, of course, was the third option: the Dare. Tell her the truth and take your chances. Suddenly, oddly, he felt almost cheerful. His mind flitted to a passage from *The Elder Statesman:*

> If a man has one person, just one in his life,
> To whom he is willing to confess everything —
> And that includes, mind you, not only things criminal,
> Not only turpitude, meanness and cowardice,
> But also situations which are simply ridiculous,
> When he has played the fool (as who has not?) —
> Then he loves that person, and his love will save him.

For the first time since he had confessed to Catharine, he admitted into his mind the thought of what it might be like to live without the burden of his duplicity. It was as if he had been on an endless forced march with a sixty-pound pack on his back. It's the kind of situation you eventually become inured to; you even forget you ever seriously hoped to get out of it. But then someone not clearly friend or foe drives by with an empty truck, stops, and waits for you to catch up. And you think to yourself, "Oh, God; maybe . . ." And all at once, in the moment before the moment of truth, you are stunned by the weight of the doubt, and thrilled by the hope of deliverance, and terrified by the fear of false hope; and you are angry and sick and sad that you have no control over any of it.

But when your case is like Paul's, it is the terror and the sadness that ultimately prevail. Somewhere else in *The Elder Statesman,* Lord Claverton observes that no one confesses where there is no hope of forgiveness. That was true. When Paul confessed to Catharine, his confession, however long it was in coming, was finally made in the hope — no, that is too weak — it was made in the presumption of forgiveness, a presumption so strong that the confession itself was hardly more than an embarrassment. The thought that absolution might be withheld never occurred to him: he knew he would be forgiven out of love. But he wasn't; and the shipwreck of that certainty had become the governing experience in his mind. In thinking of confessing to Laura, therefore, he could find no knowable reason for doing it. All he knew was that, barring some miracle of indifference or inattentiveness in her — some bizarre turning of a tin ear to his cacophony, some defect of mind that would tolerate the standing of all known values on their heads — he would simply be condemned again. Oh, yes. She had held out the promise of forgiveness: "Mortal, guilty, but to me / The entirely beautiful." But poetry never saved anybody. She didn't know what he knew. And when she did . . .

Still, what else was there? Maybe if the confession were skillful enough . . . Maybe if it were set up right, with a suitable preface about the grimness of his experience, a first chapter devoted to his hatred of the burden, and a second designed to elicit her sympathy for what it cost him even to think of reopening the subject . . . Maybe it would just be possible to wheedle — no, that would be a recognizably false note — to maneuver her into a position where she would have to see the temptation not to forgive as a potentially greater crime than anything he could possibly confess.

But that hope died too. There was no such fallback position; the act would have to be performed without a net. He would make it across the wire, or he would go down. Either she would forgive him or she would not. There was nothing else to say. So he tried for a while to believe that she would, and he thought of her goodness, her braveness, and her openness . . . But then he thought of what he would actually have to confess to her: not only an inglorious past and a dismal present but a future that would just be more of the same — and the attempt to believe simply collapsed at the feet of his certainty that no one could forgive that much.

And so it was that he came at last to what he had to do. There was a fourth option, but it was so unlike an option that he had not been able even to think of it until he had proved to himself that all the other doors were locked. It was the option of a corpse at its own funeral: lie there and get on with it. Forget the mock heroics of confessing and dying, the stagey *contrapposti* designed to convey the truth while wringing tears from the audience. There would be tears — Catharine had cried — but not at the poignancy of his repentance or the agony of his death, only at the sadness of having to deal for the last time with a life that had been dead for years. His confession was simply part of the obsequies. It could be aimed at nothing but a quick and decent burial. He could keep, if he liked, the hope of a resurrection, but only for what it was: no hope at all; just the mindless, inextinguishable flickering of the poker player's perpetual hunch that maybe, even on this last of all hands, by going shy on every bet . . .

• •

He spent the rest of the morning at dull distractions in his office. He did not think of what he would say to her; there would be time enough for that at noon. Instead, he formulated, early in the day, some general principles to govern the saying of it, and he repeated them to himself like a litany. One: no names. Two: otherwise, spell it all out: flat-out involvement where it was that, trifling where it was trifling, and make the numbers as accurate as possible. Three: don't explain, don't overstate, don't criticize; just state. Four: don't plead, don't manipulate, don't contrive, and don't hope. For once, admit you're dead; because for once, you finally are.

When Paul drove over to the restaurant, he was quiet. He knew he would do it, and that was that.

9

Laura

Paul was five minutes early; she was five minutes late. Waiting, he felt oppressed by the crass normality of his surroundings: the blacktop, the cars, the foundation planting of junipers, the brown-stained cedar shakes of the restaurant walls, the water-wheel turned by a trickle from an ill-concealed three-quarter-inch pipe. Like the crowd at a wake, they were there on their own terms, not the corpse's — standing out in the sunlight swapping gossip and jokes, magnifying the enormity of death by paying no attention to it at all.

When she drove in, he walked over to her car. "Listen. Before we have lunch, I want to talk to you about something. Do you have a minute?" His bluntness, and the foolishness of the question, bothered him; but she took no apparent notice.

"Of course."

"Why don't you drive over to the far side of the lot and park there. It's quieter."

"All right." She waited a few seconds. "Don't you want to get in?"

"Oh. Sure." He walked around and slid into the front seat. After she parked, she turned off the ignition, rummaged in her purse for cigarettes, and put them on the hump in front of the gearshift. He asked if she needed a light.

"No. Talk first."

He looked at her once, exhaled, and fixed his eyes on the glove compartment latch. "Well . . . Look. I've never done this before, so I have no idea whether there's a better way to do it or not. Just let me run it out. First of all, I love you. That's true, and there's no way I could take it back even if I had to. But I have to tell you something. It's . . ."

He started to say, "It's probably not what you're afraid of," but that sounded like second-guessing or manipulation and he broke off. Damn! He had hardly begun, and it was beginning to go badly. He could feel in his bones the old Indian-wrestling skill itching for a chance to get into action, to set her off balance with a feint at calling the whole thing off — to play on her fear of being ditched — and then reassure her before getting around to what he really had to say. Resignedly, he began again.

"All right. I'll say it as straight as I can. No commentary, no embroidery. I got to where I am by thinking of being naked with you and wanting that more than anything in the world. That's not embroidery; at least I don't think it is. But anyway, the closer I got to the actuality, the more I realized I couldn't be naked with you — with you, not with just anybody — couldn't be physically naked with you until I was mentally naked first. That's odd for me, because I've spent most of a lifetime covering up with people, keeping them in separate compartments, giving each one only as much information about me as I saw fit. I'm a hider, and my hiding has always been my armor. Nobody ever got the whole story about me, except once. Even now, it'd probably be better left hidden. But I just can't leave it that way with you."

A long, explanatory parenthesis began to form itself in his mind: some background first, perhaps; then an account of the struggle over whether to tell her the truth, and the discarding, one by one, of the three options; and finally, an exposition of the deadness he felt. He threw it all away.

"Okay. No minced words. One way or another, I've been involved in a number of affairs. For years. And not only have I been; I am now. Not that I considered — or consider — them all love affairs. There was really only one I ever did. But that makes very little difference. I mean, it's no excuse; because whatever I may have had in mind, the women concerned thought they were love affairs, and I didn't do anything to disabuse them of that notion. Well, maybe all of them didn't think so. There were a couple who seemed to take it as just friendly sex, but most of them took it as Romance with a capital 'R.' Which is why my mental reservation about having only one real love was nothing but a first-class gyp. It just meant that I was handing them a lot of attenuated devotion and allowing them to pick it up as if it were the deluxe article. Except in that one case. Being as honest as I can be, I still think I really meant that to be unqualified, even though all the messing around seems to argue against it. At least it was unqualified enough for me to confess to her what I'm telling you."

Obviously, there was an opening there for something. But what? The results of that confession? No. That smelled like a self-serving comparison — a subtle challenge to Laura to do better when her turn came. Leave it.

"Look. This may be crass, but I promised myself I'd give you numbers. All told, over the years, maybe ten. Right now, four and a half: three flat-out and three not quite, with the not quites counted as halves. It's clear enough, isn't it? I mean, that I'm confessing not just the past, but also the present and, as far as I can see, the future too? But I'm not asking for permission. I'm really not. It's inconceivable to me to ask for it. I know it sounds stupid, but I really would like to get out from under it all. It's just that, knowing what I know about myself, I can't see it happening. I want to end it, but I know I won't. It's a mess."

Laura had been watching him. She turned her head slightly and looked out through the windshield. "The one . . . is she part of the four and a half?"

He took several seconds to pick up her meaning. "No. That's all over. Washed up. A year ago."

She said nothing. In the silence he tried to think of what should come next. He felt as if there should now be some spate of words to breathe life into the dry bones he had scattered — some more telling, more damning or excusing peroration to flesh them out. But he couldn't think of a single word. Suddenly, nakedly, he had come to the end. He had done, he supposed, what he had set out to do: the corpse had been displayed. But it had been such an inadequate performance, such a perfunctory, mumbled funeral, such a tiny handful of dirt to throw on something so many years in the doing and so many hours in the repenting. But still, it had been done — and with a certain miserable consistency at that: he had slopped through his life all the way, up to and including the end. If he had omitted details, he had at least conveyed the texture of it: it was a mess. Let it lie. He settled for a last, summary stab at clarity.

"There's not much more to say. I don't know if I'm really confessing guilt at sliding between all those sheets or not. I've had too many minds on that. For a couple of years there, I thought it was all right, and maybe I still do. All I know is that now I want to give myself to you . . . God! It all sounds so corny and half-assed. . . I want it to be different, but I just don't see any way out. I tell myself that the reason for that — for the inescapability, I mean, for not knocking it off with all of them — is really kindness. You know: you've done enough damage by promising; the least you can do is suffer the consequences of your promises and hang in. But I don't know if that's a lie, or the truth, or half-and-half. To be honest, I probably think it's half-and-half. Which is just one more unacceptable idiocy. Let me shut up. All

I know is that I love you and that I had to confess — to you, nobody else — the duplicity. That's the only point. So, Amen. Christ!"

For the first time, he turned and looked at her. The sun was in her hair and on her skin: rufous, warm. His resolve not to plead trembled for a second and then collapsed.

"One more thing. I wasn't going to say this; but it's at least as honest as the rest, so I will. When I look at you right now, I have the feeling that I'm separated by only the thinnest veil from some place where everything is all right again — where I'm alive and not a mess anymore. But the veil is transparent steel or something, and there's no way I can get past it. It might as well be a stone wall. In fact, it would be better if it were, because then I couldn't see the other side and long for it.

"It's like one of those drawings of a pyramid of blocks that your eye reads one way normally, but if you master the trick of looking, you can see it with the blocks reversed, flipped into another configuration. Looking at you, I want more than anything in the world for there to be another configuration; and somewhere, deep down, I think that maybe there might be. But I can't remember the trick of looking, and I'm left only . . ." His next words would have been "with this horrible sadness," but he never got them out.

"Paul?"

He stopped and was quiet. She reached over and touched his hand. "You don't need to remember any trick."

"What do you mean?"

"You didn't have to tell me all that."

"Yes, I did. At least, *I* did. I'm sorry you had to hear it, but I had to say it. No more fast shuffles. Not with you."

"I understand that. All I meant was I didn't have to be told. I knew."

"You knew?"

"Well, not the specifics. But I did know. It's just you, you know; just who you are. Maybe someday you'll have a choice about it. I don't know. All I know is, I have no choice. Last Monday, when you held me and kissed me in the back foyer over there, I was afraid of it — afraid that I wouldn't be able to take it, that I'd be hurt and go back on you. But then that was the end of it. I love you. There's no way of sorting it out."

He put his arms around her and buried his face in her neck. After a while, he sat up and rubbed his eyes. "You're incredible."

"I have clay feet too."

He let it pass. "God! Do you realize what it's like to be able to stop trying to make yourself matter?"

She leaned over and kissed him. "*We* matter. That's all. Take me to bed."

• •

And that, finally, was that.

However, since Paul had not entertained even the possibility, it took him a minute to catch up with the fact. "You mean, now?"

"Of course."

"No lunch?"

"No lunch."

"But where?"

"I don't know. Not in bucket seats. You decide."

"There's a motel a couple of miles past the shopping plaza. Is that all right?"

"Of course."

He sat back in the seat with a dazed smile on his face. For the first time there was no more need to pretend. "It'd be better if we used one car. Drive over to mine and we'll switch. Desk clerks never ask questions, but there's no sense providing the rest of the world with more evidence than it needs."

"I adore you."

10

Resurrection

If this were a novel, it would be high time for something catalytic, if not cataclysmic, to obtrude itself upon Paul and Laura. They are almost but not quite bedded. Some disruptive or malevolent presence should now begin to hang over the proceedings; the roll in the hay that threatens so shamelessly and so effortlessly to happen should have at least a little body English put on it. A brush with discovery, perhaps, or a hint of accidental pregnancy — or, failing all else, some mindless, external evil that the reader sees but the lovers know nothing of: a thirty-foot white shark, say, cruising the moonlit waters while they skinny-dip in a secluded cove.

Unfortunately, I can give you nothing of the sort. I precluded discovery from the start; Laura's menstrual cycle is not propitious for conception; it is noontime; and I have just put them three miles from the nearest salt water. My one concession to novelistic development — the single obtrusive event in the history of their romance — has already occurred: it was the bumping of the shopping cart into the back of Paul's car. Admittedly, that was hardly galvanic, let alone catalytic; but it's all you're going to get.

And the reason is that this is not a novel. It is a parable. The protagonist of a novel can be subjected to as many crosses and contretemps as credulity will put up with; but the main character of a parable can be allowed no problems at all. "Ah, but!" you say. "What about the soul-searching of the Prodigal as he slopped hogs and sat among the husks? What about the painful screwing up of his courage to the point of repentance and return? And what, for that matter, about Paul's miserable morning just past?"

To which my answer is that you miss my point about the main character of a parable. But then, if it's any comfort to you, setting you up to miss the point of parables is the very point of speaking in parables. After all, they are told so that seeing you might not see, and hearing, you might not understand. The major ones, in fact, have been dim-wittedly misnamed: they are not at all about what the popular imagination takes them to be about. The Laborers in the Vineyard, for example, is about the Owner, not the Laborers; the Prodigal Son is not about the Prodigal but the Father.

Moreover, in the case of the latter (which is the germane one here), the popular imagination misses not one star performer but two. In our genius for preferring the peripheral to the central, we rank the Prodigal as the major figure in the story and give the Elder Brother second billing. In fact, however, the Prodigal and his sour sibling are minor players; the star billing is reserved for two others: the Father and the Fatted Calf. It pleases me that, in my version, Laura gets to play both parts.

To make her pregnant, therefore, or to toy with the prospect of feeding her to the fishes would be as idle as having the Father break a leg running down the path — as foolish as wondering whether it might not be a nice touch to have the servants rush back and report the Fatted Calf stolen. A little nail-biting and character development are allowable in a plausible, secondary character like Paul the Prodigal; but Laura, the implausible principal of the story — the divine surrogate whose role is to think the

71

unthinkable and do the undoable — must sail through her accomplishment without so much as a tangled sheet.

For at their heart the parables are about a Mystery of Grace that makes mincemeat out of plausibility. The lesser lights in them may be made as fallible and accident-prone as you like because, after all, they are simply surrogates for us. Like us, they come through hardship to the stars. But the stars themselves — lights of the first magnitude like Laura — must be securely at home in the Mystery from the beginning. It is their role to reveal the blinding, mind-boggling news that God has no problems with Sin. To give them problems, then — to hide their light under a bushel of trouble — is simply fatuous.

Accordingly, Laura's performance as the Father, so flawless up to this point, will continue to be so. And so will her tour de force in the role of the Fatted Calf. I said a minute ago that it was the co-starring role. But it is more. In some ways it is the lead. The Fatted Calf is what the Father's forgiveness is aimed at from the beginning. He wants his son home not so that they can spend their days in the confessional box but so that, having gotten past that tiresome preliminary, they can both get on with the lavish party which is the specialty of their many-mansioned house — and of which the Fatted Calf is the supreme sacrament. Grace aims at the celebration of life: "Let us eat, and be merry: for this my son was dead, and is alive again; he was lost, and is found." Indeed, Grace is the celebration of life, relentlessly hounding all the non-celebrants in the world. It is a floating, cosmic bash shouting its way through the streets of the universe, flinging the sweetness of its cassations to every window, pounding at every door in a hilarity beyond all liking and happening, until the prodigals come out at last and dance, and the elder brothers finally take their fingers out of their ears.

It would have been better, therefore, if I had not provided Laura with a sedan. Ideally, their celebrative congress should have occurred at the very moment of Grace; the music and dancing should have burst immediately upon the scene in the instant when, with a smile, *La Exigenta* turned out to be a pussycat. Then and there on the spacious back deck of a nine-passenger wagon — preferably with fireworks in the grand tradition of Cary Grant and Grace Kelly — Paul should have availed himself of what, but for his estrangéd face, had been available to him from the start.

But it was a sedan. And Laura was right to sense, in bucket seats and floor-mounted shift, impediments to proper celebration. After all, even in the original parable, it must have taken a while to get the stalled ox going properly; her intuition that the best should never be served half-baked was simply one more perfection of her role. I urge you, therefore, to be patient. Their feast will not be as long in the preparing as the Father's was.

● ●

But in the minutes it takes them to drive to their bed of green, or plaid, or whatever it will be, you and I should probably have a brief talk. I detect an ever-so-slight narrowing of your mind's eye, a small but potentially devastating question forming at the base of your brain — an incipient misunderstanding of what I am up to — which, if left uncorrected, could drive us light years apart.

You think, perhaps, that I am about to move too quickly from confession to celebration. "After all," you say, "Paul's honesty with Laura, commendable as it is, is hardly more than the first course of cinderblocks in the house of his eventual truthfulness. Might we not better wait a while — at least, say, till the raising of the roof beam? Would it not be better to hold off the rewarding case of beer until he has leveled with, if not all concerned (we understand that telling his wife might be a bit tacky), then at least with the other four-and-a-half, or six, or however many it really is, whom he has by his own admission been conning?"

Well! You raise a number of issues. Let me deal with them one by one.

First of all, your question betrays a misunderstanding of the nature of confession. It assumes that a confession, if the penitent is properly sincere, not only will make a difference in his life but will make a difference for the better — that it is a kind of transaction in which a sufficiently humble, or painful, or embarrassing act of acknowledgment is automatically rewarded by a general distribution of the wherewithal for restoration and reform — that, in short, confession is good for the soul. But at best, that is a very tricky half-truth. It must always be accompanied by a resounding qualifier — namely: *But it all depends on whom you're dealing with!*

In the popular view, confession is thought of as a process of fixing up one's own insides — of coming to one's self as the Prodigal did and deciding finally to straighten up and fly right. But in truth, anyone who honestly comes to himself comes not to the formulation of a new flight plan but to the recognition that his life has the glide angle of a Coke bottle, and a broken one at that. True repentance leads only to the conclusion that the time for the repair of one's life is over and gone and that one is in need not of a physician but of an embalmer — or *per impossible* and unthinkably, *of someone who can raise the dead.*

The point is crucial. Confession is not the first step on the road to recovery; it is the last step in the displaying of a corpse. And for that reason it can have only two natural effects on those before whom it is made: with luck, sadness; with none, disgust. But in any case, no one in his or her right mind will hang around very long. The cardinal rule of life is to have as little truck as possible with death. Accordingly, it is simply pointless to confess to anybody unless you are either prepared to stay dead or sure that the person you are dealing with is committed to, and capable of, raising the dead. Anyone up to less than that will just insist, glumly or gladly, on shoveling dirt onto your coffin.

Therefore, since no one ever knows, for sure and in advance, whether his or her confessor can really raise corpses (as Martha said: Resurrection is a neat idea, but what are the odds of its working with someone *this* dead?) — and since, in this vale of bookkeepers, the chances of finding such a wonderworker are slim indeed — the likeliest outcome of your scheme to have Paul let it all hang out in front of everybody will be only to provide him with six more pallbearers.

Which brings me to my second point. Your question belies a further confusion about the relationship between confession and reform. You seem to think that they are somehow causally intertwined — that confession will by its very nature initiate reform and, conversely, that any confession not followed by reform is no true confession at all. But that is simply false. Confession is the admission of death; and death is obviously in no position to cause anything — certainly not the conversion of its own deadness into a program of rehabilitation.

As a matter of fact, words like *reform* and *rehabilitation* should be ruled out of order. The only proper word here is *resurrection*. Confession is not a medicine leading to recovery. If we could recover — if we could say that beginning tomorrow, or the week after next, we would be well again — why then, all we would need to do would be to apologize, not confess. We could simply say that we were sorry about the recent unpleasantness but that, thank God and the resilience of our better instincts, it was all over now. And we would confidently expect that no one except a real nasty would say us nay.

But we never recover. We die. And if we live again, it is not because the old parts of our life are jiggled back into line but because, without waiting for realignment, some wholly other life takes up residence in our death. Grace does not do things tit-for-tat; it acts finally and fully from the start. Laura moves into Paul irrevocably and without condition; the tide of her rises in the wreckage of his existence and becomes his life. Not a supplement to it, not a corrective of it. Just *it*; just *everything*. In one instant, by his faith in her Grace, he becomes what Luther called the saved man: *simul justus et peccator*, a just man and a sinner at the same time. *Just*, because she accepts him; and *a sinner still*, because in her love she will not wait to do it.

Shockingly, then, it will be no skin off Paul's nose if he is still screwing around; it will be skin off Laura's. It will be nails through her hands and feet, thorns on her head, a spear wound in her side. He is saved by the impetuosity of her love, and he is saved far too soon. But he is saved.

And that is terrible. And when he sees the awfulness of it — when he finally understands the cost at which he has been loved into life — well, there is reason *there* for reform, if he wants to use the word. But the reform will be like nothing he once expected. It will be mostly tears and sorrow. Not a going from strength to strength but a lifetime of penance in the presence of the sacred, wounded head; a perpetual standing beneath the cross to mourn the well-beloved, yet thank her for her death.

Grace uses no sticks and no carrots. It just dies for our life. That is no doubt more unfair to all concerned than any tit-for-tat arrangement the world would ever make; but it is the only way we can live. If we saw it clearly, we would cry our eyes out over the sadness of it. But that is how it is: our joy comes by another's blood, and from wounds we open all our lives.

Once again, then, don't be in a hurry to shove people into confessing to everybody on the block. It's hard enough to find someone willing to forgive; and it's even harder to accept it when you do. It is quite sufficient for Paul to confess to Laura alone.

•　•

Besides. Parables are told only because they are true, not because the actions of the characters in them can be recommended for imitation. Good Samaritans are regularly sued. Fathers who give parties for wayward sons are rightly rebuked. Employers who pay equal wages for unequal work have labor-relations problems. And any Shepherd who makes a practice of leaving ninety-nine sheep to chase after a lost one quickly goes out of the sheep-ranching business.

The parables are true only because they are like what God is like, not because they are models for us to copy. It is simply a fact that the one thing we dare not under any circumstances imitate is the only thing that can save us. The parables are, one and all, about the foolishness by which Grace raises the dead. They apply to no sensible process at all — only to the divine insanity that brings everything out of nothing.

11

Beyond All Liking and Happening

Their bed, as it turned out, was indeed green. At least the bedspread was; and since it took an hour for them to get around to removing it, green was the background of their love. That, and silence.

After they were inside the room, he turned the privacy lock, tested it, and took her in his arms. His hands, at first joined behind the small of her back, parted and circled her waist. The muscles below her diaphragm contracted at the touch of his fingers. Her left leg moved forward and outward a little against his right. His first physical impression of her — his surprise at her chasteness — had been wrong. It wasn't chasteness; it was subtlety. She just began at a whisper.

He dropped his hands from her waist to her rump and, spreading his fingers as wide as he could, cupped them over the astonishing fullness of her. There was an answering contraction once again. He smiled a great, boyish grin and held her hard. Her wrists lay on his shoulders, her fingers at the nape of his neck. She half-lowered, half-turned her head and made a gesture of looking under her arm to where his hands were resting. Then she beamed back at him with the look of a child who has startled someone by jumping out of hiding.

There are people who are in touch with their bodies, and there are people who are not. But even among those who are, there is a further distinction to be made. Women of exquisite proportions are so used to inspiring reverence that they eventually begin to take themselves with a gravity that befits the keeper of the shrine. But women with features of exceptional generosity carry in themselves a mirth waiting only for some questing heart's astonishment to set it free. To make love to such a woman is to be let in on a lurking hilarity, to discover at the moment of one's own vast surprise at her pendulousness or her depth — or, in the instant case, at the grandeur of Laura's seat — a corresponding hidden laughter in her, a delicious self-satisfaction by which she answers her lover's amazement with a knowing and gleeful "Of course." Far from inviting piety, great breasts or buttocks call forth the coarse denominations of the eighth-grade vocabulary — words like *jugs* and *knockers* can hardly be kept *in pectore*; and for the learned, they make irreverent puns race through the mind: *Sedia Sapientiae; "What is the chief end of man?"*

But that is for old lovers. New ones just laugh in awkward delight and move on. Without letting go of the basis of their private joke, Paul backed her to the bed and fell on her.

Harold Ross, the first editor of *The New Yorker,* always insisted quite seriously that nothing was indescribable. There are some things, however, that are not worth describing seriously; and chief among them has to be the unrehearsed and unrehearsable ritual by which two people undress each other for the first time. Its only saving grace is that it is done *obiter* to something worth a trip through a minefield of vexations.

It begins, with deceptive ease, at the unbuttoning of blouse and shirt respectively. But then. Arms do not come out of sleeves

79

easily when bodies are lying down. The lovers disengage, therefore, and sit up. His shirt comes off with some dispatch, but her
blouse collar enmeshes itself in her necklace and their progress
comes to a grinding halt. For the first of several times during the
rite, the sacred words "Here, let me" are uttered while she unclasps
the offending jewelry.

Next, of course, the bra. For all our supposed liberation from
inhibitions to sexual freedom, is it not odd that the twentieth
century has made but a single contribution to the female wardrobe
that can conveniently be removed? I have in mind the half-slip.
But what good is that? To liberate the lower portion of the female
body only to find the upper half left inaccessible by a brassiere
hook of a design unimproved since the time of Boss Tweed . . .
why, it is easier for a camel to pass through the eye of a needle
— no, more aptly, it is easier for a woman to knot a boy's tie from
behind than for a man to undo a woman's bra from the front.
Again, the only solution is "Here, let me."

By this time, however, the point of the exercise threatens to
recede to an infinite distance; so they make such love as is possible
in their intermediate state until the *terminus ad quem* begins to
heave into sight once more. But then they have no choice but to
resume, all thumbs, the interrupted interruption. Her skirt must
be addressed: zipper and button must be found and conquered.
Next, his pants: first the belt buckle; then a pause while, one-
handedly, she worries the hook fastener in vain. Finally, "Here,
let me."

In the end, however, they reach the end. Or at least one of their
ends. But by such means! After five thousand years of recorded
civilization and twenty Christian centuries, the ultimate step in
undressing a contemporary woman is a gesture worthy only of a
caveman: skirt, half-slip, pantyhose, and panties are seized as if they
had one common waistband and hauled off in a single motion. The
motion is such, however, that while it achieves the immediate end,

80

it places the achiever approximately six paces from the end ultimately desired — and standing on his feet at that.

While he is up, therefore, he sits himself down on the corner
of the bed, takes off his shoes, removes his pants, and in frustration at what can only be a conspiracy on the part of the universe
to kill enthusiasm with the boredom of routine, stops short at
that and makes love with his socks on.

Laura gasped a little as he entered her, then took him home.
As far as he could tell from the soft, high whimper, she climaxed
immediately.

The exaltation of simultaneous orgasm as the Best Of All
Possible Ways to make love is another obfuscation foisted on us
by the modern world. There are times and places, of course, when
it is a nice, surprising touch — an interesting minor variation in
the enjoyment of a great and complex good. But to insist that
two people cannot truly do justice to the feast of feasts unless
they proceed through it in a contrived equality — she, not finishing the last grape on her *Sole Veronique* until he has eaten his;
he, not consuming a single *pomme soufflé* except in perfect syn-
chrony with her; and both, holding off the enjoyment of the
ultimate spoonful of *fraises à la creme fraiche* until they can go
down together and say, "Ahhh!" — why, it reduces the feast to an
Alphonse and Gaston routine. It is fun if it just happens; but only
people who are a little funny ever try deliberately to bring it off.

Laura, therefore, was through her first course before Paul
had done much more than touch his wine. But, sane man that
he was, he was pleased at her pleasure and, without asking,
fetched seconds.

The entrée, when served, was apparently even better than
the *poisson,* and he lost count after her third helping, delighted
only that the kitchen was able to keep up with her appetite. But
in the hour it took before she finally rested, he also lost something
more than count. He lost his lifelong preoccupation with counting

81

— and with all the other self-conscious conjurings by which the shaky sexual ego tries to instill confidence in itself. For in that hour, he found himself at last, and for the first time, gladly beyond the whole subject of sex. He was sustained not by his own efforts, which heretofore had been frequently in vain and often short-lived, but simply by her. She held him in her, she moved upon him, she surprised him with himself. And when he finally realized after long love how different it all was with her, he tried to tell her. But all she said was "I love your body." She kissed his chest and his neck, his eyes, his lips, and the cleft of his chin. "How do you shave in there?"

It was a line from an old Cary Grant movie, and it pleased him that she apparently thought of it without realizing. "You just work at it — and you cut yourself a lot. Actually, it was only half as deep when I first started shaving; but over the years I've excavated it into a real archaelogical dig."

She held herself close to him.

He ran his hands through her hair, his palms close to her head, the chestnut fullness of it gripped in the roots of his fingers: "You astonish me, Love."

Some words hit like cold water. The easy, neutral endearment — the word *Love* — reminded him with a shock of who and where he was. Like the philanderer in the Italian movie who called all his mistresses *"Tesora,"* Paul had made a point of seldom using any woman's proper name for fear of crossing wires. But here he was now, using the old, cagey generality in the arms of the new and saving particular — a sinner in the very thick of his justification. He was not past his death, as he had first imagined; he still carried the disparate collection of former lives within him.

What to do, then? Rinse out the offending mouth by working the name "Laura" into the conversation a certain number of times over the next five minutes as a kind of penance? He decided not. Let it pass, at least for now. Eventual congruence with the new

order was inevitable of course; but faking out a present congruence was just earning brownie points for himself. And cheap,
misleading ones at that. She had said, "It's just you; just who you
are." If she didn't have to sort, neither did he. His fidelity, at last,
was no longer to himself.

They were quiet for a long time. Paul stroked her hair and
said, "What are you thinking?"

"I was thinking how I like it when you say, 'You astonish
me.'"

"You really do. God! You really do."

•   •

Eventually they separated and lay side by side on the bed. She
pulled up the edge of the bedspread and tried to cover herself.

"You cold?"

"A little."

"Here, sit up." With a series of trampoline bounces, they
pulled off the spread, turned down the top covers, and slid in.
He pulled the blanket up and tucked it around her neck. "Better?"

"Much."

"Too bad I didn't bring some wine. But then, that wasn't
really a possibility, was it? And anyway, I'm not *very* sorry."

A joke ran through his mind, a mock statistic about American
men: after intercourse, fifteen percent light up a cigarette; ten
percent reach for a drink; and seventy-five percent get up and go
home. He didn't tell it. Why? Too offhand? Too cynical, too close
to home for her sensibilities? No. The reason was not in her but
in him. This time he caught the old man before he threw out the
line; or, better said, he caught the old hider before he pulled his
famous disappearing act and jumped behind a joke to avoid the
consequences of closeness. Instead, he put his arm around her
and drew her to him.

83

She lay her head on his shoulder and spoke against his chest. "You know? All my life, I've known I would be here . . . Well, maybe not all. Maybe just since I was seven or eight."

"How do you mean?"

"I don't know. I just always knew that I was never at home anywhere, but that I would be someday . . . and this is it."

What occurred to him to say sounded extravagant, but he said it anyway. No man, having put his hand to the plow, and looking back . . . "You're *my* home, Laura."

She repeated his words slowly "I . . . am . . . your home. And you are mine."

They lay still. He kissed her eyes, her face, her mouth. Suddenly she lifted herself on one elbow and spoke: "I know this sounds funny, but for a long time I just couldn't believe that I was a body. I don't mean not anybody. I mean not a body at all. And that's weird, because I really am in touch with my own body — I sense when anything is out of line. I'm almost never sick, but when I am, I hate it. And when it's not just one thing that's out of line, but sort of everything — when it's not just being ill, but a kind of not being there at all . . ." She faltered. He waited for her, saying nothing. "When it's like that, it's like being dead. But that's over now. You're my life."

He kissed her again. "That's hard to believe. As far as I'm concerned, it's the other way around. And when it comes to your thinking you're not a body. God! You are the most bodily woman I ever knew. Every move says so. It's just inconceivable to me that you could sense yourself the way you obviously do and still not know that."

"That's only sense. It works two ways. If you can't believe in your own being, it makes you feel worse — like going through the motions with no hope. It makes you feel like a mourner at your own funeral."

"I know."

84

She said "Good," slid herself to a sitting position against the headboard, and lit a cigarette. She put her right hand under his head and smoked in silence for a while. "You know why I think you give me back my body? I read somewhere that in the order of nature, places create persons, but that in the order of grace, persons create place. I'm not sure what that means, but it seems to fit. Before you, everything felt as if it was nowhere, so I was nothing too. But with you . . . we create a place."

"And the place then proceeds to create us. Right? Nature to grace, and back to nature."

"Yes. That's really true, you know. The last step is to discover what you were from the beginning."

He waited till she finished her cigarette. "What time do you have?"

"I don't want to look."

"You're being a brat. By your own admission."

"That's right."

"All I want to do is be sure we don't put ourselves in the position of having to tear unceremoniously out of here. There should be a leisure about it. But since we do have to leave eventually . . ."

"I don't want to leave. Why should we?"

"You're right. There are a dozen reasons why; and there's no reason. But we will. So what time is it?"

"Two-twenty-five."

"Perfect. I don't have to be back till four. Come. Take a shower with me."

She slid down and kissed him. "That's better. I love you."

12

From Noon till Three

Paul adjusted the water temperature, pulled up the bypass on the spigot, and when the shower was running properly, spread a towel on the bottom of the tub. "Safety first. Who needs a broken hip to explain?"

She smiled and said "You're marvelous," as if she were admiring some vast wisdom. She seemed to take only pleasure in his obviously practiced savoir-faire, perfectly aware of the circumstances of its acquisition yet somehow unbothered by the awareness. One can imagine the Father of the returned Prodigal with such a smile. The Elder Brother, perhaps, has turned up with yet another of the prim, business-school types he insists on picking for girlfriends; and the Father, sitting on the verandah with his younger son, shakes his head in silent sadness as he watches the couple leave. After they are out of earshot, the Prodigal shakes his head too and says, "Christ! She'll probably keep books on him even in bed." And the Father smiles and thinks to himself, "At last! Who cares where he learned about women? Finally I've got somebody who knows what the score is."

They stood in the shower and soaped each other. Once again,

the ritual is not indescribable, but it is slightly overrated. What is memorable about it is not the operation itself. That is simply a mixture of routine and fuss: it takes time to lather two bodies, the soap drops at least once, and their freedom of motion is strictly limited by the necessity of keeping her hair dry. What stays in the mind is only the smoothness with which two bodies slide upon each other, the sense of liberation from the drag of friction. That, and the chasteness of the rinsing.

They got out and dried each other, but when they opened the door into the room, the blast of cold air set her shivering hard, and he took her back under the covers.

She lay in his arms till the chattering stopped, then sat up a little with the blanket pulled around her. "It's a voluntary cruci-fixion, you know."

The phrase came at him out of nowhere and made him distinctly uneasy. But he was learning fast to wait her out, and he did. She had a knack for misleading opening lines.

"I know I'm a brat about leaving you," she said. "But that's exactly what I ought to be. Men and women are different, I think. Men don't think about being separated from someone they love until the minute it has to happen. I guess they feel it just as much after that, but a woman feels it all the time, even when she's making love. She carries the pain of separation inside her, always feeling it but just deliberately ignoring it. That's why I react the way I do when you ask what time it is. For you, knowing the time is a way of figuring how much longer you've got before the pain starts; for me, it's just a recognition of the pain that's already there, and the beginning of the wait until it kills me."

"I never thought of it that way. Too bad there's always sadness."

"But that's all right. The sadness is inside the joy. At least it is as long as you keep it there — as long as you keep telling it it's not allowed to be the main thing. That's why it's a *voluntary*

87

crucifixion. And it's all right to complain about it. Jesus was a brat in Gethsemane."

God! he thought. You really did have to wait her out. Jesus, of all things! And at a time like this! He had expected her opener about crucifixion to be a lead to some second thoughts about his unreliability; but he had heard only the word *crucifixion,* not the word *voluntary.* If he had said anything he would have missed her point by a mile: she wasn't afraid of pain, at least not once she willed it. And apparently the only pain she was having trouble accepting was not the pain of possible hurt from him: that, she really had accepted for good in the back foyer of the restaurant. It was simply the pain of separation.

Which reminded him of something. "You know that passage from the *Horae Canonicae* I said I'd memorize for you? Well, I did; but there was something in it I'd forgotten about, and it bothered me when I came across it. The whole poem is about Good Friday; but the verse I was quoting had the words 'what happened to us from noon till three.' I don't know; I guess it was just that that was the time we spent at lunch on Monday, and I didn't want to bring up anything that mentioned the possibility of pain coming out of it. And today it just never came up till you said 'separation' — that's in it too — and suddenly it all fell together: Monday and Friday, from noon till three. Crucifixion. Separation. Weird."

"Not really. It's another validation. Anyway. I looked the poem up myself while you were gone. That's probably why crucifixion came into my head. Recite it for me."

He sat up and tilted his head back.

> "Nothing is with me now but a sound,
> A heart's rhythm, a sense of stars
> Leisurely walking around, and both
> Talk a language of motion

I can measure but not read: maybe
My heart is confessing her part
In what happened to us from noon till three,
That constellations indeed
Sing of some hilarity beyond
All liking and happening,
But knowing I neither know what they know
Nor what I ought to know, scorning
All vain fornications of fancy,
Now let me, blessing them both
For the sweetness of their cassations
Accept our separations."

He made a small wave with his hand. "Now that I hear it, the coincidences are more verbal than substantive. Still, they're coincidences."

"And therefore they still work — they still validate."

"You know something, Love? Your mind sails a course that comes within one degree of being just plain kooky, but I have never yet caught you crossing the line. Sometimes I think I have, but when I try to prove it, I end up agreeing with you. Of course, that could mean nothing more than that I'm over the line too. Who knows?"

"What did I say?"

"Oh, the business about the coincidences still validating. It sounds as if you're just hell-bent to get validation, and you'll take any liberties you need with meaning in order to get them — like those Shakespeare nuts who find astrological cryptograms in the sonnets. But then I think of some things I've said about the imagination — how the power of images isn't confined to the discursive framework but operates all over the lot, sometimes parallel to it, sometimes not — and I say what the hell. Auden isn't talking about the same separation we're talking about; but separation is separation, and every example of it, once admitted by name to the mind, has the full power of the image. So it perfectly well could be a validation, and therefore you're still sane. Or at least you're no crazier than I am."

"Good. While you're being a compulsive pedant, what's a cassation?"

"A serenade. Actually it has two meanings, and the pun is intended. Cassation as *serenade* comes from the German *Gasse, street* — a 'street song.' But it also has a French derivation, from *cour de cassation,* a final court of appeal: a cassation, therefore, is also a quashing, a settling, a cessation, an ending. So: the poem is called *Compline;* it's about the last Canonical Hour of the day — about going to sleep, which is an image of death. But it's also about Good Friday, so this is sleep under the shadow of the crucifixion, another image of death. But then the cross is the image of reconciliation as well:

> Garlic and sapphires in the mud
> Clot the bedded axle tree . . .
> Below, the boarhound and the boar
> Pursue their pattern as before
> But reconciled among the stars.

"And there you have the constellations singing — the music of the spheres harmonized into hilarity again — and I've gotten Eliot into the act for good measure. But it doesn't matter whether he or Auden came first, because once the images are in the mind their powers are concurrent and the voltage just builds and builds till it starts arcing all over the place, validating any damn thing you please." He pulled her down on the bed, rolled over on her, and kissed her. "You win, Love. I give up."

"How come you're on top, then?"

"Because you put me there."

"I did?"

"Of course. Don't try to be logical. It doesn't become you."

● ●

They gathered up their clothes and dressed separately, she in the bathroom, he in the room itself. He put on everything except his shoes and socks, then sat in the armchair and lit his pipe. He thought about having called her "Love" again. He didn't like it: Why, in this whole afternoon, did he call her "Laura" only once? He let it go. Dead is dead. Once you're raised, it doesn't matter.

She came out of the bathroom combing her hair, dressed except for shoes. "You got me wet."

"*We* got you wet. That's the biggest charge I'll plead to. Anything more and I call my lawyer."

"All right. *Guilty!* What do I sentence us to?"

He winced again. He thought for a moment, and then said, "Life."

She said nothing. Instead, she went back into the bathroom and fussed some more. Damn! Independent kookiness was one thing; but not to respond to a line like that . . .

Eventually, though, she called out to him. "You know? I knew we'd be lovers. A year ago."

Hell! She had him by the short hairs. "How'd you know that?"

"At the end of that first course of yours I took . . . There was this sort of sad girl who always seemed to be on the edge of everything . . . I think her name was Meredith or something dreamy like that, which just made her extra sad, because it sounded so romantic, but all her romances were nothing but disasters . . . Well, she asked me — I remember it was the last day of the course — 'Hey, are you and he lovers?' And I just said

91

'No.' But I also thought: 'Someday though, if you ask me again, I'll have a chance to lie to you.'"

She came out of the bathroom and quietly, almost gravely, went and knelt in front of him. Sitting back on her heels, she looked at him, then bowed herself to the floor and kissed his feet.

He bent over to raise her. "Hey! What's that for? I can't vouch for my feet."

She sat up. "Your feet are clean enough. I'm yours."

In silence he touched her face, her lips, her hair — and finally, *post longa tandem exsilia,* he cried.

She took his head in her hands and kissed his tears. "It's all safe, Paul. Call me before six."

> *Nostrum est interim mentem erigere*
> *et totis patriam votis appetere,*
> *et ad Jerusalem a Babylonia*
> *post longa regredi tandem exsilia.*

13

Morality vs. Grace

I t is a good place to leave them for a while — and it is the best of all possible last lines to leave them with. I apologize for the Latin, but it is a stanza from the hymn *O quanta qualia sunt illa sabbata* by Peter Abelard. The theme is heaven's endless Sabbaths, and he wrote it for use at Saturday vespers in the Convent of the Paraclete — of which Heloise was abbess. So if you are upset with me for crossing sexual and theological wires, reconsider your position. Better men than I have done it before — at higher prices, and with greater effect. Apparently, they found it worth the effort. If you doubt my word, however, reread the last chapters of Rose Macaulay's *The Towers of Trebizond*. It will make your hair stand on end.

In any case, though, it is a superb last line. I hate to give you the usual translation of it, because it isn't faithful to the joyous immediacy of the Latin — to the sense of participation even in separation. All the business about "yearning" and "sighing" just isn't in the original; it was forced in by the exigencies of English rhyme and meter. Nevertheless, I shall give it to you. As I write this, it is the feast day of blessed John Mason Neale, who translated it. It would be unthinkable not to give him equal space:

PARABLE

Now in the meanwhile, with hearts raised on high,
We for that country must yearn and must sigh,
Seeking Jerusalem, dear native land,
Through our long exile on Babylon's strand.

Neale did pretty well, considering; and some of his other translations are gems of correspondence. But just to get the taste of this one out of the mouth, let me give you one more stanza of the bright and luscious Latin:

> *Quis rex, quae curia, quale palatium,*
> *quae pax, quae requies, quod illud gaudium,*
> *hujus participes exponant gloriae*
> *si, quantam sentiunt, possint exprimere.*

There, that's better.

• •

You notice, of course, that suddenly you and I seem to have no company but each other's. Paul and Laura have been suitably launched: the vessel of their romance has slid down the ways and out onto the face of the deep. If it did not happen without some friction and heat, it at least came off without untoward event — which was, if you will recall, all I promised you. So here we are.

(You note also, I hope, that within the limits imposed by a personality which I would be the first to admit is an acquired taste, I am trying to be nice to you. That Neale translation really galls me. I would not have included it except for my desire to do as little as possible to antagonize you any more than I have. We already have quite enough gaps between us.)

Let us begin, therefore. If I assess your mood correctly, you are still of two minds. On the one hand, you wish Paul and Laura well (as who would not?). You see clearly, in your heart of hearts, that the brave really do deserve the fair, and vice versa; and that there is no other way of bringing about the eschatological realization of that proposition — given the case histories of the brave and the going price of the fair — than by the foolishness of grace. You are glad, in short, as any sinner would be, that Laura did not stick at being stuck — that she was to Paul what the Gospel tells us God himself is to us all: the gracious and ultimate stuckee.

On the other hand, however, you carry in your head, at a respectful if not infinite distance from your heart of hearts, a Resident Professor of Moral Theology who politely but firmly takes continual exception to your gladness — who suggests that surely something more than my parable of wishful folly is necessary if we are to plumb the depths of the mystery by which we are finally restored. In short, you have an in-house ethicist who cannot stand the fact that before long, Paul is probably going to climb into bed with one of his previous partners.

Let me review for you some of the devices by which your personal moralist approaches this problem. He is not an unreasonable fellow, and he makes at least some effort to reach a compromise with your heart.

He first argues that the situation might be rendered acceptable if Paul undertook, successfully, to do no *new* screwing around. He very nearly perfects a line of argument which holds that lapses into sexual congress with former colleagues between the sheets can be viewed as occurring under a kind of adjournment *sine die* — and accordingly may be, if not recommended, at least seen as included in the death to which Laura's grace triumphantly brings the power of resurrection.

But then he makes some errors typical of the moral theologian. First of all, he begins to harp on the word *successfully,* which he improvidently included in his reasoning. He forgets that from Laura's point of view, her grace was antecedent to *all* the un-

95

successes Paul laid before her and would, so long as it remained grace at all, have the same attitude toward subsequent lapses as it had to preceding ones. But second, he subtly insinuates into his reasoning the idea of a *minimum condition* and lodges it in the very concept of grace. Thus he leads himself to postulate that while Laura may reasonably be expected to put up with Paul's recidivism vis-à-vis Janet (to take the next-to-the-most-difficult case) or, in the most difficult case of all, with Catharine (this is a tremendous concession on his part, but he does understand the power of the buried past; he does have a heart — located, unfortunately, in his head), he is not about to let grace write out a permission slip for Paul to sleep with some stripper in a motel in Monticello.

However, having introduced this note of condition, he has effectively lost sight of grace. It is only a matter of time before he arrives back at law. Next, therefore, he includes a further condition: not only must Paul sleep scrupulously alone in Monticello; he must, on some reasonable timetable, begin to phase out Janet & Co. Congruence with grace — and please note what a contradiction in terms that is: congruence with the ultimate incongruity — becomes the condition sine qua non of its bestowal. And so our theologian comes to his inevitable emendation of Romans 5:8: "But God commendeth his love toward us, in that, while we were yet sinners, Christ died for us, *on the condition that after a reasonable length of time we would be the kind of people no one would ever have had to die for in the first place. Otherwise, the whole deal is off.*"

The gentleman in your head, you see, is a menace. At least I consider him so, in spite of his good intentions. Accordingly, there is nothing for it but for you and me to sit here and grapple in earnest with the text which is the *locus classicus* of this whole guilt-edged, blame-filled business — Romans 6:1-2: "What shall we say then? Shall we continue in sin, that grace may abound? God forbid! How shall we, that are dead to sin, live any longer therein?"

96

14

Two Pauls

Once again, let me gloss the text for you: *What shall we say then? Shall we continue in sin, that grace may abound?*

What shall we say then? The Apostle begins with a question because he has raised a question. He has said flatly, at the end of chapter five of Romans, that sin cannot hold a candle to grace: *But where sin abounded, grace did much more abound.* All Paul's liaisons, laid end to end, are not as wide as one hair of Laura's head.

But he sees clearly that in saying this, he has opened a loophole to every immoral opportunist in the world. Worse yet, he has gotten himself in Dutch with the moralists, all of whom are ready to scream "permissiveness!" at the drop of anything that even looks like an opportunity. Therefore, he puts the opportunist's gleeful spotting of the loophole in the moralist's dour mouth and boldly asks the question at its worst.

Shall we continue, he asks (the Greek is *epiménômen* — shall we stay on, abide still), *in sin?* But continue, stay, abide in what? In a pursuit of life, liberty, and happiness? In some course of action, in some possible series of choices? No. *In sin (tê hamartía* — not a verb, not an action word at all, but a noun, and in the

97

dative case): in the state of Sin with a capital "S"; in a state which for Paul the Professor was the same thing as death; in that centerless, lifeless nowhere of his former being — in that still, smashed terminus at which, after Catharine and before Laura, he had been deposited, seedy and by himself.

But consider this death of sin to which the Apostle refers: death does not rise; only life does. He does not ask this rhetorical question to tell our Paul he *ought* not to continue in sin. He does it to tell him he *cannot*. And for a very simple reason: Paul is dead. He has no "I," no living ego, no effective, vivifying, interambient self with which to make the attempt. He is a corpse, not a body; parts, not a whole. *Shall we continue in sin?* is a foolish question not because it proposes an inadvisable action but because it proposes it to a totally non-existent actor. There is no "we," no Paul, to do any continuing, whether in sin or in anything else. We have not lost our powers; we have lost our identity. Paul is not enfeebled; he is shot. There is, as he finally found when he tried to rouse himself to love Laura, simply nobody named Paul.

And therefore, when he was raised to life again by her grace, when the tide of her flowed like living water into the dead wreckage of his being, it was not the old Paul that rose but a new one: one who was the work not of Paul but of that wholly other life whose name became his soul. His screwed-up former existence — no, I want it stronger than that: even his screwed-up present situation — is no life at all. It remains death; and the Paul who brought it about remains dead for all eternity. Laura is the only life he has; his life is hid in her. "I live," he says; "yet not I, but Laura who lives in me." She is his resurrection. When she says, "We matter. That's all. Take me to bed," it is nothing less than "Lazarus, come forth."

Small wonder, then, that the Apostle mocks his own question with *God forbid!* The question is not only rhetorical; it is ridiculous — a patent contradiction in terms: "*Paul? Continue in sin?* Come now," he says. "How can a nobody choose to continue in nothing? Talk sense, man, or don't talk at all." There is only one Paul now, and when he hears his own voice speaking at the center of his life, he hears: Laura, Laura, Laura. And there is only one continuance now that sends his roots rain; and that too is Laura, Laura, Laura. As the Apostle might have said, had he written more fully of his own experience: "For me, to live is Christ. I am dead, and my life is hid with Christ in God. *You ask me about someone named Saul. Let me think. Saul? Ah, yes. I remember a Saul I knew once. But that was in another country; and besides, the poor bastard is dead. Jesus, Jesus, Jesus.*"

You still do not see? Dear me. You feel I am forcing my parable? I am not. It is you who are forcing it by trying to make it apply too broadly. Let me put it another way.

Do me the favor of focusing your mind very narrowly on the last scene between Paul and Laura. Get all the moral baggage out of the picture. And forget about whether the emotional fervor of that moment will, a week or a year hence, survive. I am trying to get you to feel the force of what the Apostle is saying, not calculate the actuarial risk of writing a policy on it.

In that moment, therefore: in that moment only, when she knelt and kissed his feet and said "I am yours" — in that one instant of recognition when at last, after long exile, he found himself alive in Jerusalem again, in that single burst of tears when his captivity was finally over and the songs of Zion were on his tongue in no strange land — do you seriously think that then and there he hankered for some corner bar in Babylon, *that while Laura kissed his eyes, he had the least interest, say, in making out with Janet?*

Of course you do not. And in your further wisdom, you see that the possibility of his future declination from that height of awareness has nothing to do with the case. You see that such a "fall from grace" would not be a fall from grace at all. At the very most it would be a fall from faith, a piece of stupid mindlessness by which he ceased to apply himself to the only life he has.

But do you also see something else? Do you see that to lose faith is not to lose grace? That to return to death is a radically meaningless act because we remain alive, even in that return, by the unlosable grace which insists on our resurrection willy-nilly? Do you see that Christ raises *all* the dead, the just and the unjust, the faithful and the faithless alike? And that he raises them *now*?

Suppose that in a week or a year, Paul does revisit Babylon. Suppose he goes back to his death. Suppose even that he does it again and again. Ah! Now you see, perhaps, why I was so adamant about not giving Laura any hang-ups: as long as her grace remains grace, she remains the only life he has — even while he is whoring around in some Babylonian dive. Whether he behaves or misbehaves, he is dead from start to finish but for her. Unchanging, unswerving, she goes on being his resurrection, the one center at which his sins are always forgiven. All he has to do the seventh time, or the seventy-times-seventh time, is the same thing he did the first time: confess, admit once more the truth of his abiding death, and trust once again the life that never left him for a second.

Only an idiot, the Apostle says, could ever confuse that with permission. Saint Paul is not talking about morality at all; morality is for the living. He is talking about death, and the only thing that makes sense when you have to deal with the dead is resurrection. He is not pointing out some possible course of action whose permissibility or impermissibility might be a matter of debate (you have, after all, always had permission, within wide limits, to go ahead and do any damn fool thing you wanted to); rather, he is pointing out a metaphysical impossibility: *you can't get away from a love that will not let you go.* When the Resurrection and the Life says "Lazarus, come forth," the rest of the story does not depend on Lazarus. He can drag his feet all the way —

100

admittedly, a hell of a thing to do — but he rises, no matter what. He just plain does.

The Apostle, however, goes even further. Not content with setting up the permission-seeking opportunist and the opportunity-hating moralist as idiots, he presses his case and makes complete fools of them: *"Shall we continue in sin,"* he has them ask, *"that grace may abound?"*

Do you see? He is tricking them into an even more glaring metaphysical impossibility than the first. He is having them suggest that there is some way in which sin can stand in a *causal* relationship with grace, some way that death, on its own motion, can produce resurrection — that Laura's love, in short, can somehow be an effect of Paul's screwing six other women. But her grace, of course, is not an effect of anything Paul does, good or bad. It is, at its root, uncaused by anything outside herself at all. Grace makes itself abound. There is no need — and no way — of forcing its hand.

Which is why, then, the Apostle begins verse two with *God forbid (mê génoito)*. There is a problem of translation here. The "God forbid" of the King James Version catches the urgency of the Greek, but the word *God* simply isn't in the original: that just says something like "Let it not happen!" Other versions render it in various ways. The Revised Standard Version says, "By no means!" — which catches Saint Paul's meaning better, but sounds far too relaxed. And the Vulgate translates it *Absit,* which means, literally, "Let it be absent!"

I propose, therefore, that we cut our losses, capitalize on the distinctive merits of each of these several versions, and combine the result in one new rendering. Let us keep the urgent negativity of the KJV's *God forbid!*, the almost Yiddish nuance of *It shouldn't happen!* in the original Greek, the refreshing note of *Get out of here with that jazz!* from the Latin *Absit,* and the sense of simple, literal impossibility in the RSV's *By no means!* — meaning, there

101

just isn't any way. The locution that seems to me best suited to combine them all is the phrase *No way!* as it came to be used in the sixties and early seventies (Would you vote for Richard Nixon? No way!). Accordingly, my version reads as follows: *Shall we continue in sin, that grace may abound? Baby, there just ain't no way! How shall we who are dead to sin live any longer therein?*

Perhaps now you see; though if you do not, it is not entirely your fault. Not only is Saint Paul's point difficult to grasp; its difficulty is compounded by the Apostle himself later in the chapter when he nods a little and lets his own resident moral theologian sneak a couple of verbs in the imperative mood into verses twelve and thirteen ("Let not sin therefore reign in your mortal body. . . . Neither yield ye your members as instruments of unrighteousness . . ."). He seems, for a moment, to slip back into mere commandment again, to be laying down the law in the old style. And since the human race can never hear law promulgated without wondering what the penalty is, we imagine the only penalty possible and conclude that the implied condition is: *". . . because if you don't behave, God will take his grace away from you."* To be sure, Saint Paul rouses himself at the end of the chapter and closes on the clear note of grace as a free and unqualified gift. But the damage is done, and the passage has sat on the page for two thousand years as a snare even to the wary.

Luther, too, got it only mostly right. Let me quote from his gloss on Romans 6:13-14:

13. *But,* here [Saint Paul] expounds the same idea even more clearly, *do not yield,* surrender or offer voluntarily, even though they may be so inclined, *your members as instruments, tools, of wickedness unto sin,* which is unbelief, so that they serve sin unto unrighteousness, *but yield,* present, even though your sin struggles against it, *yourselves,* your whole selves first, *to God as men who have been brought from death to life,* spiritually and

102

humbly, living in the spirit and not in obedience to sin, but consenting to righteousness, *and your members to God as instruments,* tools and servants, *of righteousness,* which comes from faith, that they may serve God unto righteousness. And you can do this easily: 14. *For sin will have no dominion over you,* unless you want it to. It cannot have dominion. The reason is: *since you are not under the law but under grace,* because you have fulfilled the law through faith in Christ, whose righteousness and work of fulfillment is yours by the grace of a merciful God which is given to you.

That is so close to the mark that it's almost a shame to fault it. And the fault in it is really so minor that one regrets withholding the rewarding cigar. But alas, it must be withheld. For the all-important seal between the realm of morality and the realm of grace — the ethics-tight bulkhead that every Christian theologian must strive unceasingly to build — has a leak in it. Perhaps not in Luther's own mind, but certainly in the minds of those who read him. And the leak is at the word *voluntarily* in the very beginning of the passage. Left unstopped, it slowly but inevitably lets the whole subject of morality seep back in and swamp the notion of grace.

For any talk of the role of the human will in the plan of salvation invites back into the Gospel of grace the purely moralistic distinction between sin and temptation — a distinction that Jesus once and for all tossed to the dogs when he said that thinking about adultery was as bad as doing it. It leads us to imagine that in the risen life of grace, while there may be all the trappings of our death — while there may be mental motions toward sin, nifty ideas of renewed tricks with old (or new) partners, *seeds* of possible sin — we are nevertheless still okay as long as we can say in our heart of hearts that we have not really watered the damned things and brought them to flower.

But that is simply the old law of salvation by our own integrity; and it blows the Gospel of grace to bits. In the risen life of grace, there are not just the trappings of our death, there is our death itself; not just the tinder of sin but the full, raging fire. That is simply true. To make a distinction between the unlit tinder and the blazing inferno, and then to suggest that as long as you don't get lit you're still safe, is to fly straight in the face of the Sermon on the Mount and to require not only more than human nature, even under grace, has ever been able to manage but also more than grace itself has ever demanded. It is a case of theological imagery riding roughshod over revelation. The Gospel invites us to believe not that we are safe, *provided,* but that we are safe *period.* It is not that sin *should not* have dominion over us but that it *cannot,* for its power has been destroyed by Jesus. It reigns in our death, of course, as it always did; but what is that? What is it to have sway over a valley of dry bones? The main thing is that sin does not reign over Jesus, and Jesus is our life.

And there is the crucial point: *Therefore, we are safe.* Not safe, *if* . . . Not safe, *as long as* . . . Not safe, *provided* . . . Add anything — even a single qualifier, even a single hedge — and you lose the Gospel of salvation, which is just Jesus, Jesus, Jesus.

"Ah, but!" you say. "What about faith? Don't you need to trust Jesus — doesn't Paul need to live in faith, in fidelity to Laura, in order to reap the benefits of his safety?"

All I can say to you when you ask such a thing is that, even though there is a skin of reason on what you say, I must tell you, No. Not because it is false, but because it is such a piss-poor truth, such an obvious piece of elementary blather, that you should be ashamed to throw it up to me. Of course, no man can enjoy an acceptance he denies. But she *died* for him, for Christ's sake! Do you still not see? She kissed his feet, she prostrated herself under the wheels of his great, brakeless dump truck of a life — and she did it all in advance and without proviso. His faith is trash compared to that. His hope is junk compared to that. There is, of course, still love; and it is still the greatest of the three. But even Paul's love, compared to the grace by which he is saved, is hardly worth a line of type.

Laura died — Christ died — without waiting for Paul to reduce his sins to the level of temptations. *Greater love hath no man than this, that a man lay down his life for his friends. While we were yet sinners, Christ died for the ungodly.* To work up a theology, then, in which you hold that someone who would do a thing like that is in reality still waiting to see whether you will shape up before she goes through with what she has in mind is simply to make chopped liver out of the mother tongue.

Once again, therefore, as the Apostle says no less than ten times in this epistle: *Baby, there just ain't no way!*

15

Spirituality vs. Grace

Having disposed of our Moral Theologian Residentiary, however, we must not leap too soon to the conclusion that our grip on the doctrine of grace is now secure. You and I and Paul (all of us, let us admit it freely, persons of a finer sort) have probably never taken moral theology with the seriousness that moral theologians think it deserves. Its straight-faced, strong-arm methods, its grim earnestness, its solemn insistence on the indispensability of rules from which all of us cheerfully dispense ourselves at the first glimmer of inconvenience — and above all its idiotic assumption, in the face of all evidence to the contrary, that good advice will produce good behavior — are simply and unappealingly silly. *We* know. *We* have lectured children. *We* have asked Christians for forgiveness.

But we are not yet, for all that wisdom of experience, secure. For we — we especially — carry in our heads another Reverend Gentleman, one of an appropriately finer sort himself, whose noble blandishments, while they are vastly more commendable than the moralist's pushing and shoving, are nonetheless just as inimical to a true perception of grace. This fellow is our Resident Spiritual Director, our Private Chaplain, our Personal Guru, whose forte is mucking up the doctrine of grace not in the name of ethics but in the name of Spirituality. His specialty is not commandments; it is counsels of perfection.

Let me show you him at work with Paul. Let us assume, not unreasonably, that by and by (and probably sooner than later) Paul's promiscuity tapers off — that he reaches a point at which he is indeed, physically and mentally, faithful to Laura alone.

I say "not unreasonably" because even though grace makes no conditions about reform, it does (and not always conveniently) produce the conditions that induce reform. Grace works our restoration the way the physical body works our healing: by producing a general tilt in the direction of health, by being a force for wholeness which, while it never forces, continually disposes us to become whole.

As Augustine said, "Before grace, we had no free choice about not sinning; the best we could do was *want* not to sin. But grace has the effect of making us not only want to do right, but also *able* to do it — not by our own powers, of course, but by the help of our Liberator."

Let us assume, then, that Paul has arrived at that blessed state where he is, within the limits of the admittedly different morality of this parable, a righteous man: he has one wife to whom he is attentive, duteous, and kind; and one mistress whom he loves as his own life. There are just Sarah and Laura. He is a proper romantic adulterer, happily married and wildly in love.

It is at this point that his Resident Professor of Ascetical Theology sits him down for a heart-to-heart talk about his spiritual development. He inquires whether Paul has thought, perhaps, of making a little retreat. He urges him to take time to dwell on the greatness of his acceptance by Laura, and on the shining newness of the life he enjoys through her. He suggests that Paul consider whether he has made not a proper romantic response to her — he has indeed done that — but the fullest possible romantic response.

Next, he reads a few passages of Scripture to him:

And the young man saith unto Jesus, "All these commandments I have kept from my youth up. What lack I yet?" Jesus said unto him, "If thou wilt be perfect, go and sell all that thou hast, and give to the poor, and thou shalt have treasure in heaven; and come and follow me." But when the young man heard that saying, he went away sorrowful: for he had great possessions.

If any man come to me, and hate not his father, and mother, and wife, and children, and brethren, and sisters, yea, and his own life also, he cannot be my disciple.

No man, having put his hand to the plow, and looking back, is fit for the kingdom of heaven.

But then Paul's Spiritual Director, being of the newer, non-directive sort, leaves him to meditate in silence on the obvious question: "If I really love Laura, shouldn't I divorce Sarah?"

And Paul, entranced by the vision of Spiritual Perfection, goes for it like a bluefish after a tin squid. He sees that to be truly perfect, he not only would have to break with his family but also would have to do it without putting the least pressure on Laura to do likewise. And the vision expands. He contemplates the offering of himself, and looking on while the Romantic Angel does wondrously and ascends in the flame of the altar. He sees himself holed up in his bachelor digs, having renounced all for love, pauperized by alimony payments, with nothing but Sunday-afternoon visitation rights and two weeks in August. And he weeps over the poignancy of it all; but finally, he dries his eyes, squares his shoulders, takes up the cross of perfection, and phones his lawyer.

108

Do you know what that is from the point of view of grace? It is a lot of malarkey. It is outrageous nonsense because what he is doing is forgetting the true Gospel of his salvation — Laura took him *without condition, before everything* — and inventing a false one. He is now concocting a gospel not of salvation by moral integrity but of salvation by poignancy and super-spirituality. He is perfecting a piece of bad news which says not only that heaven is just for good guys but that it is in fact only for good guys who can manage to go everybody else one better.

But it remains unacceptable. There is no way of tying the kingdom of heaven to anything we do. It comes because the King makes it come, not because we give it a helping hand. Paul may do any stupid or brilliant thing he wants with his freedom under grace; but whatever he does, he mustn't think it's worth a damn in the process of his salvation. Which is why, in my parable, Paul and Laura just do the graceful, sensible thing and stay lovers. They don't take on a lot of dumb, supererogatory vows.

The Reformers, you see, were dead right on this subject. They carried on — no, that's much too weak — they ranted and raved endlessly about the iniquity of works of supererogation, about the falseness of the notion that the gasoline of grace could be made to give better mileage if you put into it the additive of some more perfect performance.

Read Luther sometime on the subject of clerical celibacy. The Reformation was a time when people went blind-staggering drunk because they had discovered, in the dusty basement of late medievalism, a whole cellarful of fifteen-hundred-year-old, 200-proof grace — of bottle after bottle of pure distillate of Scripture that would convince anyone that God saves us single-handed. The Word of the Gospel, after all those centuries of believers trying to lift themselves into heaven by worrying about the perfection of their own bootstraps, suddenly turned out to be a flat announcement that the saved were home free even before they started. How foolish, then, they said, how reprehensibly misleading, they said, to take the ministers of that Word of free, unqualified acceptance and slap enforced celibacy on them — to make their lives bear a sticker that said they had gone an extra mile and paid an extra toll. It was simply to hide the light of grace under a bushel of pseudo-law, to take the sacrament of the Mystery and go out of the way to make it look as little like the Mystery as possible. And for the Reformers, that was a crime. Grace was to be drunk neat: no water, no ice, and certainly no ginger ale; neither goodness, nor badness, nor the flowers that bloom in the spring of super-spirituality could be allowed to enter into the case.

In my parable, therefore (if you insist on seeing it in the tawdriest possible light), Paul lives at home and loves on the side. For myself, though, I would rather say that he lives at Laura and loves everywhere. Because the ultimate mischief in the doctrine of salvation by spiritual perfection is its inveterate tendency toward exclusivity rather than inclusiveness, its drive to prescind rather than comprehend. In the name of a romantic purity, it takes the lover who sings in the shower before taking his wife out for a birthday dinner and tells him that the best thing he could do would be to get the hell out of his marriage. That it does its mischief under the guise of heroic generosity and total dedication is just more nonsense. The *via negativa* has its place; but not in the effecting of anybody's salvation. And even in its place, you have to watch it like a hawk: at the flick of a renunciation, it can turn just stingy, stingy, stingy.

So my parable stands as written: Paul and Laura and Sarah — and Catharine and Janet et al. — all stay where they are. Insofar as they live at all, it is by no devices of their own. They (and we) are dead, and our life is hid with Christ in God. We need not be covetous of crosses: there will always be plenty to go around, and there will be the grace that reigns over death in every one of them. We were never told that it would not hurt, only that nothing would ever finally go wrong; not that it would not often go hard with us but that *There is therefore now no condemnation to them which are in Christ Jesus.*

Take my yoke upon you and learn of me; for I am meek and lowly in heart: and ye shall find rest unto your souls. For my yoke is easy, and my burden is light.

16

Superstition vs. Grace

*There is therefore now no condemnation to
them which are in Christ Jesus.*

I think that my parable has taken us just about as far as it can. By the very fact that it is only a fictional analog to the dispensation of grace, it stops short of conveying to you the force of this ultimate proposition from Romans 8:1. It leaves you still in a merely possible world where you feel free to dawdle and dream before returning, as you see it, to the harsh realities of the daily grind. "Ah yes," you say, "a lovely story. How nice to think of what it would be like if, in the thick of my sins, I were told that I stood uncondemned by a love that would not let me go. Thank you for diverting me; it has been a pleasure meeting you. But now, alas, I must get back to the salt mine."

By its very nature, you see, my parable has brought you to the point of missing its point altogether. Saint Paul has not said to you, "Think how it would be if there were no condemnation"; he has said, "There *is* therefore now none." He has made an unconditional statement, not a conditional one — a flat assertion, not a parabolic one. He has not said, "God has done this and that and the other thing; and if by dint of imagination you can manage to put it all together, you may be able to experience a little solace in the prison of your days." No. He has simply said, "You are free. Your services are no longer required. The salt mine has been closed."

It is essential that you see this clearly. The Apostle is saying that you, and Paul, and I have been sprung. Right now; not next week or at the end of the world. And unconditionally, with no probation officer to report to. But that means that we have finally come face-to-face with the one question we have always thought we were aching to hear but which we now realize we have scrupulously ducked every time it got within a mile of us. It was the question I raised in the very first chapter, and it has been lurking all along: *What would you do with freedom if you had it?* Only now it is posed to you not in the subjunctive but in the indicative: *You are free. What do you plan to do?*

And Saint Paul means really free. Free forever. And not just because the salt mine has been closed. For who knows? The local authorities might change their minds in a day or a year and re-institute the prison system of blame and guilt. Heaven knows, they have never left it in abeyance for long in the past. No. You are free not because they have promised not to prosecute you but because they could not prosecute you even if they wanted to. And for a very simple reason: You are dead. You have fallen under the ultimate statute of limitation. You are out from under every-thing: Law, Sin, Guilt, Blame — it all rolls off your back like rain off a tombstone.

But (and this is the crucial point so easily missed) the Apostle says more than that. He says *you are dead to the law by the body of Christ.* Do you see what that means? It means that it is not only you who are dead and beyond the orbit of blame, but God too. God himself, the Supreme Lawgiver, Blamefixer, and Guiltspreader, has died to the whole sorry business in the death of Jesus.

There is therefore no condemnation for two reasons: first, there is nobody left to be condemned; and second, there is nobody around to do the condemning. And likewise, there is therefore *now* no condemnation for two reasons: you are dead now; and God, as the Lamb slain from the foundation of the world, has been dead all along. The blame game was over before it started. It really was. All Jesus did was announce that truth and tell you it would make you free. It was admittedly a dangerous thing to do. You *are* a menace. But he did it; and therefore, menace or not, here you stand: uncondemned, forever, *now*. What are you going to do with your freedom?

• •

I shall not — because I cannot — answer that question for you. I have enough trouble answering it for myself, so I shall just wish us both well. But, having warned you already about your Resident Moralist and your Private Chaplain, I feel I should also warn you of a third tempter who, even though you are now free in fact, will continue to work day and night to put you back in the only prison left: the prison of your mind. I shall call her the Old Party.

You have known her all your conscious life. She is your Resident Gossip, and she has had your ear so long and so success-fully that even though none of the superstitions and old wives' tales she has regaled you with have ever proved to be true, you still believe every word she says and tremble at the power of her tongue. It was she who, when you were five, told you that a cut in the flap of skin between your thumb and forefinger would give you lockjaw: she left you convinced for life that at the first, slightest scratch, your teeth would clang shut like a prison gate. When you were seven she informed you that wearing galoshes indoors would draw your eyes: to this day, even in ripeness and perfectness of age, your eyes grow heavy if you keep your boots on in the house. At nine, she warned you that stepping on a crack would break your mother's back; at twelve, that masturbation would turn your brains to mashed potatoes and grow hair on the palms of your hands; at eighteen, that fellatio would give you fever sores; at twenty-five, that you probably had an asymptomatic case of syphilis; and at forty, that adulterers always get caught. But all along and above all, it was she who persuaded you that even if every one of these dire metaphysical linkages between your actions and her version of the constitution of the universe should somehow fail, *God would still get you in the end.*

My parable is over. But were it to continue, the Old Party would now go to work on Paul with all the resources of her big, ignorant mouth. In the face of the overarching fact of his forgiveness, she would try to talk him into functional impotence with Laura just because, at some time subsequent to his confession of death, he strays for a moment and actually acts dead — just because, in plain English, he happens to screw around again. Or, stealing a page from the Spiritual Director's devotional manual, she would try to talk him into functional impotence with his wife on the grounds that the universe, which for years has paid no attention at all to his sex life, has suddenly set up an inexorable metaphysical connection between Sarah and Laura.

She will, in other words, worry him with any gossip she can find about what other people think, regale him with any fairy tale she can confect from astrology, psychology, magic, or religion, fill his head with whatever folk unwisdom, ancient or modern, she can lay a hand to, in order to convince him that the fictions which flourish in his death are somehow stronger than the fact which is his life. And all to one end: to get his mind — and yours, and mine — off that only fact.

Which is, of course, that we are dead and our life is hid with

Christ in God. Dead. Out of the causal nexus for good. Dead. Not on trial. Dead. Out of the judicial process altogether. Not indicted, not prosecuted, not bound over, not found guilty. Just dead. And the lovely thing of it is that we were dead even before they came to get us. We have beaten the system. In Christ, we have cheated the cosmos and slipped the bonds of every necessity the Old Party will ever wave in front of us. *There is therefore now no condemnation.* It doesn't matter what the universe thinks. It doesn't matter what other people think. It doesn't matter what you think. It doesn't even matter what God thinks, because God has said he isn't going to think about it anymore. All he thinks now is Jesus, Jesus, Jesus; and Jesus now is all your life. You are, therefore, free: spit in the Old Party's eye; it's the only language she understands.

17

The Picnic

I do, however, owe you two things. The first is an admission. I grant you that I have, in this parable, been working only one side of the street — that in my effort to do justice to grace, I have neglected justice itself. I am fully aware that in doing so, I have laid myself open to the charge of granting not only screwing licenses but also franchises for far worse things: for pride and prejudice, for torture and exploitation — in short, for getting away with murder.

In my defense, let me point out that Scripture lays itself open to the same charge — and that the other side of the street has been worked so long, so hard, and so often that most people don't even know there is a sunny side. The Terrible Trio of the Moral Theologian, the Spiritual Director, and the Old Party — one might almost call her the Old Party Pooper — have conspired to keep us from any prolonged and serious consideration of the doctrine of grace. Every time it is rediscovered, we send in an army of moralizers, backwaterers, and scholasticizers to get us clear of it in the shortest possible time. Bad enough that even Saint Paul, even Augustine, even Luther should have retrenched, however slightly, on their insights into grace; simply abysmal, though, that their assigns and devisees, in less time than it took to compose a *commentarium,* almost invariably put the subject into total eclipse. We hate and fear freedom, in spite of all our lip service to it. My parable stands, therefore, without apology. It is just my ten-cent contribution to Liberty's sadly impoverished Eternal Vigilance Fund.

But there's more to it than that. I have expounded Saint Paul to you as saying that not only are *we* dead to sin but that God is dead to it too — that he has put himself out of commission on the whole subject of blame. And so, indeed, he has: "I will forgive their iniquity, and I will remember their sin no more."

I am fully aware that the Scriptures are paradoxical — that God speaks with a forked tongue — and that every lovely thing he says on the side of leniency can be matched by a dozen stringencies that will curl your hair. But I am also convinced that each of us has to make a decision about such utterances. When someone tells you many different things about his attitude toward you, you must first look at him long and long, and decide for yourself whether you care about him at all. But if you finally come to the conclusion that you do care, you must then decide which of his words you will take as his *governing* word. You ask me why I think God's leniency governs his severity? Why grace is his sovereign attribute? Well, all I can say to you is that having been a father who has spoken out of both sides of his mouth to six children for twenty-six years — and having all those years believed in a heavenly Father who saves us not by sitting in his penthouse issuing edicts but by sending us the warm, furry body of a Son who drank the nights away with us and died obscurely of the foolishness of it all — all I can say is that I put my bet on the left fork of the tongue. It is my best hope that when my children think of everything I have said and done to them, they choose to remember the times of my severity when I just gave them a kiss on the cheek, poured myself a Scotch, and shut up. And it is my last hope that God hopes the same for himself.

So I really do make no apology for landing on the sunny side of the street. I am sorry if I have offended you; but to me there are some things that simply override everything that comes before or after. And I am sorrier still if you do not feel the same way. For without that ultimate cassation — without that final quashing of the subpoena, that throwing of the prosecution's case out of court which is the only music there is for the ears of the hopelessly guilty — you and I, Virginia, are simply sunk.

Accordingly, the second thing I owe you is some vision that will stir your imagination to go where your mind, and your emotions, and your history — and those three dreadful parasites in your head — have conspired for years to keep you from going; some image that will portray to you what the final cassation might be like; some picture to suggest at least one way in which God might avoid his own unavoidable justice, might know the enslaving truth about you and yet refuse to keep you bound: some scene that will convince at least your heart that you are free.

Imagine with me, therefore, two lovers in bed. Paul and Laura will do nicely, although this isn't about them anymore: it is about the two Ultimate Lovers, God the Father and God the Son — and about the Third Ultimate Lover, God the Holy Spirit, the Divine *Us,* who proceeds forth from their loving. Still, think of the Father and the Son, if you will, as a man and a woman in a motel from noon till three.

(I am aware that my switching of the Son's gender may bother you. You could solve the problem for yourself by thinking of all the passages where God the Son, the creating Word, is referred to in the feminine gender — where he is presented under the feminine image of the *Wisdom of God,* the *Sapientia Dei* who mightily and sweetly orders all things, the *Hagia Sophia* who was with him from the beginning — where he is called, in short, *Saint*

Sophie. Alternatively, I could solve the problem for you by making them homosexual lovers. But I have a feeling that might bother you even more than two heterosexuals in a Holiday Inn; let it pass.)

Laura told Paul she remembered reading somewhere that in the order of nature, place creates persons, but that in the order of grace, persons create place. One of the perennial problems of theology is how to imagine, how to figure to ourselves, the way in which God, having made the world and let it get out of whack, manages to get it back in shape. The problem is usually solved by thinking of God as coming down from heaven and fixing something: putting in a new fuse, or doing a valve job on the world so it will run right again.

But that introduces an impossible set of images. It suggests that God, in his deepest being, is at some distance from the world — that if he turns up at all, he comes as a kind of celestial road service doing incidental repairs after the damage has been done. But. If there is indeed therefore *now* no condemnation, it can mean only one thing: that from the most important point of view (God's), he was already on the scene before the damage was done, and he fixed it before it had a chance to do any final damage. Because if God can tell you that *now* you are uncondemned for some sin you are committing right now, or even will commit next week (and he does indeed tell you just that), then he's talking about something a lot more intimate to your being than some ex post facto visit by a garage mechanic. He's talking about something he is present to *eternally.* He is telling you that as far as his *Word* is concerned (and his Word *goes*), you have never been out of line at all — or, more accurately, that anything you may have put out of line was, in the very moment of its misalignment, realigned then and there by the suave and forceful *Wisdom* that goes through all things and is more moving than any motion. And above all he is telling you that what was announced in Jesus by that Word, what was done in Jesus by that Wisdom, was not the temporal start of the repair of your wreck but the final accomplishment of it from the beginning by the Lamb slain from the foundation of the world — by the Ultimate Beloved whose voice creates and reconciles all.

Put that together, then, and ask the right question. Do not ask, "Where is God, and how does he get here, and what does he do when he arrives?" Ask instead, "Where is the world?"

And then, finally, you see. The world is in bed with Paul and Laura, with the Father and Saint Sophie. The world leaps out of nothing into being between the lips of the Word and the ear of the Father. The world is what the Ultimate Beloved whispers to the Ultimate Lover. Creation is the Pillow Talk of the Trinity. *The world is the Place the Divine Persons create by the power of their eternal Affair.*

Do you see now? Do you see why, in that bed, *there can be nothing wrong?* Why you are uncondemned and free, just by being? It is because, if the Wisdom of God be for you, nothing can be against you, nothing can separate you from the love of Christ. For you are the very body of that love, and if Wisdom speaks you into being in that bed, she speaks you reconciled forever. Whatever in you is evil, or nasty, or stupid, or sad is not mentioned in that bed; it is taken down into the Silence of the Crucifixion of the Word that is the Forgetting of the Father. Laura unspeaks the unspeakableness that is Paul and makes all things new. She takes into herself his condemnation and sequesters it in the stillness of her own gracious death. And the world she creates in his ear is the peaceable kingdom. Within the limits of my parable, it is the one place where he really lives. And outside those limits — in the Land of the Trinity itself, in the Bed where Wisdom murmurs in the Father's ear — it is the only place where we exist at all. And all that is there, and all that there is, is love, and laughter, and the joy of having gotten away with everything.

"Behold thou art fair, my beloved, yea, pleasant: also our bed is green. The beams of our house are cedar, and our rafters of fir."

Do you see then, finally, why there is no condemnation *now?* It is because there never was any — because there is nothing more sovereign than the sovereignty of grace. If you are still so committed to working the other side of the street that you want room for hell in that bed, I can give it to you. But I will not give it here, because hell is nothing but a vain fornication of fancy in the presence of the love that will not let you go. In the end, it is only for forsaking; and the price of the forsaking is exactly nothing. To be at all is to be in that Bed; and to be in that Bed is to be free. That is where, and what, you have been all along. You are, therefore, at liberty. You may *go.*

•   •

I know. I cannot prove all that. But since it *is* what the man said, and since it sounds so much better than anything else I have ever been told — since of all the tired truths I know, it comes closer than any to sounding like the hilarity beyond all liking and happening — I just chuckle to myself and try my best to believe it. I urge you to do the same. After all, you weren't really dying to hear *bad* news, were you? Try Auden one last time instead:

> . . . It is not easy
> To believe in unknowable justice
>   Or pray in the name of a love
> Whose name one's forgotten: *libera*
>   *Me, libera* C (dear C)
> And all poor s-o-b's who never
>   Do anything properly, spare
> Us in the youngest day when all are
>   Shaken awake, facts are facts,

The Picnic

(And I shall know exactly what happened
   Today between noon and three)
That we, too, may come to the picnic
   With nothing to hide, join the dance
As it moves in perichoresis,
   Turns about the abiding tree.

*There is therefore now no condemnation to
them which are in Christ Jesus.*

PART TWO

COFFEE HOUR

18

To the Woodshed

I know. Once again, I have overstated things slightly — perhaps this time, even more than slightly; but I know no other way to separate the liquor of grace from the mash of morality. If it is any comfort to you, by and by I shall tell you another story — a highly moral one about somebody who doesn't get away with a thing. But not yet. There are still too many differences between us, and I have, I admit, papered them over with a kind of theological throwaway that inspires not confidence but distrust in your mind. You deserve better before we proceed. I shall try again, therefore, and in another way.

●　　●

When I preach a sermon that finally succeeds in going to the root of the idea of redemption by grace alone, I find that those who take it in have two successive but opposed reactions.

One Sunday, to give an instance, I set myself the task of showing that in Jesus' parables of grace, the work of redemption is done entirely by the redeemer and not at all by the redeemed. The longer I proceeded by straight exposition, however, the more

I felt that the very parables I was dealing with were keeping my hearers from seeing the truth in its naked glory. I could almost hear them worrying the tiny bones of good works in the stories rather than feasting on the meat of grace that was the main ingredient — paying more attention, for example, to the Prodigal's confession than to the Father's love that forgave him even before he confessed; giving more weight to the minor point that the Laborers who worked only one hour did at least some work than to the main truth that the Owner of the Vineyard paid everybody out of his own goodness, not in proportion to the work done. My mind hunted for some clinching illustration that would make them drop the irrelevancies and get on with the meal. Finally, it came:

"All right," I said. "Take it another way. I will show you exactly what you have to do to be saved — the full extent of what you, personally, must undertake in order to be drawn into the redeeming work of Jesus. Put yourself in the scene in the eleventh chapter of John where Jesus is about to raise Lazarus from the dead. You are standing there next to Martha outside the sealed tomb, and you hear Jesus say, 'Take away the stone.' But Martha objects. She says something that, had I thought of it earlier, I would have made the text for this whole sermon. She says, 'Lord, by this time he stinketh, for he hath been dead four days.' But Jesus makes them take away the stone just the same; and after he prays to his Father, he cries with a loud voice, 'Lazarus, come forth.' And he that was dead comes forth.

"Do you now see what you have to do to be saved? Do you at last understand the precise degree of cooperation on your part that is needed to enable you to enter into life? Do you finally recognize that all that is required of you is to do exactly what Lazarus did — which is exactly and only *nothing?* Martha spoke the whole truth not only about Lazarus but about every one of us in particular and about the human race in general: 'Lord, by

128

now we stink.' We have been dead four days, four thousand days, four hundred thousand times four thousand days. In the midst of all our life we have been in death. And in the midst of that abiding death we have been in Nothing. Knee-deep in it, waist-deep in it, up to our noses and in over our heads in Not-a-Thing. But now, in Lazarus, you see that it is just that extremity which has always been our hope — that very prison, the doorway to our liberty. Because making things jump out of nothing is God's favorite act. He creates us out of it and he raises us up from it. *Jesus came to raise the dead.* Not to improve the improvable, not to perfect the perfectible, not to teach the teachable, but to raise the dead. He never met a corpse that didn't sit right up then and there. And he never meets us without bringing us out of nothing into the joy of his resurrection: you, me, the President of the United States, and poor old Arthur down by the docks with his pint of Muscatel in a brown paper bag. We are all dead. And he raises us all. And without so much as a by-your-leave. Just be a good corpse, and he does the rest. Because his Word is the word with the ultimate bark, and when he says 'Arthur, come forth,' that's all old Arthur needs. His nothin' ain't nothin' no more."

As I said, when I preach something like that, I get two reactions. At the end of the sermon, I see smiles. I see faces light up — faces which, in spite of a lifetime's exposure to the doctrine of grace, seem for the first time to dare to hope that maybe there isn't a catch to it after all, that even out of the midst of their worst shipwrecks they are still going home free for the pure and simple reason that Jesus calls them. I see barely restrained hilarity at the sudden perception that he really meant it when he said his yoke is easy and his burden light.

But after the service, in the time it takes them to get downstairs to the coffee hour, the smiles have been replaced by frowns. Their fear of the catch has caught up with them again, and they surround the messenger of hope and accuse me of making the world unsafe for morality.

I propose, therefore, that you and I stop our progress at this point and do justice to the frowning, coffee-hour mood that my parable of grace has put you in. It is your turn to speak; let me now, cup in hand and sugar and cream stirred in, silence for a while my proper voice and bespeak, if I can, your words as you hold me at bay in this musty basement where the Word provokes us to dialogue.

●　　●

"Ah, yes indeed," I hear you say. "Speak we will. And to both the style and the substance of your argument. But not until we have first registered our displeasure at the fast shuffle you have just given us. We resent being cast in the role of the heavy. You say that by and by you will comfort us with a highly moral story about someone who doesn't get away with anything. That will not do. We have sat patiently through your parable about two unlikely (and, we might add, unlikeable) people who, in the midst of a major shipwreck of responsibility, achieve the distinctly minor triumph of overlooking one or two of each other's unappealing features. Now, however — in what seems to us a transparent attempt to make it look as if we are against success as such — you propose to mollify us with a story about failure. We simply will not sit still for that. There are deep flaws within your parable, and we will not allow you to proceed against us ad hominem simply to avoid the force of our considerable objections ad rem.

"It was not that we were against the success of their affair. We are as fond as anyone of stories of love and grace triumphant. What we objected to, to begin with, was the quite unnecessary outrage to common moral sense with which you felt obliged to lard the otherwise dry meat of your parable. Why, for example, did you insist on providing Paul and Laura with wife and husband respectively? Why could they not have been presented to us as single, and therefore marriageable? We might even — our sensibilities are sufficiently modern — have settled for your leaving them unmarried lovers if you felt that a touch of salaciousness would pique our interest. But this heavy-handed over-salting of your story is unpardonable, precisely because it is unnecessary. You intended a happy ending for them from the start. Why could it not have been an inoffensively happy one, rather than this adulterous tangle of broken promises, this shabby, car-switching, phone-calling institutionalization of delinquency that you insist we accept as the paradigm of grace?

"After all, it was not as if you were laboring under the restraints of reportage. Your story was a fiction over which you had full control. You could have brought Paul's sins to Laura's forgiveness just as well without the added offense of infidelity. We would have thought that a theologian concerned to restore our taste for the goodness of grace would compose parables less likely to set our teeth on edge.

"On the other hand and much more to the point, if you were so determined to outrage our sensibilities, why were you so pusillanimous in your choice of outrages? Why did you pick such a mild one as illicit sex? We suspect we know the answer. Was it not that, having made no serious attempt to deal with the just demands of the moral order, you instinctively shied away from any clear delineation of the chamber of horrors your one-sided story opens? You tell us, in effect, that even in the sowing of wild oats, grace springs up triumphant. Why then did you provide your characters — we can quote Auden as well as you — with 'strains of oats of such an unmitigatedly minor wildness'? Why did you not give us a Paul who deep-sixes his wife and absconds with the college endowment funds to some Caribbean country with which the United States has no extradition treaty? Why not a Laura who joins him there after lacing her husband's anniversary glass of Amaretto with prussic acid? It was not simply that you lacked inventiveness. That might be pardoned. It was that you lacked the courage to put what you were saying into words of one syllable. Your unpardonable offense, therefore, is that you have trifled with us. We are free, you claim, to do *anything*. Why did you shrink from all but the most titillating fictionalization of that freedom?

"Even supposing, however, that it was not cowardice on your part — that you can still somehow, in the further explication of your thesis, make the very reconciliation of grace and the moral order for which your parable cries out — have you not made a major tactical blunder in omitting that reconciliation from the parable itself? We grant you that the theology of grace has suffered gross neglect — that we have reached a point at which almost all people, inside the church as well as outside, find that the notion of grace stands in contradiction to everything they understand by religion. But precisely because that is the case, are you not expecting too much of most readers when you ask them to learn a theology that must offend their deficient Christianity from a story that will inevitably shock their not-so-deficient moral sense? Might not the result be neither agreement nor disagreement, but simply misunderstanding? Specifically, when you exegete your parable as you go along, and do so in an age that has come to believe that salvation consists in getting rid of hang-ups — that every easing of the psyche, however inconvenient to others, is ipso facto the Will of God — will you not be thought to do no more than approve of successful adulteries? Will you not even perhaps (setting aside that particularly attractive dereliction) be thought to advance the popular but mindless proposition that people may do anything that comes into their heads, as long as they can work themselves around to the point at which it doesn't upset their insides? As Chesterton pointed out, that justifies feeding babies to crocodiles if you have the stomach for it.

"Permit us to press the point further. We are not saying that your parable is without redeeming features. We welcome the life you have given to a number of truths that need resurrection just now. We enjoyed especially your diverting us back to a better understanding of the pivotal theological concepts of Law, Death, Repentance, and Grace. But we are left still with a deep conviction that your chosen theological method — your decision, as you put it, to work only one side of the street — is fundamentally suspect. We are divided among ourselves as to the precise nature of its questionability, but every one of us has the wind up over something.

"Some among us, put off by the very cheerfulness of your diversion (the words *breeziness* and *glibness* have also been suggested), suspect that your choice of the sunny side of the street was in reality not a choice of the mind at all but simply the inevitable predilection of a flawed character. You seem to them (others of us take exception to this formulation) 'not to have suffered enough' — to have been insulated, by nature or nurture, from that necessary graveness on the subject of evil that alone lends credibility to one who presumes to lecture others on the eschatological acceptability of what they know perfectly well to be presently impermissible. They reckon not only that you would never willingly choose to face the realities of the darker side of the street, but that you are constitutionally incapable of dealing with them even if you did. In any case, however, they are indisposed to believe a word you say.

"The rest of us take a somewhat more charitable view of your disposition but by that very fact are less willing to exculpate you as to method. We question whether it is ever proper for a theologian (you see, we hope, that we take you to be what we think you seriously hold yourself to be) to expound but one side of a paradox at the length you have chosen. When you clinch the argument of your parable as uncompromisingly as you do in your exposition of the proposition 'There is therefore now no condemnation to them which are in Christ Jesus,' do you not inevitably import into it a consistency that it does not have in the hands of Saint Paul? For one thing, while you quote the text in full, you tend to deal with it as if the qualifying phrase about 'them which are in Christ Jesus' were missing. Do you not run the risk, at the very least, of leading the unsuspecting reader to think you are expounding a general philosophical proposition rather than a specifically Christian one?

"But more than that, is not your whole approach out of balance in a way that Saint Paul's is not? In the first eight chapters of the Epistle to the Romans, not only is the truth of grace presented as inseparable from the truth of the law; it is followed, three short chapters later, by a veritable compendium of moral theology whose exhortations to putting off the works of darkness and walking honestly as in the day — whose prohibitions of chambering and wantonness consist ill, to put it mildly, with the furtive motel-hopping of your protagonists. (We spare you further detail, assuming you to be well aware of the fact that in the immediately following Epistle, 1 Corinthians, Saint Paul enunciates a standard of sexual morality which would not only put a crimp in Paul's and Laura's style but would require their excommunication on the spot as fornicators.)

"It is not our purpose, however, to cite chapter and verse against you — only to observe how different a tissue from that of Saint Paul you present: one-hundred-twenty-five pages of yours on half a paradox as against fourteen of his on the full width of the fabric of truth. One of our number remarked, somewhat facilely, that every major heretic has cut his teeth on the Epistle to the Romans. We reject that as an adequate assessment, but feel it contains a timely warning to you. The essence of heresy is not that it propounds error but that it serves up parts of the truth in the absence of those other parts without which truth cannot be kept whole. Have you not, despite all your demurrers, come perilously close to just such a lapse from catholicity? Even Augustine — even Luther — did not find it necessary to stand so far from one side of Saint Paul in order to exegete the other.

"Which brings us to our next point. We said 'exegete.' But is not your method more eisegetical than exegetical? Do you not import meaning *into* your texts rather than draw it *from* them? True enough, such a method betrays to some extent your own contribution to the subject, namely, your concern to make us think through the astonishingly radical implications of what is usually called the Pauline Tradition — a tradition with which we have admittedly been too complacently familiar. But do you not, both by your eisegesis and by your canny selection of only such texts as will be patient of it, give that tradition rather more credit for consistency than is actually due it?

"Consider with us for a moment the parables to which you so often appeal. You say somewhere that 'they are told only because they are true, not because the actions of the characters in them can be recommended for imitation.' We are uncomfortable with such a statement not only because it has that ring of sweeping generality that every careful mind learns early to distrust but especially because we suspect that neither of its assertions is quite the case. To say, for example, that parables are told only because they are 'true' is to invite either a jejune literalism or an insufficient probing of their depths. They are not, it seems plain to us, 'true' in any literal sense. They are fictions — many of them purposely exaggerated fictions — designed to be intelligible pointers to the inscrutable mystery of a divine action that lies beyond but continually intersects the ordinary and scrutinizable course of events. But by that very fact, they are not 'only' true; they are true in the deepest sense of the word: they present us, as well as any words can, with a convincing glimpse of what is actually going on. Like the best poetry, they are 'imaginary gardens with real toads in them.' They lead us, by way of a fictionalization of the familiar — by their appeal to our knowledge of sprouting seeds, trawling nets, and returning wastrels — to grasp the factuality of the unfamiliar, to recognize that crucial something or someone who, while beyond common experience, is yet its root and ground and end.

"On the other hand, can you say, as flatly as you do, that imitation of the characters in the parables is in no way intended? To be sure, there is no requirement in the Gospel that one must become a publican or a prodigal in order to be saved. But Christians live under the rubric 'Forgive as you are forgiven.' Accordingly, it seems to us implicit in the parables that, should Christians ever find themselves in a situation analogous to one presented in a parable (should they, for example, find themselves to be crooked tax collectors at prayer, or discoverers of a wounded person on the ground), they might at the very least try to understand their situation in the light of the parable — and might even, in some circumstances, do well to imitate the precise behavior of the character in question. Admittedly, the parables are designed principally to depict *God's* ways with us; but it strikes us as unnecessarily sweeping to preclude all interpretations of them which try to show their bearing upon our ways with our neighbors.

"Our point is crucial: there is no way of speaking in parables that can eliminate entirely the suggestion of imitation. Indeed, the more humanly vivid the parabolic situation, the more strongly is imitation suggested. One is not, of course, very much tempted to go out and sow seeds by waysides or among thorns — and one is hardly more tempted to pay one's help as the owner paid the laborers in his vineyard. But those are bizarre and exaggerated situations. One might indeed be tempted, however, to try to pattern his fathering after the example of the father of the prodigal — for the very reason that that parable strikes, literally, so close to home.

"That being the case, what about your parable in this regard? Obviously, you think (setting the parable to one side for the moment) that non-parabolic, common-garden adulterers are objects of grace as they are, not because of this or that action on their part. In your parable, this truth (with which, by the way, we agree) is represented by Laura's loving acceptance of Paul despite his inability to put an end to his profligate ways even after he has become her lover. So far, so good. But since you are not suggesting that successful adulteries are themselves the means of divine grace for successful adulterers (at least we do not think you are, though some of us are not so sure), have you not unnecessarily muddied the waters? Have you not, in so elaborating Paul's revivification by Laura's love — in so frequently stigmatizing the inadequacies of nineteenth-century moral theology in your comments on Paul's case — inevitably led the reader to think that your story can be taken as something more than a parable (or to call a spade a spade, as something far less)? Your story hits very close to home indeed; it invites imitation no matter what you say. Was it not mischievous, therefore, to include in your exposition of a spiritual home truth such a vivid suggestion that literal infidelity to one's hearth might have so many ingratiating and redeeming results? Have you not thereby needlessly legitimized a pattern of behavior that needs no more encouragement than it already has? Have you not indeed handed out the very licenses you speak of? You may shrug it off. To us, however, a shrug is no substitute for a reason.

"But for the time being, let us stop there. Reserving our right of rejoinder at some farther point in the discussion, we ask you now to answer us in as plain and earnest a way as we have questioned you. We are by no means unteachable. It is just that we wish to be sure that it is truth and not snake oil you are asking us to buy."

19

Sticks, Stones, and Snake Oil

*D*ear me! Things are worse than I thought. This threatens to become a coffee hour-and-a-half.

If I assess your thoughts correctly (I now cease to bespeak your mind and return to the effort to express my own), your bill against me consists of twelve particulars. For the sake of order, I list them. It is your contention that I have

- given you a fast shuffle;
- outraged your moral sense but, at the same time,
- insufficiently outraged your moral sense, and thus
- been guilty of trifling with you;
- made no serious attempt to deal with the just demands of the moral order, and
- opened the door to a purely subjective morality;
- made a fatal mistake in working only one side of the street;
- imported into Saint Paul a consistency that is not there, and thus
- fallen near, if not straight into, heresy;
- been guilty of eisegesis;
- given the parables only a cursory reading, and last and worst,

138

• handed my readers, as a result of all the above lapses, deficiencies, and miscalculations, something less than a parable and possibly not much more than snake oil.

On with it, then. You ask me to respond to you in a style as plain and earnest as that of your questions. I shall try my best — though I must say that your earnestness was more evident than your plainness. Indeed, so academic was the tone of your discussion, so rife with instances of the learned fist in the pedantic glove, so infected with the style of those quarterlies in which professors blow each other out of the water with infinite civility, that you have put me off my form. (You even have me talking like you.) I find myself itching to clothe my reply in the full regalia of Thomistic argument — to give you a *disputatio scholastica* commencing with *ad primum sic proceditur* and running on forever with the full apparatus of *concedo, nego, distinguo, praeterea,* and *obicitur.* I shall, however, resist the temptation. Curbing all such excesses, high and low, I now answer you directly, pausing only long enough to refresh the palate of my mind with one modest, taste-restoring outburst:

Snake oil? Don't knock it till you've tried it.

• •

To the charge of fast shuffling:

I did not give you a fast shuffle; I simply promised you another story. If you are not ready to let me deal that hand, I am perfectly content to stop and let you examine the deck to your heart's content. If I have taken advantage of you by making you play the heavy, I apologize. I point out only that it was necessary. Not, mind you, that *you* should be the heavy, but that the grace-fearing spoilsport in every one of us should be made to stand up and speak out. Selfishly, perhaps, I exercised my prerogative as author and cast myself in the role of the angel of grace bringing light to those in mental darkness. My only excuse is that it felt good for a while to get out from under the perpetual burden of having to play the heavy against myself.

You say you are as fond as anyone of stories of love and grace triumphant. But that statement is itself something of a fast shuffle. It is only half the truth: in addition to being fond of them, we also — all of us — fear them. We fear the quirky wind of liberty that blows through them: it will not do, in a book on grace, to leave that fear unexpressed, or to rig neatly moral endings that will take your mind off it. If, by reserving the fondness for grace to myself and parceling out the fear of it to you, I have made you feel I was proceeding against you ad hominem, I am sorry. I agree with you that the only way to argue is ad rem. You must admit, though, that it is not easy. In your own rejoinder to me you were, once or twice, less than faithful to your high principle. But then, we all live in glass houses. No more rocks.

Except perhaps one. Not thrown, though, just kicked off my lawn. My characters, you claim, are as unlikeable as they are unlikely. The first part of that charge is irrelevant. I did not ask you to like them — only to recognize that their liking for each other was sufficient to engage the clutch of love and spin the wheels of sin, and death, and forgiveness, and grace. If you are of a mind that refuses to believe in the presence of those realities unless you personally can see what two lovers see in each other, all I can say is that I hope you are able to change that mind before your teenage daughter drags home her first slack-jawed clod of a candidate for son-in-law.

The second part of the charge needs distinguishing. If by "unlikely" you mean that the probability of actually coming across two such people is so low as to be negligible, I think you are wrong. In my experience, the improbable has happened so reg-

140

ularly that I have found it unwise to predict too confidently what will not be around the corner — especially at the corner where man and woman meet. If, on the other hand, you mean that I have insufficiently portrayed a perfectly likely meeting — that I have, as it were, simply shoved two people into bed without making you feel the tension that drew them there — I concede your point. Put it down to my haste to get on with the parable and display the dynamics of grace. Or chalk it up to my ineptitude as a storyteller. Any way you like. Maybe it's even your fault. Perhaps you expect too much of my method, which is after all not much more than theology by way of entertainment — and which, for some people, is recognizable as neither.

●　　●

To the charges of outrage, insufficient outrage, and trifling:

I pass the catch-22 formulation you have given these charges and go directly to the central and serious matter that lies behind them. The crime you are actually accusing me of is *Healing on the Sabbath.* I shall be as succinct as possible.

First, a delineation of its essence. The crime always consists of three elements: the doing of a good deed; the doing of that deed in a way that violates a deeply felt ethical sensibility; and the doing of it in front of people to whom the violation seems not only unnecessary but also destructive of an entire tissue of values. It is invariably seen as blasphemy, and its punishment (allowing for minor variations in time or circumstance) must always be some form of crucifixion. Properly understood, it is the crime of crimes. Nevertheless, fully aware that a plea of guilty is equivalent to conviction after trial, I do so plead myself.

I ask you only to see what I have done against the back-ground of the Gospels. In the twelfth chapter of Matthew, Jesus, in a synagogue on the Sabbath day, heals a man who has a withered hand. Promptly and quite correctly, the Pharisees go out and hold a council against him, how they might destroy him. Notice, in order of ascending importance, the three elements of the crime. First, Jesus does an unquestionably good deed. Second, he does it in front of people who he knows perfectly well are committed to the whole body of the law — and for whom the keeping of the Sabbath is no trifle but one of the supreme sacraments of the law, an affirmation (if you take Genesis 1:1 through 2:3 at face value) of the whole divine order of creation. But third, his breaking of the Sabbath seems pointless and unnecessary. He is not doing a good deed that if delayed would become undoable. This is not a man who needs immediate rescue, not a man lying unconscious in a burning house. This is not even a man whose case is like the one Jesus cites to justify the healing: no sheep fallen into a pit who would drown if left till sundown. The Pharisees are reasonable men. Of course they would pull out the sheep. If you care to make a rather Latin-style theological argument for them, you might have them reason that since the Sabbath is the chief sacrament of the order of creation, it may lawfully be broken as long as some significant individual instance of that order is in danger of imminent and irreversible disordering.

But that is not the case here. This man has had a withered hand for years. Why in God's good name can't Jesus wait out the afternoon and cure him without flying in the face of the Torah? Why can't he sit with him till sunset and use the time to fix the man's mind on the graciousness of God? Why can't they search the Scriptures together and set the stage so that the healing will be seen in all its unquestionable rightness? What is the point of this unnecessary muddying of the waters, of this apparently pointless setting of teeth on edge?

In order to see it, you have to go back. The point that Jesus had in mind to make was the point he made earlier the same day when the Pharisees caught him and his disciples going through the corn, plucking off ears and eating them: "The Son of Man is Lord even of the Sabbath day." It is, for the Pharisees, not only a new point but one that is at odds with all the other points they accept. And while it is not the same point as the one made in my parable, Jesus' method of making it — the dynamic he uses to put it before their minds — is the same, I think, as the one I have used to put the truth of grace before yours. Consider.

Whenever someone attempts to introduce a radically different insight to people whose minds have been formed by an old and well-worked-out way of thinking, he or she is up against an obstacle. As Jesus said, their taste for the old wine is so well established that they invariably prefer it to the new. More than that, the new wine, still fermenting, seems to them so obviously and dangerously full of power that they will not even consider putting it into their old and fragile wineskins.

But now try to see the point of the biblical imagery of wine-making a little more abstractly. The new insight is always at odds with the old way of looking at things. Even if the teacher's audience were to try earnestly to take it in, the only intellectual devices they would have to pick it up with are the categories of the old system with which it conflicts. Hence the teacher's problem: if he leaves in his teaching a single significant scrap of the old system, they, by their very effort to understand, will go to that scrap rather than to the point he is making and, having done that, will understand the new only insofar as it can be made to agree with the old — which is, not at all.

Perhaps the phrase "precluding the conversion of species in an argument" will do for a name for this teaching technique that Jesus uses in healing on the Sabbath, and that I have used in presenting you with grace in the context of an adultery. Were Jesus to have waited till sundown to heal the man's hand, the Pharisees would have seen his good deed as congruent with everything else they already knew. If they had then tried to put a messianic interpretation on it, they would have envisioned Jesus as the kind of Messiah they were ready for (a victorious and immortal one) and not as the kind he knew himself to be (a suffering and dying one). He was at pains, you see, to present them with a proposition that was totally unacceptable to them — namely, that the kind of Christ he would be must suffer, and die, and on the third day rise again. The species of his argument, if you will, was that he would be a different Messiah than they expected. He must not therefore offer their minds illustrations that would allow them to convert that species into its opposite. If he heals after sundown, the very goodness of that act — the very legitimacy they attach to it — will seep back and erode his main point: they will acclaim him only as the long-awaited man on horseback who is coming to punch the enemies of the Lord in the nose.

Note too, please, that this precluding of the conversion of the species is not an incidental device in Jesus' hands; it is his chief method. He comes from Galilee, whence arises no Messiah. His disciples are a ragtag lot of outcasts, likewise from Galilee. He consorts with a Samaritan woman, he eats with publicans and sinners, he is a glutton and a winebibber, he dies accursed, hung on a tree — and so on and on. He constantly couches his announcement of the kingdom in words and deeds that are at odds with his hearers' expectations for the kingdom, precisely in order that seeing, they might not see, and hearing, they might not understand. He instructs them with a constant awareness that the one thing they must not do is see, because they would see wrong, or understand, because they would only misunderstand. For he knows that the only thing that can save them — namely, himself, in the mystery of his death and resurrection — is the one thing they cannot accept, given their present view of salvation. Accordingly, he gives them not one scrap to confirm their present view

— or, more accurately, he always includes one solidly unacceptable scrap on which their minds will gag.

This long footnote to my plea of guilty, therefore, begins to draw to an end. My parable gave you one good deed: Laura's acceptance of Paul. It gave it to you in a way that outraged your ethical sensibilities. (Whether the outrage was sufficient or insufficient hardly matters: it outraged you, and that is enough.) And it did so in a way that seemed both unnecessary and destructive of values. (It trifled, as you said, with people concerned to uphold important truths.) It is indeed, therefore, *Healing on the Sabbath*.

But I did it all to preclude the conversion of the species of grace into the species of law. For the happy, innocuous ending you want would inevitably do just that. The very congruence of it with the law would seep back into your mind and erode your perception of the point I was making. Paul and Laura respectably married? Why, that would make you see grace as a way back to the sovereignty of the law — grace as a mere one- or two-shot remission of guilt whose chief purpose was to suspend the rules for a while and give a second chance to people who now, having run out of chances, had best get back to the business that God really has in mind for them — namely, watching their step. For at the roots of our fallen being, that is what we really think. Our pride drives us to establish our own righteousness. We strive all our life to see ourselves as keepers of rules we cannot keep, as loyal subjects of laws under which we can only be judged outlaws. Yet so deep is our need to derive our identity from our own self-respect — so profound is our conviction that unless we watch our step, the watchbird will take away our name — that we will spend a lifetime trying to do the impossible rather than, for even one carefree minute, consent to having it done for us by someone else.

Were I to have married Paul and Laura, your mind would

have come to rest in the eventual legitimacy of their relationship and not in the grace that was its only root. For Paul — and you and I — remain permanently illegitimate. We need more than occasional suspensions of the rules. We need *grace*. And grace is not the offer of an exception to the rules; it is a new dispensation entirely. It says nothing about the rules (indeed, it leaves them intact); it simply says that since, because of our weakness, the rules can never be the *basis of our acceptance,* God is not going to make them such anymore. Accordingly, in my view, there is nothing in my presentation of grace via a story of two people who have excused themselves from the received sexual ethic that is not, *mutatis mutandum* (perhaps even *pari passu*), in Jesus' presentation of himself as a Sabbath-breaking Messiah. I am guilty as charged, and I find myself in very good company indeed.

• •

To the charges of not being serious about the just demands of the moral order, and fostering a purely subjective morality:

I think I have just answered your question about why I put no reconciliation of grace and the moral order within my parable itself. Let me take up these two charges, then, by commenting on your assertion that my parable, under the guise of titillation, opens a chamber of horrors in which it is just to feed babies to crocodiles, provided only that you like that sort of thing.

You seem to imply that both I, by titillating, and more seriously, God, by being gracious, run the risk of giving the impression that there is no longer any objective law against anything. Let us make some distinctions. If you mean that there are people utterly committed to doing evil who are waiting for either me or God to give them permission to proceed with their wicked designs, I deny your point. Monumental wickedness just doesn't work that way. It is always clever enough to convince itself that it is not breaking the law but keeping some higher law — that it needs no permission to destroy Cambodia, for example, because it is, in its own view, doing the cosmic order a favor. If you mean, however, that there are people with an itch to do something immoral who might draw from my parable — or from the Scriptures, I might add — encouragement to scratch, I concede the point. Shaky wickedness — the unsure malevolence of weak and fearful characters — always works that way. They will hunt for permission high and low until they find it, because they are engaged in an endless, frantic struggle to think well of themselves by believing that some authority thinks they are not a menace. That is the principle of their lives. They cannot act on their own without permission (real or imagined) because they need external endorsement like air itself. We are all used by them. If they have taken comfort from me, it is no more than they would have taken from someone else — or even from you — without me.

But, on the other hand, if you mean that they are going to get from my parable, or from the grace of God, serious encouragement to believe that the just demands of the moral order have been abrogated, I disagree entirely. Even if I trifle with those demands in a fiction — even if God in his grace is willing to trifle with them by accepting us despite our transgressions of them — there is simply no way of coming to a serious conclusion that morality has been set aside. The law remains the standard of our nature. To be what the law says we should be is the only way we can be what we really are. No one breaks the law with impunity because by every transgression we and the society in which we live become progressively and perceivably less human. But for all that, no matter how far below the level of our true humanity we sink, we retain some vision, however clouded, of what that humanity is. The law stands before us forever as a vision of the true beauty of our nature: in most instances, we go on wishing that we ourselves could have kept it, and we are in all instances fully convinced that our neighbors should have kept it. The few pleasant delinquencies for which we manage to fake out permission remain just that: few.

Therefore, the law against feeding babies to crocodiles stands. I cannot topple it, and God does not. But there is no law that stands against God's acceptance of those who break it *should God, by his own devices, choose to accept them.* The Gospel is simply the once-for-all announcement that God does indeed so choose.

While we were yet sinners, Christ died for the ungodly. It is he that reconciles me, not the law; for by its very truth, the law shows me only that I am unreconciled. My many transgressions in the past, permitted or not — and my many transgressions in the future, including, perhaps, the founding of a cult that feeds babies to crocodiles — stand against me. But the Gospel of grace says that God does not stand against me, that he is not and never will be my enemy, and that he has so arranged things by the mystery of Christ's death and resurrection that at any time — before, during, or after any of my sins, past or future — I can come to him just for the coming and find myself at home.

Do you see that what that says is far more shocking than the worst shock I may have given you — that it means that I may well be wicked at any time, but that I am free for all time of any condemnation for my wickedness? And that therefore I am free to be wicked, monumentally or shakily, alone or with others, in thought, word, or deed — and with no limits upper or lower my whole life long — *and still remain free of my wickedness?* Was there any way I could have told you that truth without some shock to your system? Indeed, I begin only just now to see some validity to your point about insufficient outrageousness. Your failure to grasp the point of grace leads me to think you may have been right. It is not exactly that I trifled with you; but perhaps I did over-entertain you. I served you a delicate little fillet of dalliance when I should have rammed a whole, uncooked fish down your throat.

One footnote. If we are ever to enter fully into the glorious liberty of the children of God, we are going to have to spend more time thinking about freedom than we do. The church, by and large, has had a poor record of encouraging freedom. It has spent so much time inculcating in us the fear of making mistakes that it has made us like ill-taught piano students: we play our pieces, but we never really hear them because our main concern is not to make music, but to avoid some flub that will get us in Dutch. The church, having put itself *in loco parentis*, has been so afraid we will lose sight of the laws of our nature that it has made us care more about how we look than about who we are — made us act more like the subjects of a police state than fellow citizens of the saints.

I have raised (nearly — my nail-biting days will never quite be over) six children. After all these years, I now think my fears that the moral order was always in imminent danger of collapse were misplaced. My children and I have spent a great deal of time doing little else than wave it in front of each other's noses: my lectures to them on truthfulness were more than balanced by their tirades against me on unfairness. But all the while, there was one thing we most needed even from the start, and certainly will need from here on out into the New Jerusalem: the ability to take our freedom seriously and act on it, to live not in fear of mistakes but in the knowledge that no mistake can hold a candle to the love that draws us home. My repentance, accordingly, is not so much for my failings but for the two-bit attitude toward them by which I made them more sovereign than grace. Grace — the imperative to hear the music, not just listen for errors — makes all infirmities occasions of glory. I rest my case for Paul's and Laura's shortcomings on Rosina Lhevine's retort to the charge that Arthur Rubinstein played wrong notes: "Yes, but *what* wrong notes!" *O felix culpa.*

149

• •

To the charge of working only the sunny side of the street:

If you like, I shall apologize for having what is on most days a sunny disposition — even, if it makes you feel better, for "not having suffered enough" — though I agree with Brendan Gill that it is a strange notion that there is a quantifiable amount of suffering which is just right for each of us. Like him, I think that anyone who reaches the age of three or four has more than likely already had all the misery he or she needs.

I do see your point, however. Evil is a grave business; and I have deliberately avoided the *horror* of wickedness — for, I think, perfectly sound reasons. My parable is an *apologia* for the doctrine of grace. Like any canny apologist, I have tried, within the limits of an admittedly flexible honesty, to present my subject in the best light. Because grace is always a shock, I had to shock you; but in the interest of not losing you altogether, I chose to shock you in a motel room rather than in a death camp. I admit that such a way of doing business does not fit the requirements of total honesty. But then, total honesty is not one of the options available to the Christian apologist. The ultimate Christian position on the horror of evil is so utterly shocking that even people who have bought the bill of goods can hardly accept it. No one trying seriously to make a sale dares even mention it, especially to those whose experience of that horror has put them on the dark side of the street.

Therefore let me lay aside my apologist's bag of tricks for one paragraph and say, as a plain Christian man, what you quite rightly fear I am really saying. There is indeed no horror, no wickedness, no evil — no cruelty, no torture, no holocaust in the whole history of the world — that is not, under the sovereignty of grace, *already reconciled in Jesus.* And there is no perpetrator of

150

any horror, wickedness, evil, et cetera (up to and including Hitler and your dreadful brother-in-law) *who is not, in Jesus, forgiven.* That is the Gospel, the Good News, without which we are all obviously dead ducks. But it is also, from where we sit, the most outrageous piece of bad news the world has ever heard because it says quite clearly that, on the basis of anything we can know or feel about the goodness of creation, God is bad. All I can say is that I know and feel that too, and that I can only *believe* in a God who asks me to trust his Word to the contrary in Jesus crucified and risen. Even with a sunny disposition, I find I can buy such an outrageous proposition only about half the time; if you cannot buy it at all, I understand completely. So much, then, for the total honesty of faith. Back to the comforts of theology.

• •

To the charges of forcing a consistency on Saint Paul, heresy, and eisegesis:

I concede the first, but plead the already-cited extenuating circumstances of the working apologist. Besides, the paradox of the Gospel is like laundry in a tub: it's hard to push up something you can't see without pushing down something you can.

I deny the second without qualification. What I pushed out of sight is still there; I know where it is and accept fully the obligation to push it up again another day.

I concede the third, but I thank you for at least recognizing that eisegesis is one way of making a contribution to the subject. I do tend to throw scriptural images at each other with some abandon. Better biblical scholars than I will have to pronounce the last word on specific instances of that tendency.

• •

151

Finally, to the charges of mistreating the parables, offering less than a parable, and offering snake oil:

As to the first: once again, I thank you for your criticism. I stand not only corrected, but enlightened.

As to the second: I am torn between concession and denial. Perhaps all I can give you is a "perhaps." So many of Jesus' parables are less than parables. The Parable of the Sower is an allegory. The Parable of the Wheat and the Tares is a piece of manifestly bad advice. And Jesus' *acted* parables — his fetching of a coin from the fish's mouth, his cursing of the fig tree, his miracles of healing — *mislead* almost more than they instruct. They tempt us to fix our hopes on free tax money, or on vengeance, or on present health rather than on their main point, which is the broken and dishonored Jesus himself as the resurrection and the life. I just don't know if your objections matter all that much. I guess I doubt the wisdom of putting the parables on a procrustean bed.

But as to the third, I remain adamant: I haven't sold you snake oil, God has — and when he sells it, it ain't snake oil anymore.

20

An Unacceptable Parable

I hear a rejoinder forming in your mind. Permit me to voice it for you. You are reluctant to accept my assertion that there is nothing in my presentation of grace by means of a parable about two adulterers that is not in Jesus' presentation of himself as a Sabbath-breaking Messiah. You feel the need to point out that while the law about keeping the Sabbath no longer stands for Christians, the law against adultery still does. The two cases, in your view, are not parallel: Jesus broke a law he intended to abrogate anyway; my characters broke a law that apparently neither he nor the church has any intention of abrogating. *Ergo falsa thesis.*

In order to spare you a long answer, I yield briefly to the temptations of scholasticism.

As to your first proposition, *I distinguish:* That the law of the Sabbath no longer stands *at all,* I deny: Orthodox Jews still regard it as binding. That it no longer stands *among Christians, I sub-distinguish:* That Christians do not apply the law of the Sabbath *literally,* as forbidding work on Saturday, *I concede.* That Christians do not apply it *analogically* to the observance of Sunday, *I deny.* That Christians, having applied it to the observance of Sunday,

153

have never applied it *univocally* — that is, as forbidding work on the Lord's Day — *I also deny*.

As to your second proposition, *I again distinguish:* That the entire received sexual ethic still stands, I am in doubt: *let it pass.* That the prohibition of adultery still stands, *I sub-distinguish:* That it still stands as *law, I concede.* That it still stands as *a basis for my acceptance or condemnation in Christ Jesus, I emphatically, roaringly, screamingly deny.* YOU HAVE NOT BEEN LISTENING! *There is therefore now no condemnation.* It is Jesus who saves us, not we ourselves. He dies for us *while we are still sinners,* not after we have managed to get our act under control. He is lifted up to draw *all* to himself, not just those who are willing to break their appointments with the compromises of their lives. His reconciliation of all things in heaven and earth is a fact, conditional upon nothing but his own free choice — on nothing but his totally one-sided act of dropping dead on the cross.

And it is ours *in fact,* conditional upon no work of ours whatsoever. It is not even conditional upon faith, because faith is not a work: we are simply invited to believe that his promise is true and trust him to work it all out.

I realize I am putting this as radically as possible; and I do understand that in fairness not only to you but to the Gospel, I owe you something more on the human response to divine grace. I owe you an adequate rendering of that *repentance* which is the inevitable biblical concomitant of faith. But you must understand that our minds are such — in fact, the whole principle of our fallen lives is such — that unless faith, and the gracious God to whom faith is addressed, are put once and for all in first place, we will go right on trying to justify ourselves by works. And since repentance, by its very nature, is always a work, I shall take it up only when I feel more confident than I do now that you are not going to use it to nullify faith. *O foolish Galatians! Who hath bewitched you?*

On balance, therefore, I am afraid that the only thing for us is to put off still further my promised story and continue to wrestle with the meaning of Scripture. The differences between us seem to be such that my method in the parable of Paul and Laura has come to hinder more than it helps. Accordingly, I propose that we put it aside completely, suspend our coffee-hour wrangling, and attend to a parable of Jesus himself. Please make yourselves as comfortable as possible. This may take a bit of time.

A Plain Sermon

on

THE PHARISEE AND THE PUBLICAN

Luke 18:9-14: *Jesus spake this parable unto certain which trusted in themselves that they were righteous, and despised others: Two men went up into the temple to pray; the one a Pharisee, and the other a publican. The Pharisee stood and prayed thus with himself, God, I thank thee, that I am not as other men are, extortioners, unjust, adulterers, or even as this publican. I fast twice in the week, I give tithes of all that I possess. And the publican, standing afar off, would not lift up so much as his eyes unto heaven, but smote upon his breast, saying, God be merciful to me a sinner. I tell you, this man went down to his house justified rather than the other: for every one that exalteth himself shall be abased; and he that humbleth himself shall be exalted.*

In the Name of the Father and of the Son
and of the Holy Spirit. Amen.

Now, then. The first thing to get off the table is the notion that this parable is simply a lesson in the virtue of humility. It's not. It's an instruction in the futility of religion — in the idleness of the proposition that there is anything at all you can do to put yourself right with God. It's about the folly of even trying. The parable occurs after a series of illustrations of what Jesus means by faith, and it comes shortly before he announces, for the third time, that he will die and rise again. It is therefore not a recommendation to adopt a humble religious stance rather than a proud one; rather, it is a warning to drop all religious stances — and moral and ethical ones, too — when you try to grasp your justification before God. It is, in short, an exhortation to move on to the central point of the Gospel: faith in a God who *raises the dead*.

Consider the characters in this parable. Forget the prejudice that Jesus' frequently stinging remarks about Pharisees have formed in your mind. Give this particular Pharisee all the credit you can. He is, after all, a good man. To begin with, he's not a crook, not a time-server, not a womanizer. He takes nothing he hasn't honestly earned; he gives everyone he knows fair and full measure; and he is faithful to his wife, patient with his children, and steadfast to his friends. He's not at all like this publican, this tax-farmer, who's the worst kind of crook: a legal one, a big operator, a mafia-style enforcer working for the Roman government on a nifty franchise that lets him collect — from his fellow Jews, mind you, from people whom the Romans might have trouble finding, but whose whereabouts he knows and whose language he speaks — all the money he can bleed out of them, provided only that he pays the authorities an agreed-upon flat fee. He's been living for years on the cream he has skimmed off their milk money. He's a fat cat who drives a stretch limo, drinks nothing but Chivas Regal, and never shows up at a party without at least two five-hundred-dollar-a-night call girls in tow.

The Pharisee, however, is not only good: he is religious. And not hypocritically religious, either. His outward uprightness is matched by an inward discipline. He fasts twice a week, and he puts his money where his mouth is: ten percent off the top for God. If you know where to find a dozen or two such upstanding citizens, I know several parishes that will accept delivery of them, no questions asked and all Jesus' parables to the contrary notwithstanding.

But best of all, this Pharisee thanks God for his happy state. Saint Luke says that Jesus spoke this parable to those who trusted in themselves that they were righteous. But Jesus shows us the Pharisee in the very act of giving God the glory. Maybe the reason he went up to the temple to pray was that, earlier in the week, he slipped a little and thought of his righteousness as his own doing. Maybe he said to himself, "That's terrible; I must make a special visit to the temple and set my values straight by thanking God."

But what does Jesus tell you about this good man — about this entirely acceptable candidate for the vestry of your parish? He tells you not only that he's in bad shape but that he's in worse shape than a tax-farmer who is as rotten as they come and who just waltzes into the temple and does nothing more than say as much. In short, he tells you an unacceptable parable.

For you would (I know I would) gladly accept the Pharisee's pledge card and welcome him to our midst. But would you accept me for long if I had my hand in the church till to the tune of a Cadillac and a couple of high-priced whores? Would you (would the diocesan authorities) think it was quite enough for me to come into church on a Sunday, stare at the tips of my shoes, and say, "God be merciful to me a sinner"? Would the bishop write me a letter commending my imitation of the parable and praising me for preaching not only in word but in deed? Jesus, to be sure, says that God would; I myself, however, have some doubts about you and the bishop. You might find it a bit too . . . vivid. There just seems to be no way of dramatizing this parable from our point of view. That being the case, turn it around and look at it from God's.

God is sitting there in the temple, busy holding creation in being — thinking it all into existence, concentrating on making the hairs on your head jump out of nothing, preserving the seat of my pants, reconciling the streetwalkers in Times Square, the losers on the Bowery, the generals in the Pentagon, and all the worms under flat rocks in Brazil. And in come these two characters. The Pharisee walks straight over, pulls up a chair to God's table, and whips out a pack of cards. He fans them, bridges them, does a couple of one-handed cuts and an accordion shuffle, slides the pack over to God, and says, "Cut. I'm in the middle of a winning streak." And God looks at him with a sad smile, gently pushes the deck away, and says, "Maybe you're not. Maybe it just ran out."

So the Pharisee picks up the deck again and starts the game himself. "Twenty-one, okay?" And he deals God an ace of fasting and a king of no adultery. And God says, "Look, I told you. Maybe this isn't your game. I don't want to take your money."

"Oh, come on," says the Pharisee. "How about seven-card stud, tens wild? I've been real lucky with tens wild lately." And God looks a little annoyed and says, "Look, I meant it. Don't play me. The odds here are always on my side. Besides, you haven't even got a full deck. You'd be smarter to be like the guy over there who came in with you. He lost his cards before he got here. Why don't you both just have a drink on the house and go home?"

Do you see now what Jesus is saying in this parable? He's saying that as far as the Pharisee's ability to win a game of justification with God is concerned, he's no better off than the publican. As a matter of fact, the Pharisee is worse off because, while they're both losers, the publican at least has the sense to recognize the fact and trust God's offer of a free drink. The point of the parable is that they're both dead, and their only hope is someone who can raise the dead.

"Ah, but," you say, "isn't there a distinction to be made? Isn't the Pharisee somehow less further along in death than the publican? Isn't there some sense in which we can give him credit for the real goodness he has?"

To which I answer: You're making the same miscalculation as the Pharisee. Death is death. Given enough room to maneuver, it eventually produces total deadness. In the case of the publican, for example, his life so far has been quite long enough to force upon him the recognition that, as far as his being able to deal with God is concerned, he is finished. The Pharisee, on the other hand, looking at his clutch of good deeds, has figured that he has more than enough to keep him in the game for the rest of his life.

But there is his error. For the rest of his life here, maybe. But what about for the length and breadth of eternity? Take your own case. Let's suppose that you are an even better person than the Pharisee. Let's assume that you're untempted to any sin except the sin of envy, and that even there, your resolve is such that for the remainder of your days you never do in fact fall prey to that vice. Are you so sure, however, that the robustness of your virtue is the only root of your unjealous disposition? Might not a very large source of it be nothing more than lack of opportunity? Have you never thought yourself immune to some vice only to find that you fell into it when the temptation became sufficient? The woman who resists a five-dollar proposition sometimes gives in to a five-million-dollar one. Men who would never betray friends have been known to betray friends they thought were about to betray them. The reformer immune to the corruption of power finds corruption easier as he gains power.

Take your dormant envy, then. From now till the hour of your death, you may very well not meet that one person who will galvanize it into action. But in eternity — in that state where there are no limits to opportunity, in which you have literally forever to meet, literally, everybody — is your selflessness so profound that you can confidently predict you will never be jealous of anyone? Is the armor of your humility so utterly without a chink?

There, you see, is the problem as God sees it. For him, the eternal order is a perpetual motion machine: it can tolerate no friction at all. Given long enough, even one grain of sand, one lurking vice in one of the redeemed, will find somewhere to lodge and something to rub on. And that damaged something, given another of the endless eternities within eternity itself, will go off center and shake the next part loose. And that the next — and so straight on into what can only be the beginning of the end. The very limitlessness of the opportunity for mischief will eventually bring the whole works to a grinding halt.

What Jesus is saying in this parable is that no human goodness is good enough to pass a test like that — and that therefore God is not about to risk it. He will not take our cluttered lives as we hold them into eternity. He will take only the clean emptiness of our death as he holds it in the power of Jesus' resurrection. He condemns the Pharisee because he takes his stand on a life that God cannot use; he commends the publican because he rests his case on a death that God can. The fact, of course, is that they're both equally dead and therefore both alike receivers of the gift of resurrection. But for as long as the Pharisee refuses to confess the first fact, he'll simply be unable to believe the second. He'll be justified in his death; but he'll be so busy doing the bookkeeping on a life he cannot hold that he'll never be able to enjoy himself. It's just misery to try to keep count of what God's no longer counting. Your entries keep disappearing.

If you now see my point, you no doubt conclude that the Pharisee is a fool. You're right. But at this point you're about to run into another danger. You probably conclude that he's also a rare breed of fool — that the number of people who would so blindly refuse to recognize such a happy issue out of their afflictions has got to be small. There you're wrong. We all refuse to see it. Or, better said, while we sometimes catch a glimpse of it, our love of justification by works is so profound that, at the first opportunity, we run from the strange light of grace straight back to the familiar darkness of the law.

You don't believe me? I'll prove it to you: The publican goes "down to his house justified rather than the other." Well and good, you say. Yes indeed. But let me follow him now in your mind's eye as he goes through the ensuing week and comes once again to the temple to pray. What is it you want to see him doing in those intervening days? What does your moral sense tell you he ought at least try to accomplish? Aren't you itching, as his spiritual advisor, to urge him into another line of work — something maybe a little more upright than putting the arm on his fellow countrymen for fun and profit? In short, don't you feel compelled to insist upon at least a little reform?

To help you be as clear as you can about your feelings, let me set you two exercises. For the first, take him back to the temple one week later. And have him go back there with nothing in his life reformed: walk him in this week as he walked in last — after seven full days of skimming, wenching, and high-priced Scotch. Put him through the same routine: eyes down, breast smitten, God be merciful, and all that. Now, then. I trust you see that on the basis of the parable as told, God will not mend his divine ways any more than the publican did his wicked ones. God will do this week exactly what he did last because the publican is the same this week as he was last: he's still dead, and he simply admits it. *God, in short, will send him down to his house justified.* The question in this first exercise is, Do you like that? And the answer, of course, is that you don't. You gag on the unfairness of it. The rat is getting off free.

For the second exercise, therefore, take him back to the temple with at least some reform under his belt: no wenching this week, perhaps, or drinking cheaper Scotch and giving the

161

difference to the Heart Fund. What do you think now? What is it that you want God to do with him? Question him about the extent to which he has mended his ways? Why? If God didn't count the Pharisee's impressive list, why should he bother with this two-bit one? Or do you want God to look on his heart, not on his list, and commend him for good intentions at least? Why? The point of the parable was that the publican confessed that he was dead, not that his heart was in the right place. *Why are you so bent on destroying the story by sending the publican back with the Pharisee's speech in his pocket?*

The honest answer is that while you understand the thrust of the parable with your mind, your heart has a desperate need to believe its exact opposite. And so does mine. We all long to establish our identity by seeing ourselves as approved in other people's eyes. We spend our days preening ourselves before the mirror of their opinion so we will not have to think about the nightmare of appearing before them naked and uncombed. And we hate this parable because it says plainly that it's the nightmare which is the truth of our condition. We fear the publican's acceptance because we know precisely what it means. It means that we'll never be free until we are dead to the whole business of justifying ourselves. But since that business is our life, that means *not until we are dead.*

Because *Jesus came to raise the dead.* Not to reform the reformable, not to improve the improvable . . . but then, I've said all that. Let us make an end: As long as you're struggling like the Pharisee to be alive in your own eyes — and to the precise degree that your struggles are for what is holy, just, and good — you will resent the apparent indifference to your pains that God shows in making the effortlessness of death the touchstone of your justification. Only when you're finally able, with the publican, to admit that you're dead will you be able to stop balking at grace.

It is, admittedly, a terrifying step. You will cry and kick and scream before you take it, because it means putting yourself out of the only game you know. For your comfort though, I can tell you three things. First, it's only a single step. Second, it's not a step out of reality into nothing but a step from fiction into fact. And third, it will make you laugh out loud at how short the trip home was. It wasn't a trip at all: you were already there.

In the Name of the Father and of the Son
and of the Holy Spirit. Amen.

Coffee, anyone?

21

Objections from the Floor

Perhaps the best way for us to proceed now would be by way of question and answer. May I also suggest, though, that before anyone puts a question, he or she give a brief personal introduction? That way we'll all be able to have some sense of the context out of which the question comes and thus a better appreciation of its force. Nothing too long or revealing, of course. Just a few lines for us to read between. Who'll be first? Ah, good! Sheila Grinch. Sheila?

"Yes. My name is Sheila Grinch. I have three girls — fifteen, twelve, and nine. My husband commutes. What I'm afraid of in your sermon, Father, is that people are going to get the idea that it's perfectly all right to do anything they want. I mean, I know it's important to talk about grace and I'm sure we all need it, but there have to be some limits somewhere, don't there, or else people will just go right on lowering their standards like they always have, I guess, but especially now with all this permissiveness. It's not an easy thing, you know, to raise three young girls in this day and age, what with pot all over the schools and people thinking they can sleep with just anybody, and even if they don't, acting as if they had a perfect right to stay out till all hours of the night no matter what their parents say or how much they worry. I mean, won't they?"

"Well, Sheila, I can think of a couple of answers to your question. Let me start with them and then go on to something that lies behind them. You're worried about permissiveness — about the way the preaching of grace seems to imply that it's okay to do all kinds of terrible things as long as you just walk in afterward and take the free gift of God's acceptance.

"The first thing I think you have to say is that while you and I may be worried about seeming to give permission, Jesus apparently wasn't. He wasn't afraid of giving the Prodigal Son a kiss instead of a lecture — a party instead of probation; and he proved that by bringing in the Elder Brother and having him raise pretty much the same objections you do. That sour bookkeeper is angry about the party. He complains that his father is lowering standards and ignoring virtue — that music, dancing, and a fatted calf are in effect just so many permissions to break the law.

"The next thing is that when you say grace gives people permission to commit sins, you have to be very clear about what you mean. The statement needs some distinguishing. It seems to me that when I commit a sin, I don't ask anyone to give me permission; I just take it. If what you're saying is that preaching grace might lead some people to do more of that, I suppose you're right.

"But that's not a *use* of the doctrine of grace. It's an *abuse.* Grace doesn't make evil good. The law about what's right and wrong comes out of our nature as God creates it. Therefore, the law is from God. He never changes his mind about what's best for us. It's just that when we don't do what's best for us, he promises not to let the *what* force him into throwing away the *us.* He doesn't back away from the law; but when push comes to shove, as it always does with us, he makes his first rule *grace.*

"And the reason for that is, he knows what the law does to

165

us: it kills us. By the rules of the law's game, we're dead. So God says, 'I'll give you a new game. It's called raising the dead.' He doesn't say to the Elder Brother, 'This your brother was bad and is good again; he was playing hard to get but now he's playing easy to find.' He says, 'This your brother was dead and is alive again; he was lost and is found.'

"The point is that Jesus is making a distinction between two things we sometimes confuse. They're both true, just as apples and oranges are both true; but they have different rules and mustn't be mixed up. I've been calling them what the Bible calls them: law and grace. Let's switch to other terms and call them *edification* and *rescue*: *edification* meaning the process of building things up to run the way they should, and *rescue* meaning the process of saving them when they don't. Once we do that, you can see that the two processes are always the same in the eyes of the builder/rescuer, but they very often seem opposed in the eyes of anybody else.

"Suppose this village had an absolutely infallible fire department. One that always put out every fire before it did any real damage and that never failed to save people from death, or even injury. Now in the eyes of the fire department, its rescue operations are directed to the very same end as all the careful building operations in the village: keeping the place the way it ought to be. As a matter of fact, the fire department is so committed to that goal that it sends out fire inspectors to make sure people aren't storing oily rags in closets and to teach them all the other rules of fire-safe housekeeping.

"But when the siren goes off and it turns out that the fire is in Mr. Smith's sloppy paint shop, which has been cited for violations twenty times and has caught fire three times in the past week, what do they do? Do they drive up in front of Mr. Smith's and read him the list of violations? Do they say, 'We're sorry, Mr. Smith, but you've done this once too often and we're going to have to let your place burn down, preferably with you trapped inside'? Of course they don't. They put out the fire as quickly as they can because, in their eyes, rescue is their first business.

"But what about in other people's eyes? What about in Mr. Smith's eyes, to start with? He's a pretty unreliable character, apparently. Isn't all this unlimited rescuing going to encourage him in his careless ways? Isn't what he really needs a good dose of the fear of fire? The answer could very well be yes to both questions.

"And what about his upright and fire-fearing neighbors? They spend time and money making their places of business fire-safe. Isn't it unfair to them, after they've shelled out for their own safety, to be taxed just so Smith the cheapskate can have his menace of an establishment saved over and over again? Again, very likely, yes.

Well, you see what I'm getting at. From anybody's point of view but the fire department's, rescue can be seen as, and taken for, permission. But it isn't. And that's that. You can make the same point with the illustration of an infallible lifeguard: the knowledge that rescue is guaranteed can and does lead idiots to go out in surf nobody should swim in. But the lifeguard can't let that consideration interfere with his rescuing. In other words, people may *take* permission, but the rescuer never *gives* it. Do you see what I mean, Sheila?"

"Well, yes. But somehow it still bothers me. Isn't the church supposed to teach the moral law?"

"Of course it is, Sheila — because it has an obligation to stand for whatever is true to God's order of creation, and the moral law is part of that truth. But the church has as its first obligation the duty to preach the good news of grace, not the bad news that the law inevitably is to us sinners. All I'm saying is that our obsession with guilt makes us spend more time on law than on grace and therefore that the church has to work harder on grace than on law. It has to work on both; but grace is the bigger job. But Norman's got his hand up. Norman?"

"I'm Norman Keep. I teach English at the University, and I find myself sympathetic to Sheila's remarks. Let me see if I can point up what I think she's saying.

"I have two children myself. Not as old as Sheila's, but no matter. I think it's the children who are at the root of her objection. Or, better said, the children's moral education. It's not enough just to say that the moral law is one of the eternal truths of God and that it goes on being true no matter what. Because besides being an eternal truth from God's point of view, it is, from our point of view, a culturally transmitted truth. We're not born with the knowledge of it; we're taught it by the society in which we live. And we're not taught it by a handful of catechetical lectures. Actually, the lecture method is probably the least effective approach to moral education. Rather, we're taught it by the entire context of word and example in which we find ourselves: by parents, peers, parsons, police — whatever.

"It's not enough, therefore, for me as a parent — or to the point, Robert, for you as a parson — to maintain that a little theological lip-service to an eternally true moral law is sufficient. I teach not only by what I *say* is so but even more by what I *give the impression* is so. It may be that for persons with a fully formed conscience — if indeed there are any such — the preaching of grace will not seem to abrogate the law. But for children?

"I see Sheila nodding her head. I don't know her fifteen-year-old, but the case of any fifteen-year-old seems to fit nicely here. Is such a person's conscience so well formed that it has stopped taking — or needing — lessons? Take the subject of the morality of sexual acts. I don't want to become mired in any particular development of the subject. Sheila and I might have some differences about that. But I think we can all agree that on the basis of any philosophical system — classical, personalist, existentialist, you name it — there will always be some moral lessons that will be judged preferable to others.

"The point is that a teenager, by her very situation in life, is receiving all kinds of instruction, good and bad, in sexual morality — no matter what system you use as a criterion. Doesn't the parent or the parson in such a case — especially one who claims to know what the *true* system is — have an obligation, first of all, to teach it, and, second, not to allow it to go untaught in the midst of all the competing instruction? Isn't even a *seeming* indifference to morality — however untrue it may be that it's a real indifference — isn't that almost as bad, from a pedagogical standpoint, as a *principled* indifference? Doesn't it just as truly, and perhaps even more subtly, teach a lesson, reinforce a viewpoint, confirm a formation?

"In a word, Robert, my question is: what about moral education? Doesn't your radical insistence on grace put the subject in the shade — or even in the dark?"

"Ah, Norman. As usual, you go for the jugular. Please note also that he always picks the best spot to spring from. I try to fix your minds on the fire department, and I lose you. Norman knows they're already fixed on sex and focuses your attention mightily.

"All right, then: moral education. Let me concede what I think are Norman's valid points.

"Yes, the moral law is culturally transmitted. Yes, it's transmitted by impressions as well as by lectures. Yes, the church has an obligation to avoid giving the impression that anything goes. And yes, the preaching of grace without the preaching of law can give just that impression. The New Testament presupposes and fulfills the Old: to present it as divorced from the Old is to present a parody of it. All granted.

"That's worth following up, however, because we're in danger of forgetting some distinctions here. We're talking as if grace were addressed to a subject called morality. And that's bound to make mischief because morality, by its very nature, must be concerned with *norms,* with standards, whereas grace by definition is concerned with *persons:* it's a refusal to allow the standards to become the basis of their reconciliation or condemnation. Thus the conflict. Morality tells you the standards you need to meet in order to be properly alive; grace tells you that all you ultimately need in order to be alive forever is to be dead: 'The hour is coming, and now is, when the *dead* shall hear the voice of the Son of God, and they that hear shall live' — which is either the world's lowest standard, or no standard at all.

"Grace and morality, therefore, are another case of apples and oranges. Morality deals with virtue and vice — with what is strengthening or weakening for human nature considered as an operational possibility. Grace, however, deals with Sin — with a condition in which human nature has ceased to be an operational possibility and has ended up a lost cause. It is, to say it once more, about the raising of the dead. In the Bible the opposite of Sin, with a capital 'S,' is not virtue — it's faith: faith in a God who *draws all to himself in his resurrection.*

"All this talk about morality, therefore, is misleading. When we get far enough into it, we begin to convince ourselves that the preaching of the moral law will, if properly done, lead people to live good lives and so make them more like what they ought to be. But that's not biblical. Saint Paul says that the purpose of the law was not to do that at all but to bring us to the awareness of Sin — even 'to make Sin exceeding sinful.' We sit here talking as if proper moral instruction to fifteen-year-olds will somehow keep them clear of Sin. But Saint Paul says that Scripture has concluded — locked up — *all* under Sin, so that 'the promise by faith of Jesus Christ might be given to them that believe.'

"That's why I called attention to Norman's choice of sexual morality as an illustration. We're so over-wound on the subject that it always throws the discussion into confusion. We somehow seriously hope — against all the evidence, mind you — that in the case of sexual behavior, our lessons will somehow arm our pupils against lapses. But that just isn't so. We never admit it, of course; but everybody in this room (no matter what his or her moral education) not only has more of a sex life, mental or otherwise, than the rest of us think, but also has been guilty of breaching whatever sexual ethics they have rather more often than they'd like us to know. That's true in other branches of ethics, too: we've all been guilty of breaches of the moral laws against anger, lying, pride, and envy. Somehow, though, we manage to be more realistic about those things. While we teach our children to tell the truth, for example, we're not terribly surprised when we find them guilty of falsehood, and we can even manage to show the little liars some grace without giving them the impression that lying is okay. But when it comes to sex, we're just so nervous we derail ourselves. For openers, therefore, I want you to concede that all the moral instruction in the world, sexual or otherwise, cannot prevent that Sin — that death — to which grace is the only answer. Or at least I want you to concede that that's what Scripture says. Or if worse comes to worst, I want simply to tell you that that's what it says and that if you think otherwise, you and the Bible have a fight on your hands.

"However. Even after you've disabused yourself of the notion that moral education has anything to do with Sin-prevention, it continues, even on its own terms, to be a problematical subject. The first thing you're tempted to say is that we need it simply because a moral society is a nicer society to live in: auto shops don't make unnecessary repairs, butchers keep their thumbs off the scale, plumbers come when they promise, and everyone tells the truth about everything. (Although when I think of the general level of human performance since Adam and Eve, I'm not so sure it would necessarily make for a nicer society to have all that truth flopping around in broad daylight. But let that pass.)

"If you like, I'll concede the point *materially*. I'll admit that, in fact, if the habit of obeying the law were better inculcated, we'd all be better off. But *formally*, I want to wave a cautionary finger. I want you to take a good look at the *principles* by which the law rules over us. Because in fact, there are two of them. The first is the principle of freely chosen obedience to a known good. You love and cherish honesty, for example, and you hate and despise cheating. Those attitudes are in the very fibers of your being — they're part of your substance as a person. Obedience to the law on that principle does indeed produce a more moral society, precisely because it produces truly moral beings: people who have made a free choice of the good. The more types like that you have around, the finer the society they'll all enjoy.

"But not everybody obeys the law on that principle. There are some who freely keep the law; there are those who freely break the law; and there are the rest in the middle somewhere who keep it for fear of what will happen to them if they don't. It strikes me that this third group is probably the largest of the three, and that in one department or another, everybody here can find himself or herself in it.

"What, though, is the principle by which the law rules over that group? Isn't it force? Isn't it intimidation? Isn't their obedience something *less* than a moral proposition? Isn't it more the response of sheep than human beings? Isn't their de facto conformity to the law (which is admittedly good for them and for society) more like the enforced order of a police state than the free order of a moral one? Order is indeed order. But not all order is arrived at on a moral basis.

"An example. When people complain about the lowering of standards, one of their favorite illustrations is the Collapse of Marriage as an Institution. Society, they say, by tolerating divorce — and the church, by allowing remarriage where it once forbade it — have failed us as moral educators. People were better off in

172

the old days, when church and society had enough combined clout to make them stay put.

"I'll concede part of that: some people who really don't need to jump the matrimonial ship jump nowadays because of circumstances their grandmothers would have put up with and possibly turned out the better for. But I deny the rest. The word *clout* was right: a lot of grandmas stayed in their marriages only because they were afraid of the shillelagh the neighbors and the church held over their heads. But it doesn't seem to me that's much of a triumph of moral education. It has very little of the smell of freely chosen good about it.

"There were plenty of people in the good old days who felt nothing but trapped. Some of them, of course, took refuge in the consolations of religion; but watch that line when you're talking morality. The Christian religion is dedicated to the outlandish proposition that God in Christ can save you out of any evil whatsoever. It must not be used, however, to advance the idea that the evil it saves you out of somehow turns into a good in itself. Keep that up long enough, and you can make a case for burning people's bodies to save their souls. Evil always remains evil in itself, and its natural results are almost invariably evil. In fact, therefore, when the inmates of the old matrimonial prison didn't take up religion, they usually made a career of what prisoners are more likely to take to: resentment, bitterness, self-pity, and just plain meanness — none of which look much like the fruits of quality moral education.

"But that's only the first problem with moral education. The second is that it very often fails to reach its goal because either the available professors are incompetent or the classroom situation is so full of psychological hang-ups that the lectures haven't a chance of being heard. My course to my children on not losing their temper, for example, or yours to your children on not cheating or not dealing in personalities — think about those.

Would we seriously like the Faculty Evaluation Committee of the University of Moral Learning to come around and write our tenure hearing report on the basis of our performances? We'd all be sacked. And even where we might have some real competence . . . Suppose (to unleash Norman's pet dog for a moment) that I am in fact unbelievably good at teaching sexual morality: how far do I get in the subject with these pupils I have brought forth from my own loins — whose whole sexual identity is scrambled up with mine, and for whom seventy years will be too short a time even to begin to sort it all out? If I can't teach my daughter to drive a car without losing the thread of instruction in a tangle of personality conflicts, how am I going to make out with a teaching assignment that takes not six half-hour lessons but literally years of daily contact?

"But enough of that. It's a dismal subject. Worse than economics. Who's next? Mrs. Schlosskaese."

"I'm Gertrude Schlosskaese, and I imagine I'm the oldest person here. What most of you are going through with your children, I'm watching my children go through with theirs. Fortunately, my husband and I can go home after they've had difficult scenes. We sometimes wish there were something we could do to help, but there's really very little room for advice-giving. My oldest son once told me that grandparents have an occupational disease called *gramnesia,* which he defines as the grandparents' tendency to forget that their own children ever did anything as bad as what their grandchildren are now doing.

"I just want to say something in favor of what Father has been saying — from the point of view of how I see my own children now. It's not so much about grace, but about the *freedom* I think only grace can give. When I look at my middle-aged children, I sometimes feel sad. It seems to me that instead of becoming freer as they've gotten older, they've gotten more and more afraid of failure — to the point where they don't feel they

174

can risk *anything*. And I wonder if that isn't due to the way they were raised — all the emphasis we put on their being acceptable, all the fear of making mistakes we drummed into them. I see them passing on the same fear. They're wonderful people, very successful and responsible. But they're so depressingly *conventional*, so tight, so tense. Sometimes I think I must be turning into a swinger. We were so afraid of their non-conformity when they were young; and now it's their very conformity that frightens us. And the sad part is, they don't seem to be *happy* in their successes; they seem to be trapped by them.

"I suppose what I'm saying is that education for freedom is the really important thing — and that the only way you can give them that is to raise them with the assurance that they're free to make all the mistakes there are and still find grace and love every time. That's why I think Father is right: there *is* something about all this insistence on law and morality that produces a slave mentality. Grace really does have to be given more attention. If it isn't, all we'll see is grown people who are more afraid than children — and who have to hide from their fear in work, or drink, or a lot of other things that, as they use them, are just . . . well, *joyless*."

"Thank you, Mrs. Schlosskaese. I wouldn't want to add a word to that. But an illustration just occurred to me while you were talking about how unhappy, how depressing, how joyless you find the results of not enough grace in our rearing.

"Our trouble is that we always fall into a *legal* framework when we try to understand grace. But that's too bad because in a fallen world, legality has got to be just about the most joyless subject there is. So let me try a completely non-legal analogy. Let me try an *aesthetic* one.

"Suppose that all of us in this room were magnificently beautiful people. Not that we haven't plenty of handsomeness right now; but give us even more: glowing health, trim bodies, gorgeous faces. And give us the manners and the style to match: make our company in this place the most desirable thing imaginable to anybody.

"And then postulate a world outside this room that's the exact opposite: ugly people, deformed people, people with their noses eaten off by cancer, people who constantly cough up blood — anything, just so you make it very, very bad. And make them know clearly that, by the measure of our society in here, they are simply unacceptable — that they are, physically, nothing but publicans who can't come in on any basis whatsoever. But also make them long to come in — to escape the hell of their existence and rest here in the heaven of our presence.

"And then give them grace. In spite of their unacceptability, go out into the highways and hedges and compel them to come in. Right now, without waiting for improvements. And with no reservations, no conditions, no holding back. Put away that dreadful coffee pot and break out the champagne and caviar. Retire these ugly steel chairs and bring couches. Get rid of those scratchy records and hire Bobby Short.

"Now, then. Ask yourself a question. Do you seriously think that in their joy at having been admitted with all their deformity, they will somehow begin to think more kindly of their ugliness? Do you imagine that poor Noseless Nathan will suddenly come to the conclusion that he has been given *permission* to have no nose? Can you believe that at this moment of unmerited acceptance, he will begin to take pleasure not in our acceptance of him but in his own noselessness? That he will, as a logical consequence, begin to advocate the cutting off of everybody else's nose?

"Of course you don't. You know perfectly well that his acceptance in spite of his ugliness will not diminish one bit his desire for a nose. You understand clearly that when Dr. Wonderful, the handsome and omnicompetent plastic surgeon among us, offers to do an infallible nose job on him, he will say yes with all speed even if it hurts. And he will say yes because he'll see no conflict between the law of his beauty and the grace that accepts his ugliness; because he'll know they're both aimed at the one and only thing we and he are agreed in loving, namely, Nathan *himself*.

"But again, enough. I didn't mean to correct you, Mrs. Schlosskaese, just to thank you and take off from your note of joy into a happier illustration than the merely legal one — to put the nonsense about permission in a more sensible, *aesthetic* light.

"One self-serving comment, though, and we can move on. Do you not now see that my parable about Paul and Laura was precisely an *aesthetic* analogy, not a legal one? I simply used the beauty of romantic love as an analogue there, just as I've used the beauty of physical perfection here. All the legal quibbles you keep handing me are simply irrelevant distractions. I won't press that, however. I promised you something more on the subject of our response to grace, and it's probably wiser to try to say it in as different a way as possible. Therefore in the interest of putting an even greater distance between your mind and my parable, let me abandon it completely for a while and ask you to sit still for another discourse on the subject — in a different voice altogether, and in the style of a century far removed from our own.

"If anyone needs to leave to put a roast in the oven, feel free to do so. Otherwise, sit back and relax once again."

22

And Having Done That,
Thou Hast Donne . . .

*T*he Chapel of the Good Shepherd. The Fourth of my Decanal
Sermons upon the Pharisee and the Publican, in finè.

. . . But now Christ speaketh in a plainesse, and for himselfe.
Dico vobis, he saith, *I say this unto you,* because I alone can say it.
The *Pharisee* doth not say it to you, for he saith onely uselesse
things, and they condemne him. The *Publican* doth not say it to
you, for he standeth with you in a like darknesse of selfe-con-
demnation, and hath not even uselesse things to say. And ye
cannot say it to yourselves, for ye, and every childe of *Adam,* are
Pharisees and *Publicans* at once, full of idle goodes and busie evils,
all alike *concluded under sinne,* so that by the works of the law,
though it be holie, just and good, *non justificabitur omnis caro,*
there shall no flesh be justified before God.

Christ alone saith to you of this *Publican, descendit hic justificatus in domum suam,* this man went down to his house justified
rather than the other. Not that they did not stand in an *equalitie*
before God; though neither knew it, for it was an equalitie in
death. Mortui enim estis, saith the Scripture to them both; ye are

178

dead, in a death, in a *deadnesse* from which, by your own power, ye shall never rise; *and your life is hidde with Christ in God. The hour cometh,* saith Christ, *when the dead shall heare the voyce of the Sonne of God, and they that heare shall live.* So it is now that *voyce,* that *verbum verbi* which speaketh to you; but it is onely the *dead* that heare it and *live.* Not the *Pharisee,* feigning life by a *wisdome* of *words;* not we by our *clamourous protestations* of *harmlessnesse;* but onely the *Publican,* by his confession of that *extremitie* from which he cannot of himselfe return. Onely of him is this *descendit hic justificatus* spoken; he alone goes down justified, because he alone acknowledgeth the *foolishnesse* and *weaknesse* of his case, that he is but *granum frumenti,* a grain of wheat fallen into the ground and *dead.* Not *mortalis,* mortall, apt to die; but *mortuus,* dead, beyonde the help of any *voyce* but One. Onely of him is it said, *multum fructum affert,* he bringeth forth much fruit.

But what now of that *fruit,* that blossoming and ripening out of death, which this voyce, this *Arise from the dead,* promiseth him as he goeth down justified to his house now *swept and garnished,* cleane and apt for life? *Mortificati estis legi,* saith S. Paul, ye are dead to the law by the body of Christ, that ye may belong to another who was raised from the dead *ut fructificemus Deo,* that we, we all, might bear fruit to God. But how are we to expound that *fructifying,* that *reformation* of our lives? For while the *Publican* will never stande againe on *triall* for his *eternal soule;* while we, by Christ's satisfaction, have been forever set free from any *necessitie* of bringing good workes for our *exculpation* (for we are *alive from the dead,* and *uncondemned in Christ Jesus*); yet that fruit must come. For we goe not down to our house justified that we may take to ourselves *seven devils worse,* but onely *ut fructificemus,* that we may bear fruit. And while we may not so expounde that reformation of our life that we undoe the parable, and attach a *necessitie* where God attacheth none, making it out that he gives us life onely tentatively, upon condition of reforme (*for while we*

179

were yet sinners, Christ died for the ungodly); still, there must be an *inevitabilitie* about it. For though *Christ died for our sinnes and rose for our justification,* yet he stops not there. He wills something better for us than a poore *half-holyday* from sinne; for *whom he justified, them also he glorified.* He first contents himselfe by accounting us righteous; but then he contents us too, and makes us holie. Our *sanctification* is as much his will as our *justification.* His mercies give not onely an *absolution* from our incursion into sinne, but an *elation* out of it as well; and they give the second as easily as the first: *For if, when we were enemies, we were reconciled to God by the death of his Sonne, much more, being reconciled, shall we be saved by his life.*

We shall be whole then in Christ, who is the *house* to whome we goe justified, the onely place we live; and we shall be so by a *double inevitabilitie:* by his grace which is already at hand, and by our death which will come to hand the minute we confesse it; for we are already *dead, and our life is hidde with Christ in God.* The reforme of our life is *his worke* alone; it is onely our *joy* to have it raised up from our death; and there is nothing now that impedeth that *joyfull work* but our sadde pretence to a life we doe not have.

Consider then the preachers dutie to you. It is not onely to tell you Christ *raiseth the dead.* It is also to convince you Christ raiseth *onely* the dead. It is to *persuade* you of your death; to *reduce* you, by whatever means he can, *physicall, morall,* or *philosophicall,* to a knowledge of that last truth of yours, and so set you free to *believe* that first of his; so to enforce this *mortui estis,* this *ye are dead,* upon your mindes, that the *scales* of this *deceitfull life* may fall from your eyes, and ye see *vita vestra,* Christ, who is your life.

I doe not choose here, though, to convince you of your *physicall* or *morall* death; the churchyard argues the one, and your conscience the other. Your fraile life here now, which once was not, will soone enough againe return to naught; and that you know. And your death in sinne, not only in fresh sinnes, lately grown and scarce repented of, but in olde and withered sinnes, sinnes left and rejoyned, and left and joyned againe and againe, is a *continuall* death, because *your times are in his hand,* and that hand holds them forever *absolved* in his death. All that is plaine, and needs no argument. But what is not plaine is that your life now, your life as you hold it, though you bear no present guilt or instant sicknesse, is still no life, but death; and to make that plaine, onely a *philosophicall* consideration will doe.

Consider then your life. I doe not urge upon you this *present moment,* which is onely a scrap, a tatter, a single weft of your whole life; but its *intire fabrique,* all the warpes and wooves of time and *circumstance* from the day of your birth untill this time and place. *In manibus tuis sortes meae;* my lot, my whole condition, is in thy hands. God hath our life indeed, and he hath it *reconciled in Christ.* But what have we? Onely *one minute* in possession; all the rest lost, or yet to come. And what a minute is that? And what a hand is it that holds it? It is but a fleeting minute; no *nunc stans,* no eternall stabile *now;* but a *nunc volans,* a poore wisp of a now, flyinge forever into a darke and endlesse *then.* And what is that hand of ours that graspes it? It is a crippled, fragile hand, more apt to drop than hold, and lesse like to be *here* than *gone* the next minute. An *earthquake,* or a *fire from heaven* in this place, would breake forever my grip upon my times. And even if, in mercie, I am spared to stande some minutes more in this *vale of teares,* how *imperfect,* how *decrepit* is my grasp of all those other times of my *pilgrimage* which of necessitie comprise most of my life? It is a merely *mentall,* not a *reall* hand. It is a holding of my past in *memorie,* and of my future in *hope;* but it is a *possession* of neither in fact. I cannot reach yesterday but in my minde; and in my minde, yesterday is but a shadowe of itself: halfe of what I saw, I did not notice; halfe of what I noticed, I forgot; halfe of what I remembered, I have falsified; and halfe of what I did not falsifie, I misremembered. But none of it, true or false, culpable

181

or harmlesse, can I touch at all. That *calumnie* upon a friend, which yesterday I spread abroad for all to heare, I cannot now sweepe up and hide; that *slothful neglect* of office, when I said, *my Lord delayeth his coming,* and began to *eat* and *drink* and to be *drunken,* I cannot now supply; that angrie devastation of my childrens *soules* by which I *provoked them to wrath,* I cannot make as though it never were. I have no more *capacitie* to reach those times, though I stande here, spared and living, *a thousand years,* than if I lay here dead beneath some smoulderinge beame. And therefore *I am dead.* For all those times, *I have no hand.* And if I think of *future* times, my case is worse: I am *twice dead,* for my grasp of them hath a *double infirmitie;* it is a *misapprehension,* and it is that of things I neither saw nor see. If I should say, to-morrow I will not rage against my *children,* I cannot know the *certaintie* of that. I said as much the day before yesterday; and it was then but what it now is: a false hope against a to-morrow my hand can never reach.

Therefore my times are in Gods hands *alone.* The reformation of them must be his worke, for I am *dead,* and *he onely* holds them as they should be. To mee they are but *dreames* of *memories.* While I live, I suffer them, but onely in a dreamers *incapacitie* to escape the *shipwracke* I have wrought; and when I depart this *dreaming life,* I lose even that. If ever, then, what good they held is to be raised; if, at long last, their evils are to be *reconciled,* he alone must doe it. If my *sinnes* and *iniquities* are to be *remembered* no more, they must be *obliterate* in *better hands* than mine. For while my selfe lives here, it cannot touch them; and when I die, I onely lose *myselfe.*

But as that work of *reformation* cannot be mine by reason of my *death,* yet it is mine nonetheless by reason of *his life.* For I am dead *now,* and my life is hidde with Christ *now,* and though the Scripture saith *cum Christus apparuerit,* when Christ who is my life *shall appeare,* then shall I appeare with him in glory; yet the same Scripture saith, *nunc autem semel in consummatione saeculorum,* now, once for all, in the *very present end of all the ages,* Christ hath already appeared; *per hostiam suam apparuit,* by his offering of himselfe upon *the Crosse* hath he appeared; and though we be dead in our sinnes, yet God *convivificavit nos in Christo,* he hath *quickened* us together in Christ, *et conresuscitavit,* he hath raised us up together in Christ, *et consedere fecit in caelestibus in Christo Jesu,* and he hath made us sit together in heavenly places in Christ Jesus; and he hath done all that *nunc,* now. It is an intire work, *now;* and we have it in possession, *now. Nunc filii Dei sumus, now* we are the sonnes of God, and while it doth not yet appear what we shall be, we know that when he shall appear, we shall be like him, for we shall see him as he is. The *last day of the world* will not show us what he will doe *then,* but onely make plaine that which he did when he chose us *ante mundi constitutionem,* before the foundation of the world. All times are his times; therefore *now* is the accepted time; *now* is the day of salvation. And *now,* therefore, is that *reformation* ours.

What saith the Scripture then? How doth it invite us to that work which, while it cannot be of us, is yet ours? How doth it call us *who sit in darknesse and in the shadowe of death* into the light of that *Dayspring from on high who hath visited us? Si consurrexistis cum Christo,* it saith, if ye be risen together with Christ, *quae sursum sunt quaerite,* seek those things which are above where Christ sitteth on the right hand of God, and where ye also now sit with him in heavenly places. For ye have *died already,* and your life is *hidde with Christ* in God. *Mortificate ergo,* therefore mortifie your members which are upon earth. *Mortifie* them for that reason onely; not because, as the *Manichees* doe teach, they are living, evil members; but because, though they be good, and from the hand of God, they survive now onely in a *death* from which no power of yours can raise them. *Mortifie* them, let them die, for die they will, whether you let them or not. Put them to death,

183

for they are already as good as dead, whether you know it or not. They are dying pieces of a dead hand; snapped wooves, frayed threades upon a broken loom. But in Christ the whole cloth of your dayes hath been made *seamlesse* againe now, and *woven againe from the top throughout* now, and *made white in the Blood of the Lamb* now. Goe now therefore to that Lamb. Not to those things *propter quae venit ira Dei super filios incredulitatis,* on account of which the *wrath of God* cometh upon the children of unbeleefe; but goe onely *to him;* and goe onely *by beleeving.* For that wrath cometh upon *Pharisee* and *Publican* alike, and upon all men who in their *incredulitie* seek to stand, whether in innocence or guilt, it matters not, upon those things. But it cometh upon no *childe of beleefe,* if onely he confess that he is dead, and that his life is hidde with Christ in God. *Nihil ergo nunc damnationis,* there is therefore now no condemnation to them that are in Christ Jesus. We are saved by a free and boundlesse gift *now,* we are reformed in him *now;* if onely *now* we will beleeve.

But in our *incredulitie,* we halt, and feare, and think per-chance we shall fall short somehow. We imagine that some *failure* on our part, some *inabilitie* to embodie his reformation of us, some *declination* into sinne againe, will next time cut us off from him for good. But how should it? If *naught can separate us from the love of Christ;* if no past sinne, nor any concatenation of past sinnes could doe as much, how shall any link or chaine of future sinnes doe more? Our former futures to this present day are past; and all our future dayes from now will soon themselves be over, too. How are those two futures different, but to our *unbeleefe?* Doe they not stand all under that one rubrique, *To-day, if you will heare his voyce?* Was there ever, will there ever be any day, any time, which is not *to-day* to him, and is not a *soverain occasion* of that *voyces speaking?* Was Peters sinne in *thrice denyinge* Christ his *first* sinne? Was he not rebuked before of Christ in that saying, *Get thee behind mee, Satan?* And was *that sinne* his last? Did not

184

S. Paul *withstand him to the face,* because he was to be blamed for *dissemblinge* with the Galatians? Were not all those dayes *to-day* for Christ? Were any of those times *not* in his hand? Was even one of them not a *day of salvation* to an unhardened heart? Was that *voyce* ever still?

Cantavit gallus, saith the Gospell, the cock crew; *et flevit Petrus,* and Peter wept. In that brief compasse is the whole of our condition. The cock singeth, for the *sixth day,* the day of mans creation, hath dawned againe, and it is the onely *Good Friday* since that first. And he singeth for *every creature. Cantabunt canticum novum,* it is said of the saints; they shall sing a new song. And the cock singeth with them, in the *lawfulle pride* of his *un-fallen nature,* rejoycinge at their restoration from *Adams fall.* He singeth for *Peter,* who in this dawne can onely *weepe.* He singeth for *you* and *me* who to-day, or to-morrow, or at the *houre of our death* will have our teares as well; but he singeth because, in the *fulnesse* of our life in Christ, *God shall wipe away all teares from our eyes.* He even singeth, in a *mysterie,* for Judas, gone into a *darknesse* of his owne devising because he could not beleeve that dawne, but not gone from that *Dayksprings voyce* that holds him still.

And so we live, weepinge for our sinnes *by the waters of Babylon,* unable of ourselves to sing the *Lords song* in the *strange land* of our *dilapidation,* but hearinge alwaies that *new song* sung over us at every dawne. And as there was no space between that *gallicinium,* that *crowinge of the cock,* and *Peters weepinge;* so there is none betweene us and our reformation in the *Sonne of God.* He wills us *whole,* and he holds us so now. That we fall short of what he wills for us is but the *sadnesse* of our *death;* it is not our *life.* Our life is *Christ,* and *he,* if we *beleeve,* is our onely joy. If we must *weep* our way to *heaven,* then let us weep and be on our way, for he who is *the Way* wept too, and despiseth us not. If we can have no more than *teares* in our *reformation* now, it is enough, for he holdeth our reformation fast, and will not suffer us, *for any paines of death,* to fall from him. And so the *preachers* work is done. There wee leave you in that *blessed dependancy,* to *hang* upon *him* that *hangs* upon the *Crosse,* there *bath* in his *teares,* there *suck* at his *woundes,* and *lie downe in peace* in his *grave,* till hee vouchsafe you a *resurrection,* and an *ascension* into that *kingdom* which hee hath *purchas'd for you,* with the *inestimable price* of his *incorruptible blood.* Amen.

23

As Pants the Hart
for Cooling Streams . . .

"Alas, Norman, our coffee-hour crowd appears to have wandered off. It seems there are just the two of us left."

"I'm afraid, Robert, that the market for seventeenth-century sermons is a bit limited. Though I must say, I enjoyed it."

"Any criticisms?"

"Oh, perhaps a few false quantities here and there, at least to my ear: some of your quotes from the Latin may be a bit longer than John Donne would have liked. And an anachronism or two: your use of the words 'grip' and 'grasp,' for example. I'm not sure that's something Donne would have done. 'Purchase' sounds more likely to me. But all in all, a very pleasant conceit indeed."

"Good."

"What do you mean, 'good'?"

"That's all I ever say to comments about sermons. I never thank people who thank me because if I do that, I set myself up either for the smarmy piety of telling them they should actually be thanking God or for the hypocrisy of having to thank them when they tear me apart the next time around. Much better just to say 'good': if the sermon really was good, then that's good; if it was really bad, then it's good someone spotted it. And if the comment is simply off the wall, 'good' ends the conversation as mercifully as possible. Perfect all-purpose response."

"Good."

"Hey! I've got an idea. I'm batching it this weekend. My wife's out visiting her sister, and the kids are off to the four winds somewhere. Why don't you come over to the rectory and let me stir you up something a little more festive than coffee?"

"Marvelous idea. It's dry work all around. I'm with you."

• •

"All right, Norman. First stop, the kitchen. I've got sweet vermouth, dry vermouth, vodka, most of a fifth of Tanqueray, Heineken (if my sons haven't cleaned me out) . . . you name it."

"What kind of dry vermouth?"

"Boissiere."

"Awfully perfumey. Tanqueray on the rocks, I think. Time enough to do battle with the Boissiere when we get to the vodka."

"Good enough. Take the can of Bremner Wafers and that slab of Gorgonzola and settle yourself in the living room. I'll be right with you."

• •

"Gorgeous cheese, Robert."

"*Cristoforo Colombo.* Nothing but the best, Norman. The milk of the *bufala* and the milk of human kindness. *Salute!*"

"Cheers! You know? As a matter of fact, I do have a criticism of your Donne sermon — though it's rather more from the point of view of your department than mine. When you were pounding home all those *nows* back there, I was thinking you hadn't got it quite right. Or better said, perhaps, you got it right but you never dealt with the questions it raises — some of them rather nasty questions."

"What do you mean?"

"Well, you were quite convincing about the Scriptures' requiring us to believe in the present reality of resurrection, or reconciliation, or reformation, or whatever — about the impossibility of making them out to be simply future events. But suppose I accept that. Doesn't that straightway give me a problem about God I didn't have before? Look at it this way. Suppose you were to come to me and say, 'Norman, I'm in trouble; I need two million dollars.' And I say to you, 'No problem, Robert. I've got it right here in my pocket; it's all yours.' And you say, 'Oh, thank you, Norman, thank you.' But then, when you put out your hand, I say to you, 'Unfortunately, Robert, you can't have it just now. You'll have to wait half an hour.'

"Do you see the problem? What's the point of the delay? Doesn't it seem to be some kind of cat-and-mouse game on my part? If I'm so good and so obviously in a position to help you out forthwith, why do I string you along?"

"But Norman. My point was that it really is ours now. In a *mystery,* perhaps, hidden in the pocket — but really and truly ours by the irrevocable gift of God."

"That doesn't quite do it. Let me tinker with the illustration a bit. Suppose I have miraculous powers of healing, and you come to me with some loathsome and horribly painful disease and say, 'Norman, I can't stand my life. It's all I can do to keep from screaming in agony; please heal me.' And I say, 'No problem; consider it done.' And you say, 'Oh, thank you, Norman; when will the pain stop?' And I say, 'It's stopped already as far as I'm concerned, Robert; in fact, I've made you as sound as a dollar.' And you say, 'But it hasn't stopped for me; how long do I have to wait for it to be a fact that I can experience?' And I say, 'Half an hour.'

"Do you see it now? What kind of person am I if I can spend those thirty minutes enjoying your good health while you sit there in front of me racked with pain? Isn't my performance just Elisha and Naaman the Syrian all over again? I mean, Naaman was right, you know. Why didn't Elisha just strike his hand over the place and recover the leper? Why all the stagey delay involved in washing seven times in the Jordan? Or if washing had to be part of it, why not just one good dip? If you're going to do a job on somebody, you do it then and there if you can. And since there's no question that God can — he not only claims he can, he insists he already has — why doesn't he get on with the job and let us in on the enjoyment of it?"

"Well, let's see. I guess part of the reason in Naaman's case was simply stylistic or cultural: that was the way you staged things in those days, dragging them out to heighten the effect — like Elijah dousing the sacrifice with water three times before calling down the fire from heaven. But there's something else to it. Naaman comes with his own scenario in mind: a flashy, magic-wand performance — or at least, if it's got to involve a dip in a river, some really deluxe river like Abana or Pharpar, not this two-bit Jordan. What Elisha is saying, in effect, is that God acts upon obedient trust; and that if you have trust, all you've got to do is perfectly ordinary stuff. Because Naaman really is already healed; all he's got to do is take a long swim while his health comes back. So you're right. It really is Elisha and Naaman all over again. But what you're overlooking is the fact that Elisha and Naaman is faith's response to grace all over again — faith's response to an already present reformation wrought by grace. Thank you, Norman. I hadn't thought of an Old Testament illustration for it till you gave me one."

"Entirely too fast, Robert. Forget Elisha. If you're going to give me a serious theology of grace, you're not going to be allowed to put stylistic and cultural limitations on the Divine. The prob-

190

lem, frankly, is the sadism of God. The question isn't where he learned his bad manners; it's why he doesn't reform them. And you're not going to be able to plead mystery either, because God has gone public, as it were, in Jesus. He's come out and said flatly that the job is done — *nunc semel* and all that sort of thing: *now, once for all.* He's made known the mystery, let us in on the Good News. And once he's done that, you can't plead him not guilty to the charge of cruelty. He has to answer for the world's apparently unnecessary half-hour of agony. What you've really got on your hands, you know, is the book of Job all over again: the theologian as miserable comforter."

"True, true. But then somebody has to play Job's friends. It's just my bad luck to get the thankless parts; you question to your heart's content and then get all those sheep and camels at the end — plus three daughters who are knockouts."

"No matter. My complaint's not about the happy ending. It's about your assertion that the happy ending is already present in the rotten middle of the play where you've got all those supposedly healed Jobs sitting in ashes scraping their boils with potsherds. That's my idea of a really thankless part. You simply have to deal with the problem of the half-hour wait. You've got God's camera grinding while real flesh and blood is being lacerated. That's blood he's filming, not tomato catsup. You've got a world that's a snuff film."

"You know what just occurred to me? Your half-hour wait. In the book of Revelation, when the Lamb opens the seventh seal, 'there was silence in heaven about the space of half an hour.' Odd."

"It's not odd at all. Just more divine bad manners."

"All right. Let me take a crack at it. The question is: Why, if our restoration is accomplished now in God, do we have to sit around for a lifetime with no observable restoration whatsoever? It's more than the problem of why God permits evil in the first place; it's the problem of why, after he assures us he's solved the problem of evil, he still leaves us mucking around in it."

"Right. Now deal with it."

"Well, for openers I think you have to talk about the dynamics of creating. When you make something, you make a thing that's other than yourself. On the one hand, precisely because *you're* the cause of it, it exists mentally, ideally, intellectually *in you:* it exists *eminently,* as we say in the theology trade — in a nifty, high-class way suitable to your nifty, high-class style of being. But on the other hand, by the very fact that it's a *real being,* it also exists *in itself, by itself:* it's a substance, a thing, something that exists *per se,* not just *in alio,* in something else.

"To put it another way, there are always two grips on the being of every created thing. The first is the creator's grip on the creature; but the second is the creature's grip on itself. There's only one *thing,* of course — I don't want to get into positing the creature's existence on two levels; but there are in fact *two grips* on its one being. If I make an omelet, for example, I myself hold its being in one way: in a way appropriate to a cook — in my mind, *ideally;* in my omelet pan, *causatively;* and so on. But the omelet holds its own being in a way strictly appropriate to an omelet. It doesn't *know* it's an omelet, and it certainly isn't able to *cause* itself to become one.

"For instance. You know the laws of my way of holding the omelet. You don't think — at least I hope you don't — that if you took off the top of my skull, you would find a headful of cooked egg. But you also realize that the omelet nonetheless does exist in my mind — and that as it exists there, it is always perfectly browned, flawlessly folded, and never less than piping hot. In short, as it exists in me, it is perfectly obedient to the laws of my way of holding it.

"On the other hand, you know that as the omelet holds itself, it is just as obedient to its own laws. If I answer the phone after turning it out onto the platter, it will get colder every minute I am on the phone — or it will be savaged by my cat and come to the table with one of its ends missing. In other words, it can suffer as many sad declinations from its perfection as the law of its own eggy way of holding itself makes possible. And therefore, precisely because I have made a real omelet — and even more precisely because, even though there are two grips on it, there is only one omelet — I am stuck with both sets of laws and, in particular, with the problems that arise when the omelet's set differs from mine. Unless, of course, I destroy the omelet. But then, that's not an option when you're talking about God: he threw that one away early on, when he put up the rainbow at the end of the Noah fiasco. Does any of that make sense to you, Norman?"

"Some. You're saying that God is stuck with creation's way of holding itself, and that's the reason for the half-hour wait — because time is one of the laws of creation's grip on itself. It all seems a bit *external,* though. I mean, isn't God's way of holding things supposed to be more intimate and immediate than that? Isn't he, unlike a cook who answers the telephone, never away from what he makes? I hope you're not saying he simply phones in our restoration."

"That wouldn't be all bad, Norman. I have a suspicion that, lurking in your last remark, there might just be an analogy to both the Good News of grace and the fact that faith comes by *hearing.* But let it pass. Let me try another illustration. I knew a civil engineer once who worked for a while on the DEW line — someplace way above the Arctic Circle, and in the middle of January at that. Well, one night he'd spent about three hours setting up a theodolite in forty-below-zero weather so he could take a reading. When the time came to make the actual sighting, he removed the cap from the eyepiece and, by a purely reflexive action, blew on the lens to remove any dust. Result? One ice-coated lens, and a whole night's work down the drain.

"That's got the note of intimacy, you see. What could be more intimate to what a man is doing than his own breath? What could be more an expression of his immediate intention to get on with his work? But it wasn't only his grip on his breath that counted. His breath's moisture-laden, imminently icy grip on itself counted just as much. It had its own laws; and at forty below, they just worked out."

"Come now, Robert. That happened only because he paid no attention to those laws — because he forgot about them. Supposedly, God doesn't do that: he's always got everything in mind."

"Doesn't make any difference. The point is that he's stuck. Sure, the engineer could have decided to withhold his breath — his *spirit* — from brooding on the face of the lens; but in fact he didn't. He turned it loose. The point of the illustration lies in the actuality of what he did, not in the consideration preceding it. We don't know *why* God created — for all we know, he could have made a mistake, just like the engineer. But he *did* create, and that's that. And therefore he's stuck with the laws of what he's made."

"But how does all this insistence on God's being stuck square with the idea that he's all-powerful? Don't you leave him looking rather like a lame duck?"

"That doesn't matter, either. The biblical view of the omnipotence of God simply says he gets everything his way in the end. It doesn't demand that he get his way in every instance by sheer power. Sometimes — and above all at the most important time, on the cross — he does it by weakness, by being a *dead* duck."

"Still though, Robert. Apart from that totally unserious line about God's having made a mistake, you haven't gotten him off the hook on the subject of evil. You've only said that *if* he decides to create, he's got to put up with his creature's grip on itself. I'll give you that if you like. But what I won't give you is that it's an answer to my question. It just puts it back one notch. My question now becomes: Why, if he could see all this bleeding agony coming, did he go ahead with his insistence on making a substantial world — especially one with such an unreliable purchase on its life and times? Why couldn't he have settled for a purely mental world in his divine head, one only he would have a grip on — a kind of endlessly enjoyable unwritten novel? Even the worst writer in the world is less guilty than you're making God. If some hack corners himself into having to run a locomotive over his protagonist, at least he doesn't do it in reality. A bad book is a pardonable ineptitude; a bad world is a deliberate crime."

"That's good, Norman. And I'm tempted to make God's own reply to it right now — which is that he *is* a criminal, and that he admits it by dying as one in the death of Christ. But there's a little more to it than that, so let me fetch the wine jug and the Tanqueray first. 'As pants the hart for cooling streams, when wounded in the chase . . .' As you said, it's dry business, all this thirsting after righteousness."

●   ●

"There you are, Norman. Help yourself. Now, then: *God is bad.* Okay, granted. Given the evidence, the best plea I can enter for him is *nolo contendere.*

"But you seem to be implying that God is somehow worse than we are — that at our best, we wouldn't permit the kind of cruelty he does, that we would either stop it before it got started, or else (if we had somehow got it reconciled in ourselves) not require anyone else to go through it for a minute.

"That's not the case, however. Oh, sure, with small children we'll intervene to stop mayhem. But what about with grown children? What about Mrs. Schlosskaese and her forty-five-year-old Freddy drowning his fear of freedom in a pint of gin every

195

night? It's not just her creaturely limitation that keeps her from coming on heavy with him. It's her knowledge that he really *is* free, and that however much he may mismanage his own freedom, there's simply no way he can be himself unless he's *left free* by her. It's wisdom, not weakness, that keeps her from putting the arm on him. Or, better said, it's the foolishness of God which is wiser than men that keeps her from it. So God at his worst is at least no more guilty of criminal neglect than Mrs. Schlosskaese is at her best. He even goes through the same passionate sadness she does."

"All right, Robert; but it's still not enough. Gertrude Schlosskaese *bore* a free creature. She went to bed with her husband one night, made love, and took the consequences. She didn't invent Freddy and his damned freedom; she just found him ready-made nine months later. But God did invent him; so it was none other than God who set Freddy and Gertrude up for whatever tears they've shed for forty-five years in this vale of freedom. And therefore there isn't a court in the country that wouldn't dismiss God's vaunted claim of innocence by reason of divine foolishness and find him guilty of reckless endangerment and criminal neglect. And if he's got old Freddy all reconciled now in Jesus, he's only compounding the felony by dragging the two of them — plus Mrs. Freddy and all the kiddies and God knows who else — through one minute more of his totally unnecessary shirtiness about freedom."

"Good, Norman, good! Right on target! The final theological answer to your question, therefore, is that there is no answer. Not to your last and deadliest formulation of it, at any rate. Why freedom? Why a substantial world with such a slippery grip on itself? Why such a transient, blind-staggering, mortal grip? *No answer.* All the threads of reason disappear into the inscrutable knot of the eternal counsel of a God whose ways are not our ways.

"There's only one slight softening of the harshness of that. On a good day, when you've just fallen in love and your lungs aren't acting up, God's ways, while they're not yours, look awfully like the very ways you'd choose if you were God. We love freedom, Norman. We really do. But on a bad day, when the consequences of it catch up with us and we're coughing up the blood of our self-destruction, we curse it for not being the sovereign cough syrup we thought it should have been.

"But it's not cough syrup, and that's that. Freedom is death, and the Passion, and agony and bloody sweat. And why it has to be that, nobody knows. And why it goes on being that for us after God has gotten it all turned into cough syrup for himself, nobody knows either. The only thing you can say is that if you love him, you go on being a damn fool and trust him anyway."

"'Though he slay me, yet will I trust him.' That's it, is it?"

"Unfortunately for the apologist, Norman, yes. All he can say is that at least he's not guilty of misrepresentation. His product is strictly as advertised: as you said, it's the book of Job all over again. Or, to expand the reference a bit, it's *My God, my God, why hast thou forsaken me?* sandwiched in between noon and three, along with *Consummatum est* and *Happy days are here again* — believe it or not. There may or may not be grace. But it's certain that if there isn't, there simply isn't a scrap of finally Good News anywhere. And it's still more certain that even if there is grace, the only way to it is faith. There's something more to say after you've passed the point of faith, of course — something like, 'So what if God made a "mistake"; if the Someone who set up the world so that evil is possible is willing to *commit suicide* over his mistake rather than blame *you* for it, then *trusting* such a person doesn't seem like an altogether bad idea.' But you can say that only at the price of shutting up about the unanswerable question. The question, you see, is not 'Is he competent?' but 'Does he *care?*'"

"That's rather a hard sell."

"That it is, Norman, that it is. However, if you've got a little more time and patience, I do have something else I'd like to bounce off you."

"My patience can hold out as long as your Tanqueray does. What is it?"

"The story I promised you. Fetch some more ice, and I'll get the manuscript."

PART THREE

THE
YOUNGEST DAY

24

Rub-out

It was quarter to one on the same Friday afternoon in April that found Paul making his confession in Laura's car. Unnoticed by either of them, a gray Cadillac dropped off two passengers at the entrance to the back foyer of the restaurant and parked at the corner of the building. Two more men got out of the front seat and looked around the parking lot.

"You sure we shook them, Bobby?"

"Yeah, I'm sure. You haven't seen them since they got stuck at that light in Corona, have you?"

"No, but maybe they caught up and we didn't see them."

"No way. Why the hell do you think I took Northern Boulevard instead of the Parkway? They'll never figure it out. Relax, Dominic, relax."

"I still don't like it. Hey! There's somebody in that yellow Volvo over there."

"For Chrissake, don't make a federal case out of it. It's probably just what it looks like; you spend more time making out like that, and the boys won't call you 'Fat Mickey.' Get your ass inside without acting like it's gonna fall off."

They walked in, went up the back stairs to the banquet manager's office, and knocked.

"Who is it?"

"Roberto."

The door opened into a room about ten by twelve. One desk covered with papers, three chairs, five men. No one sitting but the old man behind the desk in a swivel chair. He waited with his eyes down and his hands folded until the door was closed. With the blinds almost shut, the half-darkness left only his face clearly visible, lit by the light of the desk lamp bouncing up off the papers. He lifted his head.

"Well, Roberto?"

"It's good, Boss. We shook the only tail we had in Queens. Just to be real sure, I killed an hour cruising around side streets in Manhasset."

The old man looked around the room. "What about outside?"

"Bobby and me saw somebody in a yellow Volvo on the other side of the lot when we came in."

"Shut up, Mickey. I already sent Rudy to check if they're locals. Just keep your ears open and your mouth closed. What about the rest outside, Franco?"

"Nothing, Boss. All empty cars. Just the usual lunch crowd."

The old man looked down at the desk again and half-closed his eyes. "Okay. Still, we wait for Rudy."

Minutes passed. No one spoke. Finally, Rudy knocked and came in.

"Well?"

"It's some guy and a broad, Boss, just sitting there talking. He drove in just before twelve-thirty. She came ten minutes later. He got in her car and they went over there and parked."

"Anybody know them?"

"The captain says the guy comes here a lot. University type. The dame was here only on Monday. They had lunch, then made out a little in the back hall before they left. If you ask me, he's out there trying to talk her into a real lay this time."

"I didn't ask you."

He looked up across the desk at a man roughly his own age. "It's too bad, Vito. Too bad. You got anything you wanna say?"

Vito wiped his forehead with the back of his hand but otherwise remained still.

"Nothing, Vito?"

"What's the use, Angelo? You got your mind made up. I could ask you for old times' sake, but I know better."

"Just like I could ask you for old times' sake why you let Riggio use you to sucker my nephew into that car." He put his head down again and breathed hard. "But I'm tired, Vito, and we both know you got no answers I can afford. Let's get this over with. All of you get out of here. Except you, Bobby."

When the others were gone, Angelo stood up and faced Roberto. "Bobby, you got everything straight?"

"Yeah, Boss. We go to . . ."

"Skip it. I can read that in the papers. Just don't blow it."

"Have I ever, Boss?"

"Bobby, you're a smart kid. But 'Have I ever?' is the dumbest question in the world. Up till two weeks ago, Vito could have asked it. Just watch your step. The record doesn't count — only what you do for me today. Just do it quick and painless. And you do it, not those other bastards." He reached into his pocket and handed Bobby a pair of cotton work gloves and a nylon cord. "Shit! Forty years . . ."

Roberto waited, but nothing came.

"Okay, Boss. Just the way you say. Is that all?"

"That's all. Now go. And tell Rudy he's driving me back to Jersey. I hate this dump."

• •

Mickey pulled the Cadillac up to the rear entrance. Franco put Vito in the front between him and Mickey. Roberto got in the back seat. "You drive where Franco tells you, Mickey, and don't talk. And stay under the limit, for Chrissake. Franco, you remember what I told you."

They drove east on the highway until they were past Port Jefferson and then headed down the back roads toward Ridge. Nobody spoke except Franco, giving directions. After about half an hour he said, "Okay, Mickey, take the next right." He turned himself a little and looked at Roberto. "We're almost there."

Roberto took the pair of work gloves out of his pocket, put them on, and wound the ends of the garrote around his hands. He sat forward on the seat, checked the deserted road ahead and behind, braced himself, and threw the cord over Vito's head onto his throat. Vito's hands came up but Franco grabbed them and forced them down with his full weight. Roberto pulled the garrote tight.

"Hold his fucking feet, Franco!" Mickey yelled. "I can't keep the damn car on the road with him all over me."

"Shut up, Mickey," Roberto grunted. His arms were trembling, but he held the cord tight until Vito slumped. Then he loosened it, wound it once around Vito's neck, and pulled it tight again. "Okay . . . two minutes more . . . just to be sure. Slow down, dammit . . . slow down! Where's the fucking place, Franco?"

"Maybe a hundred yards. On the right. It's an old path. You can't see it till you're on top of it."

Roberto checked the road behind again. Sweat was running down his face. Mickey started to pull the car over onto the shoulder.

"Stay off the fucking dirt, you jerk," Roberto shouted, "or you'll leave tire tracks. Keep your wheels on the road."

"This is it," Franco said. "Stop!"

The car came to a halt, and Franco opened the door. Roberto held the cord tight a little longer, then let go of it and climbed out of the back seat.

"Take him under the arms, Franco. I'll get his knees. And don't let him drag. Mickey, you stay in the car. If anybody comes down the road either way, drive off and come back for us when it's clear. You got that?"

"Yeah, Bobby. Just get him out of sight."

The two men lugged Vito's body through the undergrowth at the entrance of the path and went about fifty yards into the woods.

"Far enough, Franco. Let's put him on the other side of those bushes."

"Good. He's a heavy bastard."

They lumbered into the brush for a few feet and dropped him on the ground.

"You sure he's dead, Bobby?"

Roberto knelt over the corpse and listened against the chest for a heartbeat. He felt for a pulse. Then he sat back on his heels and stared at a dark, damp spot at the crotch of Vito's trousers. "Yeah, he's dead, all right. He's had his jollies."

They scrambled back to the path. Roberto brushed his knees with his coat sleeve and picked up a small branch from the ground.

"What's that for?" Franco asked.

"Just watch. Start walking back to the road." He went down the path backwards, using the branch like a switch, raking over their footprints as he went. When they got to the car, Mickey threw open the door and Franco slid into the front seat. Roberto took a deep breath, looked slowly up and down the road, then finished raking the sand on the shoulder with the branch. He threw it into the woods and got in next to Franco. "Move over, Franco. That's a nice seat for you, huh?"

Franco shot him a look.

"Franco's got no sense of humor, Mickey. Maybe we better go."

Roberto sat back, took off the work gloves, and put them in his pocket. After the car was headed west on Route 25, he rolled down the window and tossed out the nylon cord. "There, Franco. You feel better about your seat now?"

"Very funny, Bobby, very funny. Gimme a smoke."

●   ●

Vito found himself standing in a crowded bar. The place was full of smoke and the stink of stale beer. Somewhere, on the other side of the room, he could hear a fight heating up. He edged his way to the back door and went out into the alley.

The light was blinding at first. When his eyes got used to it, he started to walk down a long, grubby corridor that looked like the USAir section of the Washington airport, counting the departure gates as he went: Nineteen, Eighteen, Seventeen, Sixteen, Fifteen. Except for a couple of people in Fifteen, the place was deserted. He went up a short flight of stairs, wandered across a motel lobby, and went to look for his room.

The door was partly open. He expected to find the maid, but instead Theresa was there. She was wearing spike heels. That made a difference. She had short legs. When she had her shoes off, he had to do a half-knee bend to get against her. He wondered for a second if anybody was with her, but then forgot about it when she pressed herself against him. He didn't like the feel of her stiff, teased hair against his face, but he forgot about that, too.

Outside again, it was darker now, and he was running. He had no clothes on, but his legs felt heavy, and he couldn't make any speed. There was a long row of trees by the side of the road; and somewhere, down at the end, he knew he'd find Angelo if

206

he could only make it. But his damn legs! It was like trying to run in deep water. He thought of swimming, and did a couple of strokes, but his arms were even heavier than his legs, and he hardly moved at all. He gave it up and fell down on all fours, struggling to get there before it got completely dark.

Angelo was standing just beyond the last tree, about twenty yards ahead of him, waiting. Vito tried to talk, but nothing came out. "Got to save my strength," he thought. "Just keep crawling." But he was slowing down and he knew it. He went about ten yards with his head down, hardly able to see the pavement in front of his eyes; he could feel some round stones in the macadam with the palms of his hands, but only a couple of white ones were visible.

Five yards more. He passed the last tree and looked up for Angelo. It was so dark now that all he could see was the outline of him, but even that wasn't clear. Angelo seemed to have no shape anymore, no head or arms or legs; he was just a fat, black stone standing there in the darkness. Vito looked down again. It wasn't just his arms and legs that were heavy now; his whole body was pressing itself down to the pavement. He made one more effort to move, but nothing happened.

•   •

Angelo was sitting in the afternoon sun on the back patio of his house in Tenafly. His daughter came to the doorway. "Papa? Roberto's here. He says he has some news."

"Tell him to come in. And close the door when you leave."

Roberto walked over to the old man's chair and handed him a copy of *Newsday* folded open to page five. The headline read, *"N.J. Mobster's Body Found in L.I. Woods."* Angelo read the lead: "The partially decomposed body of Mafia chieftain Vito Scorso was discovered yesterday in a wooded section just north of Ridge, in Suffolk County. Police said he had apparently been strangled several weeks ago. . ."

Angelo dropped the paper on the floor. "That's that, Roberto. I was beginning to wonder a little."

"*You* were beginning to wonder, Boss! I was beginning to get scared shitless. Christ! That was the longest three-and-a-half weeks in my life."

25

Afterlife

"Well, Norman?"

"I think I see where you're going, Robert. It's a boiled-down *Pincher Martin,* isn't it? A little putative history of what happens between the moment of death and the ultimate deadness that sooner or later sets in."

"Yes. Except Golding stretched his story into a whole novel and let you in on the fact that the protagonist was dead from the start only at the end. I reversed the procedure, and got it over with in a hurry. I wanted to preclude any of those religious, life-after-death interpretations some people put on *Pincher Martin.* As far as I'm concerned, Golding was just being cynical — saying it all comes to nothing — which is just fine for my purposes."

"Which are, precisely . . . ?"

"Well, having done death among the living with the story of Paul, I want to go on and do death among the dead via the story of Vito — to fulfill the rest of my theological contract on the doctrine of grace by taking a crack at the eschatology of it all. I want to take a look at the ultimate disposition of everything in heaven and earth in the light of the notion of grace raising the dead. But without using the death-denying imagery of an afterlife."

"Can you bring that off, though? I mean, after all, it's scriptural imagery, isn't it? You can't just drop it."

"I have no intention of dropping it permanently. But the idea of life after death is more a Hellenistic extrapolation from biblical imagery than straight biblical imagery itself. You know: people take the authentically biblical images of Christ's second coming and the general resurrection of the dead at the end of time, and then proceed to speculate about the logistics of what the dead are up to between the time of their death and the day of judgment. My point is that while that's permissible, it's been done for so long that it's pre-empted a lot of other biblical images that present all the eschatological realities as facts *now*. The 'afterlife' has gotten a monopoly on the Christian imagination; and monopolies always make for bad theology. Christian truth is paradoxical, two-sided at least. The cardinal rule therefore is that when you've got two competing sets of theological images, you've got to keep them both going, working one set on Monday, Wednesday, and Friday, so to speak, and the other on Tuesday, Thursday, and Saturday — and taking Sunday off to thank God you're not saved by theology anyway. But when the Monday-Wednesday-Friday set — the *now* imagery, the imagery of something that happens not at some future *then* but *today,* between noon and three — has been put as much in the shade as it is for us right now, then the only thing you can do is to work twice as hard on *it* and take the others for granted for a while. You can't redress an imbalance without putting more weight on the light side, at least for the time being. And that's all I propose to ask my reader to do — that, and to bear with me while I try to do it myself. Unfortunately, Norman, that will require some fairly earnest and direct dialogue between me and my reader."

"Why do you say 'unfortunately'?"

"Alas, Norman, I'm afraid your usefulness to me is just about over. In the words of Angelo, you got no more answers I can afford: I'm going to have to drop you out of this book. Don't worry, though, I won't do a full-dress Roberto job on you — just a quick exit after a phone call from your wife announcing the sudden arrival of your sister, your brother-in-law, and all five of their ankle-biting children. She won't even ask to speak with you; she'll just tell me to send you home forthwith so you can play host."

"I almost think I'd rather play Vito."

"Too late, Norman; too late. There's the phone."

●   ●

I know. That was ruthless. You don't like authors who simply explode characters out of a story when they become inconvenient. But you mustn't be so sentimental. Things explode every day. Anyway, old Norman wasn't really that likable. I gave him good lines, and all he did was insult my taste in vermouth.

●   ●

As I see it, we have a couple of preliminaries to get out of the way before we can proceed. The first has to do with my assertion that Vito, on his own, has no afterlife. Let me try to argue that for you, beginning with his life as he held it before he died.

While he lived, Vito could be said to have a life in two ways. On the one hand, he was alive. That is, at any given moment of his existence, certain physical and mental processes necessary to his being were in fact going on, just as they are in your case and mine right now. In that sense, we all have life. But please note once again (this time in twentieth-century English) what a poor possession of life that is: it is a holding of only one moment at a time, and it is a holding that is tenuous even as regards that present moment. Roberto's nylon cord was quite sufficient to

211

break that grip; and so are a million other changes and chances of this mortal life, any one of which — someday, somewhere — will do just as good a job on you or me as the garrote did on Vito.

But on the other hand, "being alive" is only the smallest part of what we have in mind when we talk about a *life*. Boswell's *Life of Samuel Johnson,* for example, is an account of something more than the good Doctor's vital signs. Likewise, when we think of the way Vito held his life, we have in mind his grip on something more than just his aliveness. We are addressing ourselves to his holding of the whole tissue of his days from birth to whatever point in his life you care to select — all the way up to his death.

Consider carefully, however, the nature of that grip. How did he hold all those days? Mentally? Yes. But that's a severely limited holding, isn't it? Did he remember being born? Was his recollection of, say, Theresa adequate to the wholeness of her being or was it only a caricature drawn by his particular brand of macho fetishism? Even at best, wasn't his life, as he held it in his mind, only a selective remembering of his experiences?

And how long does even that grip last? Experts will differ, of course. I gave it six paragraphs after the application of the garrote. Golding dragged it out for the length of a novel. A physiologist would probably give it the time it takes for all evidence of brain activity to disappear — however long you need to get a completely flat EEG. But we will all agree that in a relatively short time, Vito will have no more *mental* grip on his life after he dies than he did ten years before he was born — for the simple reason that the physical equipment by which he was able to achieve that grip just isn't around in one piece: Mentally, Vito doesn't live here anymore.

But what about his other grip upon his life, his *physical* grip — the way his body held itself simply by being a body? Vito had a scar on his left cheek from a fight with broken bottles when he was eighteen. His hold on that will last a good while after his death. Even after three-and-a-half weeks in the warm spring woods, the scar was no doubt still visible on the decomposing tissue of his face. But however long his hold on it might last, it will never last long enough to be anything more than a loser's grip. Between the crows, the worms, the sexton beetles, and natural forces of decay, his physical record of that night in a bar in Hackensack will soon enough be gone.

And the rest of his physical grip on his life will be gone even sooner. At a family party two weeks before he died, he picked up a mandolin and found that without any conscious mental activity on his part, his hands still remembered how to play "O Sole Mio." No doubt some of that eye-ear-hand coordination, ingrained in the fibers of his brain, nerves, and muscles, survived his death for a while. But how long? Make any estimate you like. In any case, his hold on it won't last as long as his hold on the scar on his cheek. Another loser's grip; one more proof that the Vito who, however imperfectly, had his life all together while he lived simply isn't there to hold it when he's dead. He has come utterly unstuck. Vito has no afterlife because there's no Vito to have one.

But you object. What about his soul? My answer is the same as before: I don't want to use the word. It's misleading. Most people conceive of the soul as some kind of *substance,* some finer, spiritual me that temporarily inhabits my body but goes on to better things after I die. But that's hardly biblical. For most of the Old Testament, that idea of a soul simply never came up, any more than it does in Judaism even today. And as far as the New Testament is concerned, it's just as unnecessary. In the first place, the Greek word *psyche* (sometimes translated as *soul*) is a perfectly ordinary word for *life* — for that quality, characteristic, or force by which we distinguish living beings from dead ones, bodies from corpses. Accordingly, it strikes me as more scriptural to talk about Vito's *life* rather than his soul.

213

But in the second place, when the New Testament does get around to talking about whatever life Vito has "after death," it speaks not about the immortality of his soul but about the everlasting life of his *risen body*. It says he is dead, and his life is hid with Christ in God. It says *Christ* is his life. It most emphatically does not say that some vaporous part of Vito goes floating up to heaven or wherever. It insists that his whole life — the entire fabric of his days and years that even at his best he had only the briefest of times to examine — is somehow held in Christ for Vito's *endless exploration of it*. Vito, if you like, will get a second, or a third, or a thousandth crack at every scrap of it — even at that one-way ride he was taken for. I doubt seriously, for instance, that he paid much attention that afternoon to the clouds in the April sky, or the chevrons on the red-winged blackbird that flew by as they turned the last corner — or to anything but the smallest fraction of what was available for his examination.

In short, Christ has it all for him, even after he's lost the grip he had on it himself. There is therefore only one life for Vito, and that's the one he lived from the moment of his conception to the moment of his death. If you look at that life from the point of view of *Vito's* grip on it, it's his mortal life; if you look at it from the point of view of *Christ's* grip on it, it's that *very same life* held for him eternally in Jesus. One life. Two grips.

The point is crucial, because of the almost overpowering temptation to solve the problem of the relationship between mortal life and eternal life by making them out to be two different lives. A life before death, for example, followed by a bigger, better and essentially different life after it. One life here, eating, drinking, and making love; another life there, sitting on clouds, outfitted with paper wings, pipe-cleaner halos, and tin harps. Or one life down here, pooping along in the half-reality of a material world, and a niftier, really real life waiting "up there" somewhere to break through to us in the future.

But none of that does justice to Scripture. *Christ* is our resurrection and our life throughout the whole of the one and only life we ever have. He doesn't take us from one life to another; he just holds our one mortal lifetime *eternally.* When we die — when we lose our grip — we don't "go on" to anywhere else; we walk smack into where we have always been. We "come to ourselves" as held in Christ.

Take the raising of Lazarus, for example. Lazarus's problem with his life was that as far as he was concerned, he'd lost his grip on it. Somebody had walked by and kicked out his plug. But when Christ comes to raise him, he doesn't say to Martha, "I've come to put your brother's plug back into the outlet for a while, just to show that I can be a red-hot wonder-worker if I choose." He says, "I am the resurrection, and the life: he that believeth in me, though he were dead, yet shall he live; and whosoever liveth and believeth in me shall never die." Jesus says that as far as his way of holding Lazarus's life is concerned, Lazarus was never unplugged at all — that when Lazarus died, he lost only his own power to hold his life. He emphatically did not lose Christ's power to do so. And therefore when Lazarus comes blinking out into the sunshine, the Mystery of Christ's holding is all he has — which is exactly the right way to put it, because if Christ really has Lazarus, then "all Lazarus has" is nothing less than everything Christ has. Furthermore, in the Mystery of Christ's holding, Lazarus always had it all — and he had it already reconciled, before, during, and after those four days in the tomb. All the miracle did was to proclaim, to *sacramentalize,* the presence of the Mystery that was always there and to invite Lazarus and everybody else to believe it.

●   ●

That, however, leads to the other preliminary consideration we have to deal with. Like Martha, you are used to thinking of the resurrection of the dead as something that will take place in the future, at the last day. Like her, you cannot conceive of eternal life as something present; like her, you are mystified by Jesus' flat assertion that the resurrection is already here and that eternal life is right now. But what about all the biblical imagery of the Second Coming and the End of the World, you wonder? Do we just write that off as so much folklore that Jesus swallowed uncritically as a child of his times?

No. There is no way of getting that kind of imagery out of the biblical view of things — and there is not even any necessity to balk at a literal interpretation of it. But it is essential to see it in balance, because it's only half of the paradoxical fullness of the Bible's imagery — it's only one of the two ways that Scripture talks about our relationship to the Mystery that holds us created and reconciled from start to finish. Therefore, let me first distinguish them for you, then try to harmonize them.

At first sight, they seem utterly contradictory. On the one hand, the Bible talks as if the relationship between us and the Mystery were merely historical or horizontal. The work of creation and reconciliation is laid out on its pages as if it occurred along a time line: God makes the world; but then when Adam and Eve mess it up, God begins the long process of straightening it out. First, he calls Abraham, Isaac, and Jacob. Then he leads the children of Israel into bondage in Egypt and out again in the Exodus. He takes them to Mount Sinai, gives them the Law, brings them to the Promised Land, provides them with Jerusalem and the Temple, sends them the Prophets, leads them into Captivity and back, and finally, in the fullness of time, becomes incarnate himself in Jesus, dies, rises, ascends, pours out the Spirit on his church — and at the end of the time line, he comes back to make the final disposition of all things. All strictly historical: a horizontal series of operations, building toward a climax that doesn't appear until the end of the world.

On the other hand, the Bible says just as clearly that the operation is also a vertical one, an immediate one — that the reconciling climax is somehow present at every moment of the historical process, that the end is in the beginning and the beginning in the end, and that the Christ who shows up for the first time in the middle is the Alpha and Omega as well. Jesus, when he is finally crucified on a Friday afternoon in twenty-nine A.D., for example, is spoken of as the "Lamb slain from the foundation of the world." His sacrifice, which looks for all the world like a specific transaction at a specific time, turns out to be a very odd transaction indeed: forgiving all sins, at all times — before, during, or after the crucifixion and the resurrection. We are told that we are *already risen* with Christ, that we are already fellow citizens with the saints in the City of God.

In other words, the historical, step-by-step, horizontal imagery in Scripture is continually intersected by a much more immediate and vertical kind of imagery in which both creation and reconciliation are a single step for God — a step in which, at the deepest level, he never shifts gears, never plugs in new circuitry, and never adds previously missing components. He's just got it all together from the start.

But how do you harmonize those sets of images? How do you prevent the one you happen to be working on at the moment from making you forget the one you've got in your pocket? For that happens all too easily. If you take the horizontal imagery the wrong way, for example — if you begin to think that the *real* resurrection of the dead occurs only at the end of the world — you'll begin to stop thinking seriously that you're dead and risen now. And when you do that, you not only deny the Bible's vertical imagery of death and resurrection *now;* you also cut yourself off from the only authentic root of Christian living.

Or, on the other hand, if you affirm the vertical imagery too exclusively, if you put yourself in the bind of having to say that resurrection *now* — in a Mystery, as a spiritual truth — is the only real resurrection, you will quite promptly find yourself writing off resurrection *then* as just so much mythology incapable of literal interpretation.

But that kind of cutting up of truth by truth is totally unnecessary. The way to avoid it is to invoke one of the prime rules of both textual criticism and dogmatic theology: *the more difficult reading is to be preferred.* In criticism, it means simply that the unusual, or hard, or obscure variant in the text is more likely to be the work of the author, and the easier, intelligible readings are usually the work of second-rate editors and copyists trying to make simplified sense out of inspired insight. The usual illustration is from Jacques' speech in *As You Like It:* ". . . sermons in stones and books in the running brooks" — which some German critic is said to have sensibly and stupidly emended to read, ". . . sermons in books and stones in the running brooks."

As the rule applies in theology, it means that you start with the set of images you find it harder to take seriously and force yourself to concede the utter reality of that set. Then, when you go to the other set, you almost invariably find that the work of harmonization is all but done. Let me illustrate by using the doctrine of the Sacrifice of Christ on the Cross.

As always, you have two sets of images before you. On the one hand, you have the historical, horizontal set — the images of the event of the crucifixion, of sacrifice by way of literal bloodshed and real death at a certain time and in a certain place. But on the other hand, you have the immediate, vertical set — the images of the Lamb slain from the foundation of the world and of the eternal Great High Priest and Victim taking away all sins, at all times, all at once, in one Mystery of Heavenly Intercession.

Which of those two is the easier reading of the Good Friday revelation? The horizontal set, of course. But watch what happens if you go with that set first in trying to make theological sense of both sets of images. You very soon find yourself in trouble. You begin to be compelled to build Rube-Goldberg theological contraptions to make the vertical set work at all. For example. Jesus was crucified in twenty-nine A.D., and that very act is the key to the salvation of the whole human race. Well and good. But what about some poor Jewish peasant who died in twenty-eight A.D.? How does Jesus' sacrifice get to absolve Ezra's sins — and how does the poor fellow surmount the obstacle of his untimely death so he can get a chance to relate himself to the Cross? Well, the way it's usually worked out is to put a lot of weight on a rather small biblical base (Jesus, between Good Friday afternoon and Easter morning, goes and preaches to the "spirits in prison") — and to say that when Christ thus "descended into hell," he went and paid calls on all those who died too soon for the main event and gave them rain checks.

But that solves only Ezra's problem. What about an even poorer Norwegian peasant who died in two-twenty-eight A.D. — before the missionaries got as far as Scandinavia? The vertical set of images insists that you tie him into the operation, too; but how do you do it? Well, you say that he can get in his innings because Christ arranged to have his sacrifice on the cross repeated every day in the Mass, and once Olaf's great-great-great grandchildren have been Christianized, they can get themselves to the altar and earn indulgences for him so he can have the benefits of it all.

But then, what about the English peasant who died in sixteen-twenty-eight A.D.? By that time, Geoffrey's relatives were all Protestants and didn't believe in the sacrifices of masses. So if Geoffrey hadn't made his act of faith in Christ's sacrifice on the cross by the time he bought the farm, there wasn't much they thought they could do for him. The theologizing, you see, is not going very well: our jerry-built Ark of Salvation is beginning to spring leaks. And what about the pagan Chinese peasant who

219

died in nineteen-twenty-eight? Poor old Chang seems to be out of luck completely. The Ark begins to look a bit like an enemy gunboat cruising shark-infested waters, perfectly content to leave most of the human race out in the drink.

You might, of course, get them all accepted if you could make Christ's descent into hell into a kind of permanent money-changing operation by which, the minute people die, they get a chance to trade in their natural good deeds for specifically Christian legal tender and so enter the Heavenly Country with coin of the realm in their pockets. But then that's hard, because it begins to make the crucifixion itself look a bit like window-dressing for an operation that's really going on somewhere else — and which is in fact based on something rather less than the sole merit of Jesus.

But enough. I just wanted you to have a little demonstration of what happens when you start theologizing with the easier reading first. Watch now what happens when you start with the harder one.

Christ, the Word of God by whom all things are made and offered to the Father, is also the Lamb of God by whom all things are reconciled — from the very foundation of the world. That means that the Mystery, the hidden, ever-present act by which he perpetually causes all things to leap out of nothing, is matched at every moment by another Mystery, another hidden, ever-present act by which he perpetually reconciles all things to the Father. And that means that the Creating, Reconciling Word himself is perpetually present to every single created thing at every moment of history, B.C. or A.D.: Ezra, Olaf, Geoffrey, Chang, and all the stones in all the running brooks from A to Z. He has them all together from the start, without their lifting a finger.

But how is the world to know about that distinctly good piece of news? How, in the midst of the mess it has made of itself, can the world even guess at it, let alone recognize it and enter into the enjoyment of it? For after all, it is indeed a mystery — and therefore invisible, inaudible, intangible, and unsmellable. As it turns out, however, there's no problem. God may work in a Mystery, but luckily for us, he's incapable of keeping a secret. So he takes the Mystery, which is present everywhere but out of sight, and puts a visible sign on it on the Friday of the Preparation of the Passover in twenty-nine A.D.

But what does that do to the crucifixion as the central redeeming event in time and space? Does it turn the cross into mere window-dressing? It does not. It says that the cross is the Mystery itself in *visible operation.* It says that the horizontal image is nothing less than the *sacrament,* the real presence, the visible outcropping of the Mystery that the vertical image insists is going on everywhere anyway. It is the *acting out* under the sign of one historical moment of what is immediately given at every moment. You don't have to fuss about either its historicity or its ability to bear the full theological weight the Bible puts on it. The whole apparatus is solid as rock.

All right, then: the end. How does this general principle work when you apply it to the resurrection of the dead? Well, to begin with, the resurrection is also proclaimed to us in two sets of images: resurrection *now,* and resurrection *then* — resurrection presented under the imagery of *immediacy,* and resurrection pre-sented under the imagery of *history.* Which is the harder reading? Resurrection *now,* obviously. Accordingly, take that reading first: make resurrection now utterly real. Insist that, in him, we have always been as risen as we're going to get — that there will not be a single truth of our life at the end of the world that wasn't present, in the Mystery of the Word, from the foundation of the world. Say flatly that he's always had it all together, and that in him we've got it all together too *right now.* In short, take the vertical imagery of the Mystery at full force.

But then ask yourself: How would we have known that

221

Mystery unless, for one thing, he actually gave us a sign of it in his own resurrection in twenty-nine A.D., and for another, he gave us an assurance of our participation in it by promising us a resurrection of our own at the end of the world? Do you see what that means? It means that the sign in twenty-nine and the sign at the end of time are no problem. They are not, either of them, *when* the resurrection happens; they are simply two times when the eternal happening of the resurrection is *sacramentalized* — historically manifested — as really present. They are simply two points at which the truth under all points is thrust up for our attention in faith.

There is therefore no conflict between the two sets of images, if only you take the harder set first. In technical theological language, the imagery of history shows you the *sacramentum,* the *sign* of the Mystery; and the imagery of immediacy shows you the *res sacramenti,* the *reality* of which the sign is the true sacrament. In plain English, the resurrection of the dead underlies all the moments of time; but God has picked out two of those moments and put a label on them.

And there you have it: a dramatized resurrection for Jesus on the first Easter Day, and an even more spectacularly dramatized resurrection for all of us on the youngest day of the world — complete, if you like, with angels scurrying around with dustpans getting all the scattered bits of Vito, you, and me ready for the final curtain call. But nothing new. Just the same old act by which the Lamb slain from the foundation of the world draws all things to himself for the praise of the glory of his Father's grace. Which, it pleases me to say once again, is nothing more or less than what the man actually said:

Blessed be the God and Father of our Lord Jesus Christ, who has blessed us with every spiritual blessing in the heavenly places, even as he chose us in him before the foundation of the

222

world, that we should be holy and blameless before him. He destined us in love to be his sons through Jesus Christ, according to the purpose of his will, to the praise of his glorious grace which he freely bestowed on us in the Beloved. (Eph. 1:3-6)

It works, you see. With the right method, the lights begin to go on instead of off.

26

The Four Last Things

But enough preliminaries. The subject, as before, is grace raising the dead. Now, however, instead of having a lover restored to warm and panting life as the basis of our theologizing, we find ourselves with nothing but one dead mobster on our hands. We have arrived abruptly, and with no return ticket, at the bizarre realm of eschatology — at the end of the line where the consequences of grace, already extreme enough under the cozy images of Fathers falling on Prodigals' necks and mistresses kissing lovers' feet, become flatly ultimate and reveal themselves in the forbidding landscape of the Four Last Things: *Death, Judgment, Hell, and Heaven.* If you thought we had problems before . . .

But never mind. Let me begin by asking you to go back to the afternoon of Vito's execution on that deserted road north of Ridge. Fix your mind on the interior of the gray Cadillac: Mickey, Vito, and Franco in the front seat, Roberto in the back. Now, then. Remembering that I am working strictly as a dogmatician, not an apologist — that, with Norman finally gone, I no longer have the least interest in proving that a word of this is true, only in seeing if the images that faith accepts can somehow be *figured* to make sense — do me two favors. First, join me for the moment in assuming that the events of the faith-story about Jesus might just possibly be related to reality — that even if you doubt some of them to be facts, they might nonetheless be about a Mystery of reconciliation that could indeed be a fact. In other words, make believe (even if you find it preposterous) that the historical fact of the death of a Galilean nobody on a cross outside Jerusalem in 29 A.D. actually has some connection with the final disposition of the cosmos. Second (and less of a mental stretch), make believe that the events in my story about the one-way ride in a Cadillac were likewise historical facts — that someone (who might as well be called Vito), somewhere (which might as well be north of Ridge), was actually garroted on a Friday between noon and three. If that's not too much to ask, we're now ready to proceed with the exercise that will occupy us for the rest of our time together.

•   •

First of all, acting on the assumption we just agreed to that all the stories in this book, biblical and homemade, might at least possibly be true — and promising ourselves (in accordance with the dictum about preferring the more difficult reading) to avoid the less difficult interpretations of those stories as much as possible — let's make a list of the hard things these "facts" require us to say.

First, about *Death:*

- As far as time and space are concerned (that is, from the point of view of history), all the earthly "events," biblical or otherwise, occurred only in their own times and places: in Jesus on the cross, with Paul and Laura in the motel, and on the road down to Ridge — all on their given Fridays, all between noon and three. Jesus Christ may hold them some-how in a Mystery; but you and I, Paul and Laura, Roberto

225

and company — we can go back to them only in memory.
And Vito, in the shape he's now in historically, can't go back
to them at all.

- All of us, eventually, will be in the same shape as Vito.
- Nevertheless, by virtue of the believed "fact" that every moment of our history is held in being by the eternal Word of
God, each and every one of those moments or episodes exists
really and eternally in Christ. As far as God is concerned,
they are in no sense past; they are forever present. And they
are present down to the last detail: every motivation, every
thought, every cell, every thread in every shirt, and every
atom in everything else from the nails in the wood to the
vinyl on the roof. Christ has them all in one eternal now.
- That means two things. First, it means that in the year three
thousand, for example, when the cross and the bedspread
and the Cadillac are all dust and rust, Christ will still have
them all. If Roberto and Vito care to reinvestigate their
episode in the car as Christ holds it, they may do so ad
libitum. But second and more difficult, it means that at the
moment when Roberto is dropping the copy of *Newsday* in
Angelo's lap — when Roberto, obviously, cannot get back
into the Cadillac except in memory — Vito, in Christ, can
get back into it in fact. In other words, everything, no matter
how nicely or badly it may have happened in history, is going
on all at once, *as it really was,* in Christ who holds it.

Second, about *Judgment:*

- Nevertheless, we are also required to say that as Christ holds
those moments in the Cadillac eternally, he somehow holds
them *reconciled.* By virtue of something real he has done
(name it any way you like: for the sake of simplicity, let's say
"by virtue of his death and resurrection"), there is now

226

nothing wrong with anything in the whole episode. Christ's final judgment on it at the Youngest Day will be only and always a judgment of *approval*. Whatever was wrong with that episode when Roberto's and Vito's times were in their own hands, there is nothing wrong with it now as those times are held in Christ's. And when the two Mafiosi have finally both lost their grip on themselves and have entered into Christ's grip on them, they are going to be able to sit in that car in the heavenly places and do whatever they please: talk about girls, rehash the murder, sing psalms, or have a good laugh. Or, alternatively, as things are now (where Vito is able openly to enjoy Christ's reconciled grip, but Roberto is still struggling along in his own unreconciled one), Vito is going to be able to deal with Roberto in Christ even if Roberto doesn't choose to do the same with him.

• Nevertheless (you note, I hope, that *nevertheless* is practically the word-of-all-work in eschatology), the "fact" of which the Last Judgment is the image requires us to say that even though Christ holds those times in the car reconciled, he in no way approves of what Roberto did to Vito. However Christ gets it all together, he does not do so by adopting a sappy attitude of indifference to good and evil. The reconciliation sacramentalized by the Youngest Day is not a suspension of value judgments. It is a vindication of the goodness of creation — for the simple reason that Christ is the one and the same Word who creates and reconciles. It just makes no sense to expound the two activities in a way that requires him to welsh on the one in order to bring off the other.

Third, about *Hell*:

• On the other hand, hell also must be taken at full force. Our exposition of Christ's eternally reconciled holding of Vito

227

and Roberto must leave room for the possibility that either or both of them may refuse to explore that holding — that, having lost their grip on themselves by death, they may yet decline, by a kind of second or eternal death, to lay hold of and enjoy the grip that Christ has on them.

• Nevertheless (once again), even if they so refuse, we must expound their "second death" not as a separation from the eschatological picnic but as somehow taking place in the midst of it — though in a way that doesn't spoil everybody else's fun. This would seem to be difficult, requiring some better imagery than the old picture of the saints up in heaven laughing at the agonies of the damned down in hell; but it must be done if we are to do justice to the job before us.

Fourth and finally, about *Heaven:*

• Nevertheless (one last time), the imagery of heaven must also be given full weight. The picnic must come off. The Word of God has got to win. The Father must get his eschatological druthers: not a ramshackle, whitewashed City of God in which he settles for accommodation instead of perfection but the very New Jerusalem he had in mind from the beginning — his *bride,* adorned as the apple of his eye. No matter where the hell of it all may be, heaven has got to be Heaven: not a hair out of place, not a single detergent spot on a single wineglass, no soggy rolls, no collapsed soufflés, no heartburn, no *crise de foi,* and above all, no more love that turns out to have been something else altogether.

● ●

It is, admittedly, a tall order. I propose, therefore, that we take this list as a sufficient if not exhaustive catalog of the problems at hand (anything omitted can be picked up in the exposition), and go to work. Remember only the precise nature of what we are doing. I am not trying to tell you what the ultimate Mystery is really like. I have no knowledge sufficient for that, and you wouldn't have any way of judging it even if I did. We are simply going to sit down in front of the images under which the Mystery is presented to us and see if we can get them to shed a little light on each other. It is a modest venture, despite the tallness of the order. The name of the game is *Paul and Laura and Roberto and Vito, All Reconciled Nevertheless by Jesus; or, Through the Youngest Day with Cross and Camera*. And it is, of course, only a game. It is not, for all that, either unserious or unimportant; but it *is* only a game, and don't forget it. The first mark of a theologian is a deep awareness that his pack of cards is not what gives him life.

27

Tracking the Mystery
of Reconciliation

I think the best place to begin is at the notion of *reconciliation,* precisely because it's the most difficult one of all for us to imagine. Anything else comes easily: *death,* we figure pretty well; *judgment* has been our cup of tea for so long that it all but preoccupies our minds; *hell* is a cinch; and *heaven,* while it may seem too good to be true, still seems the kind of thing we'd like to be true. Taken one by one, the eschatological images are not problems. The rub comes when you say that by the power of Jesus' death and resurrection, all the realities comprehended under those images are somehow perfectly reconciled to each other and to God. Note well: *are* reconciled. Not *will be* (though there is promised a youngest day when their reconciliation will be *sacramentalized* by being made public); but *are* reconciled, and *always have been* in Christ, the Word of God, the Second Person of the Holy and Undivided Trinity.

Let me make sure, however, that the problem is sufficiently *aggravated* in your mind — that you see its enormity. I'm asking you to imagine that all the items in the list that follows are held in Christ in *one eternal now;* further, that they are held by him precisely *as they are or were* in history; and finally, that without ceasing to be the evils that they were and are, they are nevertheless *reconciled* in the Peaceable Kingdom of God. Here, then, is the list of reconciled unreconcilables:

- Roberto and Vito at the moment the garrote was applied;
- Vito and Angelo;
- all torturers and all their victims;
- Paul and Catharine the day after the shipwreck of their affair of ten years;
- all lovers in all their betrayals of each other;
- all battered children at all the times of their mutilation, physical, emotional, and mental;
- the Cardinals of the Inquisition, the Czars of Russia, Stalin, Hitler, and all the Jews they persecuted;
- the weasel and the hen he stole from the chicken coop; and
- you, me, and Jesus at the moment we put the nails through his hands and feet.

The list is not exhaustive, but it will serve. My point in making it is simply this: it will not do to expound the reconciliation by means of theological devices that in effect get rid of history. The Christian revelation has the *incarnation* as its central image: God manifests himself in the historical process itself; this world, as it is, is his cup of tea. As I see that radical earthiness of the Gospel, it must be taken to mean that it is precisely *our history* he came to reconcile. And our history as it was, and is, and will be *in him*. We must swear off, therefore, any interpretations of the imagery that require us to abolish events in order to get rid of their troublesomeness, or to confect a heaven in which history is superseded by some non-historical, purely spiritual order.

Let me illustrate by citing the course of my own thinking

about the reconciliation. I began, as most Christians do, with the image of Christ's death on the cross as a sacrifice: Jesus the Great High Priest offers up to God his death as the Saving Victim and thereby makes a perfect satisfaction for the sins of the world. But for a number of reasons, I found that image less than satisfactory. For one thing, it conjures up the notion of a bloodthirsty God. For another, it sounds awfully like a merely divine transaction: God doesn't really help us out much; the Trinity simply fixes up its own internal relationships so the Father isn't mad at us anymore. For a third, when I came to take seriously the idea that all times and places, however unreconciled in themselves, are held eternally in God, all I could come up with was either a very large hell (which is, admittedly, one of the images of Scripture — but *that* large?) or a very unsatisfactory heaven, full of unrelieved agony.

Consequently, I found myself casting about for some imagery that would either shrink hell to reasonable theological proportions (thus allowing the divine Success to look a little less like cosmic failure); or alternatively, clean up the New Jerusalem so it wouldn't look so much like the South Bronx. What came to hand was the image of the dead human mind of Jesus between the time of his death and the day of his resurrection.

It struck me that if you took the utter deadness of that mind (as dead as Vito's was after three days in the woods) and posited *the sheer oblivion of that mind* as an eternal fact, you came up with a kind of universal black hole down which all the unreconciled evil of the world could be dumped. God says he will remember our iniquities no more; the dead human mind of Christ seemed to provide a way for omniscience to do just that: Jesus takes all the badness down into the forgettery of his death and offers to the Father only what is held in the memory of his resurrection. Christ as eternally dead (if he was dead even ten minutes, those ten minutes are still held eternally) provides you with someplace to put evil — with a hell *inside Christ's human death,* so to speak. And correspondingly, Christ as eternally risen provides you with a "place" for heaven: heaven is the actual, historical world that he offers, eternally reconciled, to the Father. The world the Father sees and loves is the world he sees in his only-begotten Son. All the evil is sequestered in the forgetting of the dead human mind of the Word; all the unspeakable things go unspoken at the picnic by the Word who in the resurrection speaks them only to himself, in his death.

Best of all, the image of the dead mind of Christ seemed to give me a way of getting rid of my own evil, of "coming to the picnic with nothing to hide." Because in my own death, I would be provided with an access to that same black hole. I could leave my sins and iniquities where Christ unmentions them, and come out into the Party as he holds me reconciled and mentionable to his Father. And if I chose not to come out, I could stay down in his unmentioning forever — which gave me a real enough hell but one that was more proportionate to the Party, one rather congruent with the biblical image of the *second death:* a nice, quiet, sequestered hell that couldn't spoil the eschatological fun.

After a while, however, that imagery of forgetting and un-speaking and unmentioning began to look no more satisfactory than the other. There's just too much of me that is eternally unmentionable. My sins are not appendages that can be lopped off and dropped into silence; they were, and are, *me* in action. Indeed, properly speaking, my problem is not my *sins* at all but my whole centerless life, my corrupted *way of being* that the Bible calls *Sin* — a condition from which not one shred of my history is exempt, except in Christ. If he's going to tidy up the universe by dropping Sin into the divine forgettery, *I'm* going to have to go down there with it. And all of me, not just chunks. You see, then, what I had done with my theology of the black hole: at the price of a smaller, quieter hell, I had figured out an even quieter, practically empty heaven.

Let me illustrate. The image of the divine oblivion requires us to say that when Vito and Roberto reinvestigate the inside of the Cadillac in the Heavenly City, they will be not only unwilling but unable to recall a single thing about the garroting. But that's impossible. If Vito's history is reconciled, how can its climactic moment be omitted? How can a reconciliation be real and leave out the one thing the people involved most need to accept as reconciled?

Or, to take another instance, when Paul and Catharine come across each other of a long, eternal afternoon, is it in any way helpful to our understanding of their reconciliation in Christ to have to say that they will sit down and chat forever with no mention of the ten betrayed years of their lives? How useful is it to have them talk only about ten years' worth of *New York Times Book Reviews?* How possible, in any real heaven, for them to avoid the one question neither of them ever answered in their lives — and which, unanswered, made their lives hell — namely, "Why? Whatever on earth went wrong with the most glorious thing we ever did?"

The answer, of course, was that the imagery of forgetting, when pressed like that, became unhelpful and impossible. It was almost enough to drive me back to talking about propitiatory sacrifices to an angry God again — or even about ransom to the devil. At least those notions left you with some whole beings to put in heaven. If they didn't shed much light on the Mystery of how Jesus got us straightened out, they still stopped short of consigning the greater part of our lives to oblivion.

But there seemed no way back to that, either. The only open course was to go hunting for some imagery that would figure the work of reconciliation as being more intimate to us than it was under the image of sacrifice, and less destructive of us than it was under the image of forgetting. Accordingly, I began to look for new clues.

The first lead was one I'd taken seriously enough all along but which I now wondered if I'd taken correctly. It was the old, bedrock statement that we are reconciled solely by God in Christ, not by anything we do — that the work of reconciliation, however it is figured, is God's, not ours. At first sight, that seemed to lead nowhere. *All* the images of reconciliation took it at face value: if you talked sacrifice, you said only Christ's sacrifice did the trick; if you talked forgetting, you said only his forgetting brought it off, and so on.

But the very fact that they all used it — and that they all used it pretty much the same way — was curious. All the images of reconciliation agree that the operative element in it is something internal to God himself, some kind of fixing up of the inside of the divine head. (I had, of course, used that language before, rather glibly: it's fascinating how often theological throwaway comes back to haunt you.) I decided, therefore, to go with the idea of some "alteration" in the divine knowledge as the next possible lead.

"Alteration," of course, couldn't be the final word as far as God himself was concerned since, at least according to the classical view, God doesn't change. But you can't fuss about such things so early in the hunt. You simply make a note to clean it up later and work with whatever legitimacy it has for the time being. And it does have some: whatever it is that God does with his own insides to reconcile us, he invites us to believe that it results in a definite alteration of *us*: we go from being badly unstuck to being nicely pasted together. Even if we can't say that *God* alters, we can at least say that he makes a difference.

It was something about the divine knowing, then, that was the clue. And that clicked. Because the divine knowing — what the Father knows, and what the Word says in response to that knowing, and what the Spirit broods upon under the speaking of the Word — all that eternal intellectual activity isn't just daydreaming. It's the *cause* of everything that is. God doesn't *find out* about creation; he *knows it into being.* His knowing has hair on it. It is an *effective* act. What he knows, *is.* What he thinks, by the very fact of his thinking, jumps from no-thing into thing. He never thought of anything that wasn't.

But that meant his knowing was determinative of the being of each and every thing. And not simply of its *static* being, its existence considered as something just sitting there doing nothing. God's knowing (the knowing of the Trinity, to be precise) had also to be seen as determinative of the *dynamics* of the being of every thing — of the way it *moves by desire* toward the Highest Good. For all things arise out of nothing for one reason only: because of the *desire* of the Word and the Spirit to offer to the Father what he delights to know. Everything that exists is a delightful present, gift-wrapped and given, at the Father's eternal un-birthday party. All creatures spring from and are borne upon a torrent of desire for the Father's good pleasure; there is a river of longing flowing from the Son and the Spirit to the Father, a river whose streams make glad the City of God.

But that in turn meant something more. Since it is the very creatures themselves that are the gifts of the Beloved to the Father, the creatures themselves are participants of that flow of desire; and they are participants *by knowing themselves* on whatever level they can manage. The apples of his eye, to whatever degree they can know and love themselves *as apples,* to that degree they really do participate in the knowledge and love of a Son for a Father who is crazy about apples.

In other words, the proper self-knowledge and self-love of every created thing is ipso facto a participation in the knowledge and love of God. The entire universe moves by desire for the Highest Good simply because every part of it loves what God loves — namely, its own unique being. The stones on the beach, the grass in the field, the rabbits in the woods, and the stars in the sky all move toward him by the most dependable of all motions: their own desire to know and love themselves. And that was another click. It was Gerard Manley Hopkins all over again:

> Each mortal thing does one thing and the same:
> Deals out that being indoors each one dwells,
> Selves — goes itself; *myself* it speaks and spells,
> Crying *What I do is me; for that I came.*

Putting it all that way, however, gave me a few minutes' pause. Comprehending every motion of everything in the world under the single rubric of desire for the Highest Good *through self-knowledge and self-love* was a pretty sweeping generalization to begin with. But in addition, two more objections came immediately to mind. The first was to its anthropomorphism. Applying concepts like desire to things like stones and grass and rabbits and stars puts some people off. I thought about that for a while but finally decided that since it wasn't really my own objection (the people it would bother were mostly those who would have fits anyway over anything that sounded out of date), I'd go with it nonetheless. When all is said and done, using the old analogues of desire and knowledge to describe why the so-called lower orders move is more helpful than misleading. As far as the animals are concerned, it's very close to the mark indeed: the ox knoweth his owner, and the ass his master's crib. And it works with the vegetable order as well: plants have a nice sense of their own identity; and, in desiring it, they move themselves to be precisely what God makes them to be. Tomato plants please God by insisting on being tomato plants, sunflowers by knowing enough to face the sun. The only hard case is the mineral order, but even there the analogy serves: a stone, especially a large one right in the middle of your projected vegetable garden, seems definitely to have some rock-hard mind of its own about where it wants to

be. It moves only reluctantly in the gravity of its stony self-knowledge, doing its willful best to remain the immovable object God
wills it to be when he decrees its lifelong love affair with the great
mass of the earth.

The second objection, however, was less easily dismissed —
though in the end, when I properly understood it, it turned out
to be the biggest lead of all. It was that when you applied the
grand rubric to human beings — when you said that every motion
human beings make is a motion toward the Highest Good and
works by means of our desire to know ourselves as the totality
that God knows — you had to include Sin in the equation. All
the horrible items in my list — Roberto and Vito at the moment
the garrote was applied, Paul and Catharine at the fatal lunch in
the Italian restaurant, and so on — had to be said to fall under
the same rubric. Even those acts of knowledge that end up desiring what God does not desire had to be seen as expressions of
the desire for the Highest Good by means of a desire to know
what God knows. Perverted desirings, perhaps — knowings-in-
contradiction, inconvenient and dangerous alterations in self-
knowledge — but still that same desire to know which is the only
root of all motion and which, despite its perversion, is still a desire
for the Highest Good.

Obviously, that was the most difficult reading so far; but
there was no point in reneging on the principle now, so I stayed
with it. I had no idea what the solution might be; but at least it
was beginning to look as if the problem could be stated by going
back to the story of the original alteration or contradiction in
human knowledge — back, that is, to the garden of Eden itself.

28

Re-membering the Garden

The story of Adam and Eve in the second and third chapters of Genesis fitted nicely with my suspicion that it was something about the alteration in human self-knowledge that lay at the root of all the un-reconciliation in the world. And it began to give me hope that if I could just get the imagery right, it would shed at least a little light on what lies at the root of the final reconciliation.

As I read the story up to the end of chapter two, it struck me that Adam and Eve had, to that point, been doing very well at the job of moving themselves toward the Highest Good by means of their desire to know themselves. Two instances in particular practically jumped off the page. The first one was the original solitude of Adam: he was alone in the world, with no help meet for him.

So God makes all the animals and brings them before Adam to see what he will call them. The Lord, as it were, puts an aardvark on a leash and trots it before Adam. Now God knows what an aardvark is: it's whatever the divine Spirit with his unutterable groanings and the Word with his divine fiat says it is as they speak the being of it into the ear of the Father who thought

239

it up. And the aardvark knows what an aardvark is by its uniquely aardvarky grasp of its own being. But Adam is another case: he's a rather more advanced knower than the aardvark, and what God is interested in getting from him is the unique grasp of the aardvark that Adam will come up with by doing his own adamic thing. At this point, of course, Adam does beautifully: out of his sure grasp of his own being as the priest of the world and the lord of creation — seeing clearly that it is his very nature to know all things by his own names for them and to offer them up for themselves and for God in his proper self-love — Adam comes up with the admiring and priestly *word* so far unspoken on land or sea: "Good Lord! That's some *aardvark* you've got there!"

But the second instance is even clearer. When God has finally dragged by the whole animal parade from aardvark to zzebra, there's still a problem: there is still no help meet for Adam. Human beings do indeed know something about themselves by knowing the animals, but they cannot fulfill their self-knowledge until they know *other human beings* — until they make a priestly offering of *humanity itself*. Consequently, God puts Adam to sleep, takes out one of his ribs, makes woman, and brings her to Adam — this time, presumably, without the leash. And Adam says, "This is now bone of my bones, and flesh of my flesh: she shall be called Woman, because she was taken out of Man. (Luckily, the English preserves the play on words in the original Hebrew: man, woman: *ish, ishshah.*)

What Adam says, you see, is that he finally knows what he is: he is this other that is yet the same as he. He now knows *himself*. He has come to himself as God holds him, and without contradiction he knows both himself and the God who holds him: except for his naming of the animals, Adam doesn't speak a coherent sentence, or even address God, until he realizes who he is in his perception of woman. And everything is just dandy: "And they were both naked, the man and his wife, and were not ashamed." The Bible is silent at this point about whether they had sexual intercourse, but I can't see any way around it. I don't think that knowledge of each other's flesh should be prescinded from that fullness of knowledge which the story is so obviously at pains to depict. I insist on a Paul and Laura act before the Fall. In a world moved by desire, it just has to be.

Next, however, comes chapter three, with the story of the temptation. But, appropriately enough, the fall of human nature is depicted there as nothing less than the introduction of an *alteration* in Adam's and Eve's knowledge of themselves — a pursuit of the path of desire for the Highest Good not by the true self-knowledge of chapter two but by an attempt to know themselves as something they are not: "Ye shall be as *gods*," says the serpent, "knowing good and evil." Once again, several particulars fairly leap off the page.

The first is the way they have to gussy up their perception of the Tree of the Knowledge of Good and Evil in order to achieve what they have in mind. Up to now, it was all straightforward. They could walk up to the tree and say, "That's a nice tree; but God says it's not for us, so let's go pick mangoes." But now they proceed to do a con job on themselves: ". . . the tree was good for food, and . . . pleasant to the eyes, and *a tree to be desired to make one wise*" (italics, Eve's). They put, you see, the central thing about themselves *outside themselves*. It was by knowing themselves that they were supposed to desire the Highest Good; but instead, they parked that knowledge in a dumb tree and forsook their own center.

And that was fatal. Because the next thing that jumps out at you is that when they did try to know themselves again, they found they couldn't do it anymore: "And the eyes of them both were opened, and they knew that they were naked" — a discovery, of course, of nothing at all, followed by the stupidity of prancing around in aprons stitched up out of fig leaves and by the ultimate embarrassing question from the mouth of God: "Who told you you were naked? Where did you get this egregious piece of non-knowledge? You've been mucking around with your self-knowledge, haven't you? And look what it's got you: one giant head trip about a lot of stuff I haven't the least desire to know. And since what I don't want to know just doesn't count, it's going to make you nothing but misery until you lay it down and get back to thinking about what I love to think about."

But as you know, they couldn't lay it down, and neither can we. And so their story and ours simply unravels into the untidy drama of human life as we know it, with all the sad results of the alteration in our knowing: man's knowledge of himself in woman precluded by the subservience he forced upon her; the ground cursed for our sake; a flaming sword between us and our self-knowledge; the invention of religion to close the uncloseable gap; and the first of many murders because we're afraid God likes somebody else better than us. After the most promising of all starts, we quickly find ourselves helpless and hopeless. In our blindness, we can only stand and wait for an inconceivable further alteration in knowing — which, if it comes at all, cannot possibly come from us.

●　　●

That, then, was the problem. But true to form, the principle of stating it the hardest way paid off: the shape of the solution began to unfold.

The first thing I noted was that in the whole biblical account of creation, there is not a single evil *thing*. Everything that comes from the hand of God, including Adam and Eve — and, most important, everything that is available for Adam and Eve to know — is solid, twenty-four-karat *good*. Even the Tree of the Knowledge of Good and Evil. Even the serpent, about whom the worst thing said is that he was more subtle than any beast of the field.

But that meant that evil could come neither from God nor from things, but only from the human race's penchant for knowing the good in contradiction — from that same nasty alteration in knowledge and self-knowledge I had been tracking all along. Put that way, of course, it was a theological commonplace as old as the Scriptures — lifted practically verbatim, moreover, out of Charles Williams. Still, it's nice to sight a known checkpoint. My chosen theological method — heavily heuristic — is very much like navigating a shallow bay in a small boat. When you're out of the main channel, all you've got for markers are the saplings stuck here and there in the water by the locals. They, of course, know which side, port or starboard, to keep each marker on. But when you're a stranger, you simply have to guess, and then strain your eyes in the fog to spot the next one. Until you see it, you expect to run aground any minute; when you do spot it, you breathe a definite, if temporary, sigh of relief.

This particular theological marker, however, turned out to be more than a temporary reassurance. Just beyond it, the outline of the dock itself began to take shape. For if the origin of evil lay in the alteration of human knowledge, then the end of evil — the quashing of it, the reconciliation of all its disastrous consequences — must lie somehow in a second alteration of that same human knowledge.

But that sent me straight back to the one available image of that second alteration: the human mind of the incarnate Word of God — the mind of Jesus, dead and risen. Only this time it offered itself not as a black hole down which vast sections of everybody's historical existence had to be dropped into oblivion but as the device by which all the perverted alterations in human knowledge could finally be terminated and our full historical existence be seen as reconciled in the unaltered remembering that the Word of God offers to the Father. For our sake, Christ dies not simply to the law but to that whole contradictory way of knowing the good for which the law condemns us. By the deadness of his human mind and ours, we are literally *absolved, set loose,* from the unreconciled knowledge of our times as we held them in our hands. And in the power of his resurrection, we are lifted up into nothing less than the reconciled knowledge of those times as they are held by the Second Person of the Trinity in both his unaltered divine mind and his risen human consciousness.

And as Christ holds us risen in himself, the deadness of our own human minds — yours, mine, Vito's, anybody's — works the same way. All the horrible alteration, perversion, and contradiction in Vito's knowledge, for example — the one and only root of all the evil in his life — is absolved, dissolved, in his death. Because in his death he loses everything that was his, good and bad. And when he comes out of his death into the power of Christ's resurrection, he comes out with the full knowledge of everything in his life, good and bad, restored to him from the hand of God — held by him as it is in the risen mind of Christ. He sees it all with a knowing untainted by alteration, perversion, or contradiction (because the mind that knew it that way is dead forever); and he grasps it no longer as the evil it once tried to be but as the desire for the Highest Good it always was in the offering of the Word to the Father. If our Fall was our re-cognition, our re-knowing of the *good as evil,* then our Reconciliation is our re-cognition in Christ — our re-knowing in the risen humanity of the Word — of evil as *the good he has made it once more.*

And there finally stood the dock, clearly visible. The grand image of it all turned out to be nothing other than the great sacrament of the reconciliation itself, the Eucharistic Offering: "Do this in remembrance of me. . . . As often as ye eat of this bread and drink this cup, ye do show the Lord's death till he come." *Do this,* he says, for my *anámnêsis,* for a remembering, a re-cognition, a re-knowing, a re-presenting of *my death*. Take, he commands us, the worst thing you ever did to me — that most disastrous of all the disastrous alterations in your knowledge — and see it now, face it now, accept it now as I see it in my resurrection: as the best thing that ever happened to you. Take this worst of all the world's Fridays in thankful *anámnêsis* and *recognize* it now, *celebrate* it now as the Good I always meant and saw — and that you meant, too, but could never achieve in your contradiction. By the grace of my unaltered risen knowledge, see even the disasters of your history as the inexorable desire for the Highest Good I always knew them to be.

Nothing, therefore, is lost. Not a scrap of history. Not the smallest, whitest lie or the greatest genocidal holocaust. It is all held in a renewed knowledge — in an *anámnêsis,* in a *re-membering,* a *re-cognition* by the grace that raises those whom death has absolved. The lethal imagery of the black hole was finally out of the way. What God effects in the reconciliation does the *work* of forgetting without the *danger* of forgetting. He does better than forget: he remembers our evil in grace as *the only real thing it ever could have been.* He takes away the flaming sword between us and our self-knowledge and brings us home to ourselves.

And with that, all the images began to light up. Christ's restoration of Peter, for example, after Peter's threefold denial. Jesus and Peter, in the grace of the resurrection, sit around after a breakfast of kippers and toast and make *anámnêsis* of the only thing in the whole Bible that Peter ever cried about:

> "Simon, son of Jonas, do you love me?"
> "Yes, Lord; you know I love you."
> "Feed my lambs."

Jesus asks the question three times, once for each denial. But he does not ask it simply to rub salt in an old wound or to tidy up accounts before proceeding. He asks it three times to remind Peter that this is not the first time he asked it — that he asked it back there in the palace of the high priest by the mouth of the servants:

> Then the damsel that kept the door says to Peter, "Aren't you also one of this man's disciples?"
> And Peter says, "The hell I am!"
> And Jesus says to him, "Feed my sheep."

Do you see? Jesus' relationship with Peter — and the incarnate Word's relationship with all of us — is perpetual and inevitable even when, from Peter's side or ours, it looks like an off-again on-again proposition. Even while Peter is busy thinking he has to deny Jesus, Jesus is busy re-membering that very denial in the only way it can be held forever. Or, to take the extreme case: even while Judas is busy thinking his way through his plans to betray Jesus, the Word is busy holding that betrayal reconciled in the *anámnêsis* — in the *putting of it all back together* that he accomplished by his death and passion. The only difference between Peter and Judas, therefore, is that Peter sat around after breakfast and joined Jesus in the *anámnêsis* of his denial, while Judas did not. Judas, remembering only his own version of that denial, hung himself — even though Jesus' version of it would remain forever available to him in the remembering of the Word. But Peter, making *anámnêsis* with Jesus at the sea of Tiberias, now hears at last the only thing his denial could ever have meant *in Christ: All* our denials, however perverse and wherever given, are re-cognized by the Word of God in Christ as yes. Only hell says no to such a remembering.

Thus Peter now says in joy the yes that Christ heard all along. "I know now," he says, "what you always knew, but what I in my contradiction couldn't see that Friday morning in the high priest's palace. In your death I have died to the alteration in my knowing, and by your grace I have risen into your unaltered and unalterable knowledge of me."

Peter, of course, didn't say all that. After such a breakfast, theological heavy-handedness was simply out of place. For that breakfast was nothing other than the Mass itself under a different form — the true condition of the whole of creation displayed under another sacramental species. It was a celebration — an *anámnêsis* in joy, a re-cognition in grace — of the reality the Word has always offered up in love for the Father to know.

But that threw light on still another image: the Five Wounds in Christ's risen body, the Glorious Scars in his hands, feet, and side. They had always struck me as curious. When theologians expounded the resurrection of the body at the Last Day, they always said we would be raised in perfection: if you had lost a finger, an arm, or a leg, you were raised with the damage repaired; if you had a bad liver or a cracked head, you got yourself back as good as new and even better. Why then was Jesus himself an exception? Why were deformities left in his risen body? Well, under this eucharistic imagery of *anámnêsis,* the answer is straight-forward: the Glorious Wounds are the perpetual sacrament of the remembrance, of the re-cognition of evil as good. They are the Cross and the Passion as the resurrection holds them. They are the sign of the Word's knowledge of the world's agony after the absolution of the world's knowledge of it in death.

But the light spread even further. Even the homemade images lit up. The weasel and the hen, for instance. For both of them, of course, the knowledge of that episode in the chicken coop was unaltered, sinless knowledge; but for the hen, it was still agony and death. And yet by the very absolution wrought by her death, the hen, in her resurrection, is able to see that agony as what it really was all along. She will finally understand that in a world in which everything lives by the death of others, every death is an act of that greater love by which she lays down her life for her friend. And when she sits down with the weasel in the peaceable kingdom, she will be able to chat with him in the friendliness of it all about anything she likes: the joys of her life as Christ gives it back to her in his holding, or the nobility of her death for her late-found friend. (The weasel, of course, will have had no problem with the episode: obviously, he thought fondly of the hen from start to finish. His problem will be with the farmer who shot him on a return visit to the chicken coop. But their chat, too, will be governed by the same rubric: "All shall be well, and all manner of thing shall be well" — *in Christ.*)

Or, if that strikes you as too fanciful, think of Angelo, who (I neglected to tell you) died of a carcinoma nine months after Vito. In the reconciliation — if he accepts the absolution of his knowledge by his death — he will see that he, too, laid down his life for a friend. A cancerous and malignant friend as it then was when their times were in their own hands; but now that they are in Christ's, a rather interesting fellow with all kinds of clever tricks up his sleeve. Angelo, while he lived here, was too busy running rackets to catch even a hint of the engaging aspects of the life of cancer cells; but had he been a research biologist, and in perfect health, he might have suspected all along that there could be more between them than a merely adversarial relationship.

But, best of all, the images of sinful, altered knowledge lit up too. Take Vito and Angelo in the reconciliation: they had forty years together in this life — most of them, from their admittedly gangsterish point of view, good years. And, of course, they had those last few weeks of Vito's life — weeks of mutual betrayal and failure as they saw them then. But in the risen knowledge of those times — in the *anámnêsis,* the re-cognition of them after the absolution of their first knowledge by death — what is there to stop them from seeing even Angelo's putting out of the contract on Vito as that desire for the Highest Good which was the only thing it ever really could be in Christ? A perverted and contradictory desire, admittedly, in the days when their only knowledge of that Good was altered and fallen; but that same desire nevertheless, now known as the Word offers it to the Father in his death and resurrection. Angelo's order for Vito's execution is one more Glorious Scar — another case in which the contradictory knowledge of the good as evil becomes, in Christ, the unaltered knowledge of the only good it could ever have been in the first place.

Or, to take what is perhaps the clearest case, think of Paul and Catharine on their long, eternal afternoon. Of what must they make *anámnêsis*, what is it that they must re-cognize in their reconciliation? Clearly, the whole tissue of their relationship as Christ holds it for them. All the good years, the days of wine, and talk, and books. And all the elations of their love: "Had we but world enough, and time . . . ;" and Vivaldi; and the laughter in bed; and the stillness after. And the thousand elegies before death that were the counterpoint of their desire:

> Oh, there will pass with your great passing
> Little of beauty not your own —
> Only the light from common water,
> Only the grace from simple stone.

But then, all the passing too. All the betrayals, all the missing of each other's meaning: ". . . that is not what I had in mind at all" — down to the last betrayal, totally unnecessary and utterly inexorable, by which the light died and grace left their world. Of all that they must make *anámnêsis* if they are to re-enter the City of their love as Christ holds it for them. The years of dead light and absent grace must be recognized as the only thing they can possibly be in Christ: Glorious Scars, the wounds of the alteration of their knowledge held forever in the re-collection by which grace gathers the dead into life.

And after them, all the rest: Laura and Catharine, Paul and Janet, Roberto and Vito, the torturer and his victim, Hitler and the Jews . . . It remains the tallest of all orders. It remains a Mystery. And in our altered and contradictory knowledge now, it remains inconceivable, even as a possibility. But then, it was never presented to us as such. It was announced as a fact accomplished without our cooperation by a grace unconditioned by our comprehension.

"No man can *know* that he is justified or *feel* that he is saved; he can only *believe* it." At the end of the game of images, we put the cards back in the box and go to bed with nothing but the trust we started with. Old Norman, you see, was exactly right. It is indeed the book of Job all over again: "Though he slay me, yet will I trust him." Another hand of cards, perhaps, in the morning; but through the dark times, only faith.

29

The Outrage of Grace

Before we proceed, I want you to take careful note of what has just happened. If I judge your mood correctly, you find yourself (perhaps to your surprise) more unhappy with this latest refinement of the theology of grace than with any of my other efforts so far. Your annoyance at my first parable of grace, with its free-swinging characters who get away with adultery, seems now a pale thing compared to the positive rising of your gorge at my exposition of an eschaton in which scoundrels get away with murder. "The torturer and his victim!" you mutter in dismay. "Hitler and the Jews! That's the most God-awful thing I've ever heard!"

"Do you know," I hear you say to me, "what you have produced? All that fancy dancing about *anámnêsis* and re-cognition adds up to only one thing: *a God who has no shame*. If the executioner can simply walk through the pearly gates like some hail-fellow-well-met, slapping six million backs and exchanging pleasantries about how nice it is that all the agony he caused is hunky-dory now, then God is a jerk. And you're a jerk, too, for even bothering to talk about it. Go back to blood sacrifice, or even to your empty-headed God with his divine forgettery. Any-

251

thing. But for Humanity's sake, don't come around here anymore trying to fob off a perfumed dunghill as the New Jerusalem."

All right, all right. Let me give you one soft answer and let it go at that.

I don't know why God insisted on allowing us to run our own history in the first place; and I don't know why he insists on leaving us free enough to botch it in the second; and I don't know why he insists on saving it in the third. Maybe he really is a jerk. But if those three insistences are the facts of the case (and if you're a Christian, you believe they are), then there's no way around the outrage of grace. By and by I shall give you something on judgment and hell, just because they're part of the imagery too. But don't hold your breath waiting for the other, score-evening shoe to drop, because it's not going to. Ever since Noah, God has had trouble keeping track of that shoe; and he finally lost it for good in Jesus. He simply doesn't keep score. History does, and we do; but as you just proved, keeping score simply ends the game. And therefore he refuses to do it. Instead, he erases all our records by death and raises us by grace with nothing but his record left. Maybe it was just the best he could do; I don't know. But I do know that's what he says he does. Your objection to it was voiced perfectly — if less vehemently — by the Elder Brother; and God's only answer to you was given equally perfectly by the Father: "It is meet that we should make merry and be glad: for this your brother was dead and is alive again. Even your rotten kid brother. Even Hitler. End of subject."

Except for one comment on my method in this book. My *Parable* about Paul and Laura was designed to shock you into an awareness of the outrageousness of grace. My *Coffee Hour* was a trick to lull you back into a little complacency again — to lead you to hope that perhaps if I would promise to stop using titillating illustrations, you would be able to see grace in a more acceptable light. This present consideration of *The Youngest Day* is meant to break that hope for good. Straight theologizing about grace is more, not less, outrageous than parabolic theologizing. The more clearly you make grace sovereign over human life, the more unacceptable become your efforts to harmonize it with life as we know it. The farther you go in expounding grace as the ultimate goodness of God, the deeper you find yourself mired in the manifest badness of God. I am sorry about that. If I were an apologist, I think I would either shoot myself or go into some business like selling used cars where people accept being gypped as the price of dealing with you. But I'm not, so I won't: dogmaticians just natter on, trying to cash in on anything and everything in the lot — even the polished-up old predestinarian heap I just tried to unload on you. I'm sorry about that too, in a way; but not very. A man has to make a living. Besides, it really wasn't driven anywhere except to church.

30

Rigged Justice

Your brief but heartfelt tirade in the last chapter will serve as a sufficient introduction of the subject of judgment — and, by extension, of its concomitant, hell. All I will add, for your comfort, is one corroborative text from the book of Revelation, chapter six, verses nine and ten:

> And when he had opened the fifth seal, I saw under the altar the souls of them that were slain for the word of God, and for the testimony which they held. And they cried with a loud voice, saying, How long, O Lord, holy and true, dost thou not judge and avenge our blood on them that dwell on the earth?

Even Scripture, you see, joins you in balking at evil unavenged. God must not finally be made a fool who puts up with everything.

And yet Scripture's imagery of judgment is so richly para-doxical (or, if you like, so blatantly self-contradictory) that it would be unwise to proceed without first setting down not only the unusually wide outside dimensions of the picture it presents but also some of the more notable details of the imagery. As before, the theological problem must be *aggravated* before it can be dealt with properly; otherwise, all you get is more of the same light and tasteless meat the world is already gagging on. Consider, therefore, the following sampler:

- And I saw the dead, small and great, stand before God; and the books were opened: and another book was opened, which is the book of life: and the dead were judged out of those things which were written in the books, according to their works. And the sea gave up the dead which were in it; and death and hell delivered up the dead which were in them: and they were judged every man according to their works. And death and hell were cast into the lake of fire. This is the second death. And whosoever was not found written in the book of life was cast into the lake of fire. (Rev. 20:12-15)
- For the Father judgeth no man, but hath committed all judgment unto the Son. (John 5:22)
- Ye judge after the flesh; I judge no man. And yet if I judge, my judgment is true: for I am not alone, but I and the Father that sent me. (John 8:15-16)
- I am come a light into the world, that whosoever believeth on me should not abide in darkness. And if any man hear my words, and believe not, I judge him not: for I came not to judge the world, but to save the world. He that rejecteth me, and receiveth not my words, hath one that judgeth him: the word that I have spoken, the same shall judge him the last day. (John 12:46-48)
- Now is the judgment of this world: now shall the prince of this world be cast out. And I, if I be lifted up from the earth, will draw all unto me. (John 12:31-32)
- And you, being dead in your sins and the uncircumcision of your flesh, hath he quickened together with him, having forgiven you all trespasses; blotting out the handwriting of

ordinances that was against us, which was contrary to us, and took it out of the way, nailing it to his cross. (Col. 2:13-14)

So much for the outside dimensions, the remarkable breadth of the paradox. Next, some notes on its qualitative peculiarities.

The first is one we have already taken account of: judgment is presented in these texts under both horizontal and vertical imagery. It is portrayed both as a historical event that will take place on the last day of the world — the *dies novissima,* the *youngest day* — and as an immediate and intimate reality *now.* The passage above from Revelation, for example, is a vision of the Mystery at work at the end of time; the one from John 12:31 ("*Now* is the judgment of this world: *now* shall the prince of this world be cast out") says just as plainly that it is at work in the present. Whatever we say about judgment, therefore, must always do justice to both kinds of imagery. We must not abolish end-of-the-line judgment in favor of judgment now; and above all (the more difficult reading being the preferred one), we must not neglect the judgment as a present reality just because the judgment as a future reality is more easily conceived.

Next, it must be noted that under either kind of imagery, judgment occurs in an intimate connection with the resurrection of the dead. In the sequential view of Revelation, the first event after Christ's second coming is the raising of the dead (of *all* the dead, please note, not just the "good" dead); it is only after the general resurrection that the judgment takes place. And in the more immediate, vertical view of John, it occurs under the same rubric: "I, if I be lifted up (on the cross, from the grave, in the ascension), will draw *all* unto me." We come before Christ, even in judgment, by the power of his cross and resurrection only; our contribution to the process, like Lazarus's, is simply our death, not our good or bad behavior.

But that means that no one comes to judgment with his times in his own hands; everyone who is drawn to Christ, whether now or at the last day, comes with his loser's grip on his own life broken, absolved by death. And that means, quite astonishingly, that Christ judges us only as *he holds us,* not as we hold ourselves. And since he holds us reconciled ("There is therefore now no condemnation to them which are in Christ Jesus"), it means that the judgment is, in some vast and fundamental sense, rigged in our favor. In the youngest day, we will all be completely acceptable.

Which brings us to the third and last peculiarity: the imagery of a divine fix being in, even before the judgment starts.

- *Item:* the *two sets of books* in the passage from Revelation: "and *the books* were opened: and *another book* was opened, which is the book of life." Perhaps it is forcing things a bit in this text to see the *Lamb's book of life* as our lives held in Christ, and "the books" as our lives held in our own hands before the absolution of death — to see the former as all our days held in reconciling *anámnêsis,* and the latter as those same days held outside it in our own (and others') dismal bookkeeping. But there are in fact two sets of books, and the temptation to do something theological with them may not be all wrong, especially since the image of the fixed trial is quite clear in other places.
- The three *items* from the Gospel according to John: in a word, the *runaround* God seems to give himself on the subject of judgment. To begin with, the Father, for whose ultimate gratification the whole business of creation and reconciliation is undertaken, *judges no one;* he has committed all judgment to the Son. Next, the Son, to whom the nasty job has been assigned, waffles mightily on the subject: "What, *me* judge? I don't judge anybody; I came not to judge the world

257

but to save the world." The Son's two comings, you see — those two historical manifestations of the one immediately vertical Mystery of the Word — are flatly contradictory: one to save, one to judge. But each of them, paradoxically, does both: his first, saving coming as the light condemns a world that loves darkness more than light; but his second coming as judge saves all those whose names he has fudged into his book of life by raising them (again, *everybody*) from the dead.

- One supporting *item* for the fudging: the text from Colossians where God in Christ blots out the handwriting that was against us and takes it out of the way, nailing it to the cross. Some judge! He confiscates the prosecution's whole case and seals it up in his death. Not a word of evidence about our guilt ever gets mentioned in court!

- And one final supporting *item,* just in case you feel sorry for the poor attorney who has to argue the case for our condemnation before such a blatantly prejudiced judge. Do you know who he is? He is the Paraclete, the *paráklētos,* the Advocate, the Heavenly Lawyer himself — namely, God the Holy Spirit, who is of one mind and substance with the Father and the Son. Utter collusion! Court-appointed counsel in cahoots with the non-hanging Judge! Sent by him, instructed by him, saying nothing but what has been determined by him, helping not the cause of justice but the infirmities of our otherwise hopeless case, and making intercession not for the system we have offended but simply and exclusively for us — with all the courtroom antics he has mastered in an eternity of unutterable groanings and other theatricalities.

If that doesn't say the fix is in, I don't know what would. Nevertheless, if you find the formulation a bit strong, I can tone it down for you. At the very least, it says that judgment is not vindictive, that God is not out to get us but to vindicate us, to show us ourselves as he holds us in his reconciliation — to put between us and himself not the shipwreck of our history but the snug harbor to which he has brought us by his death and resurrection.

Let me change the imagery a little, to make the idea of vindication stand out over against the notion of vindictiveness.

When I dream, my whole life as I hold it is available to me: the events of the party just a few hours ago; the circumstances of a two-week convention six years past; old loves not thought of for years; attitudes toward my father long since repressed by guilt. And in my dreaming, I hold — or, better said, I *suffer* — all those things in their unreconciled state. The good things simply rattle around in my sleeping consciousness like so many defenseless beings: really charming people wander off and are replaced by detestable partners; the beloved appears across a room I never manage to traverse; gorgeous views vanish and are replaced by steel staircases and locked doors. And the evil things have free rein in my dreams: my father belts me in the back of the head; I rage at my children; my friend turns me in to the authorities; I find to my horror that I have accidentally shaved off my beard.

Do you see? For all the time of my dreaming, what I most ache for, what I most need, is not some vindictive condemnation of those evils, not a vendetta in the name of those goods, but precisely a vindication of the goods as they really were and of the evils as the good they ought to have been. And when I awake, it is just that vindication which, within certain limits, I achieve. Conscious once again — my life held once again in *anámnēsis* by an ordered and ordering mind — I find it is now *all right*: the dreadful shaving off of my beard is held joyfully in the delightful and present possession of my beard; the clip on the head from my father is re-cognized in the whole tissue of my relationship with him as the good that he meant it to be in the first place; my own rage at my children is re-membered into the larger whole which is the only thing that ever could have mattered; the steel staircases are delighted in as proper steel staircases.

Indeed, if what Freud taught us is true, it is only in the *anámnêsis* of those evils that the good can be vindicated. Repressed or forgotten, whatever good there was in them remains forever under the thumb of evil; it is only in the awake and ordering mind — and, above all, in the mind that can judge accurately at last — that the things that matter can be seen to matter most. It is not, you see, that evil is winked at even for a second; rather, evil is seen as no longer having any proportionality to the good at all, and therefore as ultimately not mattering. We look the betrayals and the cruelties and the twaddle straight in the eye; and in the vindicating light of the last day, we see them finally as they are remembered in our waking and reconciling mind.

Therefore, convert the usual imagery of the judgment to the imagery of the dream, and watch what happens.

My whole history, and the whole of all our histories, are held by us as in a dream — the good defenseless, the evil rampant. There is for us no ordered and ordering mind capable of re-cognizing it in reconciliation; it remains, as we hold it, a poor, sad history, aching for vindication but never rising higher than poignancy. But when Jesus comes to that history as judge, he comes as *risen from the dead* — as the only *awake* person in the world — as the only one who sees things as they are, the only one who can afford to remember *everything*, to re-cognize without omission and so to re-order it all in his *anámnêsis*.

Which is why, when you think about it, the Gospel is presented as an object of *belief*, not knowledge — why we are asked only to make a response of *faith* to it, not to work up a bag of tricks by which we can render it effective. What needs to be done has already been done from the beginning: right from the start of every perversion of reality, all the ill-known and mis-known goods have been re-cognized and vindicated by the *Lamb slain from the foundation of the world.*

And therefore, when Christ comes to judge, he comes to judge only between *belief* and *unbelief*. Not between the good and the bad, because by the absolution of his death and ours, the bad is held only in his *anámnêsis* of it. Not between those who have cooperated with grace and those who have not, because his grace is sovereign and reconciles all things willy-nilly. He comes to judge only between those who in the midst of an undeniable reconcil-iation and vindication of all things — in the very thick of the fact of their restoration to themselves — choose or do not choose to *trust* his word that he has already done the job of reconciliation for them. The Lamb's book of life, therefore, contains not less than everything: *the entire creation* as it is spoken in love to the Father by the Son when he says, "Behold, I make *all things* new." The only sense I can make out of those "not found written in the book of life" is to construe them as those who refuse, despite the Word's irrevocable acceptance of them by grace, to believe they will find their names there if they look. Hell is the ultimate unreality: it is unbelief in the only set of facts there is.

Before going on to say something about hell, however, let me tell you a little story that ties up a good many of the loose ends of the subject of judgment.

Late one evening, I was with a group of people who were having an extended series of nightcaps after the funeral of a common friend. We had all known him well, although none of us was related to him; and as the night wore on and tongues became looser, the conversation circled back to poor old Oscar. I say circled back because, earlier in the evening, we had regaled each other with a series of fond and complimentary tales about him, and then wandered off to other subjects. When we came back to him, however, someone's casual remark about not wanting to get up the next morning with a big head turned us to the subject of Oscar's drinking. (It wasn't really all that bad; but on the other hand, Oscar's liver wasn't all that good, so it got him in the end.)

The fascinating thing about the conversation was that we found ourselves sitting there happily rehashing not only his tippling (we used to find his empties in our desk drawers) but even the resultant liver trouble that soured his disposition in his last years. In our first, pious conversation about his good qualities, we had, consciously or unconsciously, simply avoided all of our most recent experience of him. We had, as it were, confined ourselves to half an Oscar — a faked-out, prettied-up version of a man we all knew to be other and less admirable than the one we were praising. It wasn't until the second round of Oscar stories, however, that anyone realized just how fake the first one had been. Suddenly, everybody relaxed. We finally had a whole man to talk about, and for the first time that day it was possible to feel he was really resting in peace.

As I think about that evening now, it strikes me that it provides a handy, if limited, analogue to the day of judgment as I've been trying to figure it. First of all, Oscar was really judged — and accurately. Second, he was being judged in our *anámnêsis* of him — in our re-cognition of him out of the love we all had for him. Third, that love was the overriding consideration: we all wanted a vindication of Oscar, not a condemnation. But last of all, that vindication could not occur until we had stopped the pious fakery by which we tried to achieve it earlier in the evening. We really had to judge him — and all of him, good and bad alike — as he really was. Our love, since it was for the whole man, could not be operative for him until it had faced the whole man. But once it did, his reconciliation was the most obvious thing in the world. His bad liver and his grouchy disposition were no longer a problem to *him:* as far as he was concerned, his death had effectually absolved him of all such inconveniences. And they were, in our re-cognizing judgment of

262

him, no problem for *us,* either: we were finally free to hold him, with all his faults, *in the proportions our love insisted on* — and with no inconvenient, self-propelled Oscar to come around the next morning and bellyache.

Like all analogies, of course, this one breaks down. But even its collapse is edifying: our *anámnêsis* of Oscar — our re-cognizing word spoken over his history — is not like Christ's. It is not the Word's word, with a bark to it that wakes the dead into real resurrection; it is only a human word that does little more than fix up our own insides. But within those limitations, it works the same way: It comes to Oscar *in judgment, out of love;* it wills not retribution but vindication; and it achieves that vindication by seeing everything that was just as it was, but held now as what our love insists that it be. His drinking and his bad liver are not forgotten or suppressed. All the grim days he suffered as consequences are known for what they really were. But because they are over now for him, we remember them only under the rubric of the Glorious Scars: in our reconciling *anámnêsis,* they are held as a funny story about the bishop's embarrassed and totally unconvincing explanation of why empty vodka bottles kept turning up in his office closet.

If the day of Christ's judgment is anything like that at all, it will be — in fact, it already is — a great day for the world. It is indeed rigged; but it is rigged only out of love. Even though the fix is in from the start, the fix involves not inattention but the setting of no less than everything in the true proportions that his love insists on. But, above all, it is an utterly successful vindication. As Oscar, on that evening, had no power to prevent his reconciliation in our *mental re-cognition* of him, so nothing in the universe has any power to prevent its reconciliation by Christ's *real* re-membering of it — his putting of it all back together — in the resurrection of the dead.

Which is — once again, and gratifyingly — the very thing

the man said: "For I am persuaded, that neither death, nor life, nor angels, nor principalities, nor powers, nor things present, nor things to come, nor height, nor depth, nor any other creature, shall be able to separate us from the love of God, which is in Christ Jesus our Lord" (Rom. 8:38-39).

If after all that you still want a hell, I think it may finally be safe to sketch you one. But don't expect me to go back on anything I've said. Any hell I come up with now will be nothing more than a bunch of untrusting Oscars, as Christ holds them reconciled, somehow mucking up nothing more than their own enjoyment of that reconciliation. It will be a thoroughly modest proposition: very small, very quiet, and supremely unnecessary.

31

The Hell of It All

M y last remark about hell's being unnecessary needs some distinguishing, of course. If, for example, you take it as referring to the fate of any given individual, it is simply true by the very terms of the Gospel: we are saved by Christ alone who raises us from the dead — from the *absolution* of our death. We come before him at the judgment with no handwriting whatsoever against us. It's simply cheating to say you believe that and then renege on it by postulating some list of extra-rotten crimes for which Christ has to send you to hell. He, the universal Redeemer, is the only judge; as far as he's concerned, the only mandatory sentence is to life and life abundant.

Again, if you take my statement as referring to the fate of any given individual *as that individual resides in the power of Jesus' resurrection,* then hell is still unnecessary. For if, while we hold our times *here* in our own hands, all we have to do to be reconciled is *believe* he has them in his, how much less will we have to do *there* when we shall *see* they are in Christ's hand alone — that is, see them held for our eternal enjoyment as *all right?* If we are to find a second death in the midst of such a perfectly manifest risen and reconciled life, we're going to have to hunt for it by some strange and supremely avoidable *second alteration* of knowledge — a contradiction compared to which Adam's and Eve's first alteration was a children's parlor trick. We're going to have to go a totally unnecessary billion light years out of our way to avoid the risen nose on our face.

But if, on the other hand, all of that leads you to ask whether hell is not therefore *absolutely* unnecessary, I have to hedge a little. For it does have some necessity about it, at least as far as a Gospel-regarding theological system is concerned. For one thing, the imagery is simply there in the Bible. What you do with it, of course, is pretty much your own business; but the one thing you must not do is chuck it altogether.

But there's more necessity to it than that. If you remove the possibility of hell from Christian theology, even though you do it out of pure kindheartedness, you do more harm than good. You end up saying that after all the expense and heartache God went through to respect the freedom and integrity of his creatures (heartache for us as well as for him), he ultimately reneges on it by forcing everyone's hand, thus turning the whole business into nothing but a cruel charade. Further, you are forced to postulate a God who, after all the fuss to persuade his creatures to want what he wants for them, says in the end that he doesn't care if they want it or not — a God, in short, who doesn't give a damn about *them*.

But, worst of all, you come up with a loveless universe. It isn't kindheartedness that makes the world go round; it's love — and if you think they're the same thing, you've never been in love. Because if you have, you know that the heaven of the beloved's acceptance of your love comes wrapped inseparably with the hell of her possible refusal to accept it. Your gift of yourself to her is always a free and staggeringly abundant gift; and you must extend it — and she must reckon with it — with fear and trembling. Nevertheless, you and I and everybody else who hasn't gone dead or sour go right on extending love because we recognize our penchant for risky invitations as the best thing about us. All you do, therefore, if you take the possibility of hell out of your view of the universe, is posit a God who is so interested in playing it safe that he becomes unrecognizable as a lover. The theological function of hell, accordingly, is to be the sacrament of the ultimate and real element of risk by which alone we can recognize a world ruled by love. Universalism, *as an overriding theological principle,* is a false start.

On the other hand, if you ask whether there is *in fact* a hell — whether specific persons will actually go so far as to insist on a second death in the face of their resurrection by the supreme Lover himself — that's another matter altogether. And it's a matter about which I think a theologian has only four things to say:

- *One.* It is obvious that something like a second death is possible here and now: nobody, however beloved, *has to* love in return.
- *Two.* It is manifest from experience that something like it is also *actual* here and now: we have all loved people who, for a while at least, preferred their private hell of rejection to the heaven of acceptance we held out to them.
- *Three.* For the reasons already given, it seems that a similar second death may be *possible* in the *hereafter,* but
- *Four.* Nevertheless, whether it will or will not be *actual* hereafter seems impossible to conclude one way or the other: we just don't know enough about the magnitude of either God's love or our freedom to figure the outcome of a high noon between two such incorrigible romantics.

Moot question, therefore. Move on.

While we're on the subject of universalism, however, a few observations are in order. Even as a theological principle, we're not able simply to dismiss it out of hand. For while it can't be made the governing consideration (it's only a possible deduction from the doctrine of grace, not the sovereign doctrine itself), something very much like it will be found in every authentic Christian system, precisely because such a system will always proceed from the doctrine of grace. To see why, all you have to do is consider the alternative.

Suppose you start out by saying what many people actually think Christianity says — namely, that if you're good you go to heaven, and if you're bad you go to hell. Do you see what that does? It voids the work of Christ. The Gospel says that only *his reconciliation* ultimately matters, that the world the Father loves is the world he sees in the risen life of his only begotten Son. But if that's true, then he's stopped counting the world's goodnesses and badnesses as the world holds them and sees them only as vindicated and reconciled in Jesus. If you start counting them again as they are in us, you welsh on the whole idea of Christ alone as the resurrection and the life.

Therefore, any authentically Christian system is going to have to keep off the kick of human merit and demerit and stick resolutely to a universalism of grace that overrides the subject of human works. And they all do, even the systems that at first blush seem not to. Take, for example, some of the starchily Roman scenarios of salvation. Historically, they've flirted dangerously with merit and demerit — to the point, at times, of losing their grip on Christian authenticity. But where they have not, they have always ended up with a doctrine of hell that paid its respects to the universalism of grace: they've said that the only thing that can put you in hell is *final impenitence* — the final refusal of an absolutely free gift of forgiveness in the risen Lord. Sometimes, to be sure, they've defined that condition in a way that made it smell strongly of merit and demerit; but insofar as they have held to it at all, the hell they have propounded was no cosmic inevitability but precisely the weird and unnecessary trick of missing the nose on your face. The exact objection to Romanism that many people have is that it's too easy, that it lets lifelong bounders escape hell just because they squeaked in a confession before they corked off for good. But that objection comes to grief on the rock of the Gospel: if the Prodigal was forgiven before he made *any* confession, why can't even the longest-term sinner be absolved after a last-minute one?

Or take Calvinism for another example. At first sight, its doctrine of double predestination (that some go to heaven, and some to hell, for no other reason than the inscrutable counsel of God) seems one-hundred-eighty degrees away from any kind of universalism. But if you look at it narrowly — that is, if you look only at what it says about the *elect who go to heaven* — suddenly, it's plain, unvarnished universalism all over again. Those in heaven are there on the basis of no merit of their own, and no demerit of their own can keep them out of it. Indeed, it is almost a universalism of the worst sort: a freedom-negating, love-denying, drag-'em-in-by-the-head inevitability. But for all its defects, it holds inflexibly to the sovereignty of grace — and accordingly, to that high degree, it is authentically Christian.

Somehow, therefore, whatever we say about hell must be said under the rubric of a universal and effective reconciliation of all things in Christ. If we choose to say *where hell is*, it must somehow be *inside* Jesus' reconciliation. If we choose to explain *how hell can be*, we must somehow say that Jesus accepts our choosing of it *without willing us into it* in any deterministic way. If we want to try to say *what hell does*, we must somehow leave it with no detrimental effect on the universal picnic. And if we are so bold as to attempt to say *what hell is like*, we must somehow make it even more of a nothing than our first death, which is its master image. So much, then, for the preliminaries. Now for the hell of it all.

• •

Nowhere in theology is it more important to work scrupulously from the top. Hell is the ultimate contradiction, the last anomaly, the only holdout in the universal reconciliation of all things in Christ. Therefore, it must never be allowed to govern anything. That means in particular that when our exposition of a given set of theological images is going reasonably well with regard to other doctrines, the fact that it may go badly with respect to hell should not, in and of itself, be allowed to spook us into abandoning the imagery. If hell is indeed the only "loophole" in the sovereignty of grace, it will probably remain something of an exception to any attempt to expound that sovereignty theologically. I realize that sounds suspiciously like stringing a net under a supposedly daring high-wire act, but I don't think it is. It's just insisting on putting first things first.

From the top, then: Hell, as I said, is a necessity in any theological system committed to the idea that God loves what he makes — that he is not indifferent to his creatures but actually gives a damn what they do with themselves. To put it in a slightly different way, it is an inevitable concomitant of the doctrine of judgment, which in turn flows directly out of the doctrine of creation: all things are what they are because the Word speaks them into being out of love for the Father. Anything that exists can really be only one thing — namely, *what he says it is.* If he says "pussycat," then pussycat it is; if he says "Howard Cosell," then Howard Cosell.

However, if it is indeed true that human beings can, both here and hereafter, somehow contradict what he says — that we can counterspeak the Word, as it were, that we can live unreally in the midst of the sole reality we have — then the only verdict the Word can pass on that contradiction is *"That is not what I had in mind at all."* Which is literally a hell of a thing to say; and if we were actually to insist upon his saying it forever, it would be quite enough of a hell for anybody — an ultimate failure to know anything at all, stemming from an ultimate refusal to know the only real self that's left to know. And it would be doubly unnecessary. For in our case, he has added to his sovereign word of creation an equally sovereign word of reconciliation by which he contradicts even our contradictions and holds us justified in his risen life.

Keeping that firmly in mind, then, we can attempt to answer some of the questions hell raises. For example, take the question *"Where is hell?"*

I am aware that most of the scriptural imagery for hell is "separation" imagery: hell is somewhere away from heaven — *out there,* not at the wedding feast of the Lamb; *in darkness,* not in the light; in a *lake of fire* and a *second death* from which it cannot rise and come back to spoil the party. But since Scripture also insists that insofar as anything exists at all, it exists because of the intimate and immediate speaking of its name by the Word of God, there seems no way of reading that separation as an absolute divorce from God. If we're going to be resolute about putting first things first, then the presence of hell to God has to be the overriding consideration and the separation imagery has to be read as pointing to something other than a merely literal absence from God. Perhaps it might be read in a *subjective* sense, taking it to mean that those in hell, while they're at the party, are there absent-mindedly. Or perhaps it might be read in a more *ontological* sense, so that we will see them as there, but only as perpetual rebels against the party — as trying to rescind their true being by their endless contradiction of the Word who constitutes and invites them.

Therefore, the only answer I can give to "Where is hell?" is to say "It's in the same place as heaven, and earth, and everything else — namely, *inside the speaking of the Word.*" Or, to use the image

271

of the lovers in bed at the end of Part One: "Between the lips of the Word and the ear of the Father." In other words, hell is right smack in the midst of the reconciled creation in Jesus. It is nowhere else than at the picnic where all times are held in the vindicating hand of Christ.

But that, of course, raises a second question: "Why doesn't hell spoil the party? How can you have such a collection of ontological wet blankets around and not have them put a damper on the picnic?" You note, of course, that this is a question which doesn't arise if you take the separation imagery more or less literally. Hell, in those terms, is safely *out there* somewhere; there's not even a suggestion of its interfering with heaven — which may be the precise reason for not throwing such imagery away cavalierly. The paradox of hell, as the most contradiction-filled one of all, will in all likelihood be patient of no exposition but the most contradictory. A single, comprehensive insight into the mystery of iniquity is less likely to be possible here than anywhere else.

Nevertheless, an answer of sorts can be made on the basis of the imagery of *anámnêsis*. Hell doesn't spoil the picnic because as far as Christ and the saints are concerned, they make joyful remembrance of those in hell as Jesus holds them in his reconciliation. Even though the "damned" won't accept that reconciliation themselves, it remains real in Christ: all their evils and miseries are held in him as the only real things they could ever have been. If those in hell insist on an eternal exercise in unreality, that's too bad for them; but it remains an exercise in unreality and so bears no comparison with the overwhelming weight of the real.

That, of course, is pretty much the answer C. S. Lewis gives in *The Great Divorce*. Hell, as he depicts it, turns out to occupy no more "space" in the eternal theme park than a tiny crack in the ground between two blades of grass. Anyone who wants to come up out of the crack into reality is free to do so; but if he doesn't, he isn't a problem because he takes up so little of all the *real* space available. That has its drawbacks, to be sure: it's perilously close to both the imagery of literal separation and the imagery of real forgetting. But it isn't quite the same thing, and it may well be the best that can be done.

Still, I'd like to try to press a little harder on my own imagery — namely, that of Christ holding the damned reconciled in his *anámnêsis* of them while they insist on fooling around with the utter nothingness of a second death. What does that give you?

Well, to be honest, it gives you problems. It seems to put the damned at the picnic like so many well-dressed store-window dummies: they're all spruced up and ready for the party, but they're not with it. Somehow, they're absent from themselves. In one sense, of course, that's not a difficult image. Everybody has seen it in others and most of us have seen it at one time or another in ourselves: the ten-year-old refusing to enjoy his own birthday party out of pique; the teenage girl having a miserable time at her prom because she's got the sulks; the boring guest who might as well be alone for all the company he keeps.

In another sense, however, that image is difficult in the extreme. It's a poor party at which the birthday boy is a pill; the prom queen's escort doesn't have much of a time if she keeps grouching all evening; and the company at dinner keep making excuses to leave the table. It's hard to see how you can have the damned as large as life at the eternal party and not have them slow the proceedings considerably. After all, since it's their whole reconciled life that's present there — and present not only to them as Christ holds them but to all the others with whom they ever had to do — it would seem hard for those others to have them around when the one thing they most want from them — a personal response that accepts their reconciliation — is not about to be forthcoming. The imagery of *anámnêsis* worked nicely with

Oscar on the evening of his funeral, but chiefly because Oscar wasn't able to walk back in and obtrude his recalcitrance upon our joyful re-cognition of him.

What do you do with it, then? Well, I think the only thing is to acknowledge that when you try to use the imagery I've been working with to answer this second question, it begins to break down. You can save it only by shading it in the direction of C. S. Lewis: the damned are at the picnic, but they don't spoil it because somehow they are not there as large as life. They can be thought of as there only in two ways: first, in Christ's remembrance of them in his effective, joyful *anámnêsis* of all things; but second, in their own vain remembrance of themselves — that is, in a Second Death in which, like Oscar in his first death, they are not sufficiently *with* anything to interfere with the festivities.

But that in turn can be made to work only if you do one of two things. Either you read their remembrance of themselves into a smallness — into a crack in the ground or a darkness outside; or you take it as a retreat into a vaporous self-knowledge that precludes their having any adverse effect on the party — that is, into an insistence on knowing something that's no longer there to know (namely, their life as dead), which is therefore incomprehensible to any real knower. In Christ's *anámnêsis* of them, they remain — like Oscar — as large as Jesus' knowledge of them wills them to be; and *that* knowledge of them is available to the saints. But since they insist only on their *own* knowledge — since all the agency they can manage to exercise at the party is only the agency of a dead mind — they obtrude themselves on the party as no more than the dead nothing that is all their minds can come up with. Like Oscar, they just don't make any *real* waves.

If you find that a bit tortured and want to go back to straight separation imagery, I can't say I blame you. The *anámnêsis* ball, on this pitch, doesn't look like much to hit. Still, since I'm the one standing out here on the mound, I just keep pitching, hoping only that maybe I can get somebody to swing at something — or that even a walk would be acceptable if I could manage it without beaning the batter. So here goes one final pitch that's a combination of two images I've already used more than once: I have in mind C. S. Lewis's *crack in the ground* from *The Great Divorce*, and the creating, redeeming *hands of Christ* that hold all things in being — hell included.

Lewis suggested that all of hell could fit into a tiny crack in the soil of the heavenly country (and therefore that hell was *within* the heavenly country, no matter how far away its inhabitants felt themselves to be). But I'm going to suggest that all of hell will fit into the hands of Jesus — and specifically, into one of the Glorious Scars of the crucifixion, into the nail wound in the left hand of his risen body. That, you see, goes Lewis one better. It puts hell not under the floorboards of the eternal party but in the palm of the hand of the host who is passing the drinks and hors d'oeuvres. So if a wedding guest at the Supper of the Lamb is curious to see what a particular resident of hell looks like *from the point of view of the party*, she can peek into the nail print and see old Adolph as Jesus holds him in the midst of the festivities: re-cognized, re-membered, and reconciled. But old Adolph himself can't see that. All he can see from *inside* the Glorious Scar — from inside that narrow opening into which all the horrors of time and eternity have been fitted with room to spare — is the Hitler of his own dread history. Do you see? Jesus has managed to accommodate everyone. As far as he and the saints are concerned, the damned are nowhere *but* at the party. But as far as their deeds are concerned — and as far as they themselves are concerned — they are *nowhere* at the party. They are precisely a chunk of nowhere that happens to have been drawn into the party and given houseroom in the left hand of Jesus. So there, finally, is the pitch I've been leading up to with all the long, slow curves I've thrown at you.

Maybe it solves your problems with me; maybe it doesn't. In any case, two more questions, and we're at an end.

Given the imagery so far, wouldn't it be wiser to say that we make our own hell and not get into the business of having God damn us? If he wills life and life abundant, why should we set up a system in which we obscure that truth by having him somehow will the utterly contradictory second death as well? The question, obviously, is "Who wills hell?"; and the answer, I think, has to be "Both God and human beings." If you want to make a nice, canned theological distinction, you say that the *proximate* and *effecting* cause of hell is the human will, while the *remote* and *enabling* cause of it is the divine will. God makes hell *possible,* but not necessary; human beings, unnecessarily, make it *actual.*

It remains important, however, to steer clear of the flat-footed assertion that hell is nothing but a subjective state of our own devising — that God has no relationship with it and no particular feelings about it. Those in hell are as much the apples of his eye as those anywhere else; if they are so cantankerous as to refuse to see that forever, then God can only look on them forever and stamp his foot. He just has to say, "Oh, damn!" If he can't get mad, he's not much of a lover. His wrath, of course, is vindicating, not vindictive; but precisely because it's nothing other than his love in the face of contradiction, he wills it in the same act by which he wills his love. And therefore he wills hell simply by being unwilling to stop loving. No doubt annihilation would make for a more pleasant eternity; but annihilation, apparently, is not one of God's options. Re-enter here, therefore, all the imagery of the worm that dieth not and the fire that is not quenched, and of weeping and gnashing of teeth — none of which is a bit too strong for any lovers' quarrel, let alone an eternal one.

And that brings you to the other question: "Is hell eternal?" The Bible, of course, says rather plainly that it is; and most theologians who have taken the matter seriously have said the same thing. A few, like Origen, have been moved by the vision of the sovereignty of grace to postulate an eventual closing up of the infernal shop; but until recent times, the church has almost too enthusiastically acted as if hell would be in business forever.

My own answer to the question is "It all depends on how you set it up." Nowhere more than in answering posers like this is it so obvious that theology is a game. About the facts, nobody knows anything; therefore, all we do is juggle our own perceptions. Here are mine:

Grace is forever sovereign; hell is forever unnecessary. As far as any persons now in time and space are concerned, we believe that nobody, however evil, has to go to hell because Jesus has erased the handwriting against everybody: all anybody has to do to enjoy that freedom from damnation is just trust that it's true — because it already is. A question still remains, however, about the condition of those who have passed from time to eternity: Can those who have eternally refused to believe Christ's gracious reconciliation of them ever take back that refusal? Can there ever be a "moment" or a "point" in their eternal contradictoriness at which they get fed up with their stupid sulking, look finally at what Christ has in hand for them, and, with a huge, sheepish, all-relieving grin, just cut out the nonsense?

As I said, it all depends on how you set it up. The usual answer (namely, it's *impossible* for that to happen) is based on a sharp distinction between time and eternity. Time, being a succession of moments, allows you to choose something in one moment and unchoose it in the next; eternity, being one single unending moment, leaves you no such room to maneuver. Eternal choices, therefore, can't be rescinded.

If, however, you make time and eternity less mutually exclusive, the usual answer doesn't have to be given. Watch.

Time (along with space) is a condition of creation as we hold

277

it *in our hands;* eternity is a condition of that same creation as it is held *in Christ's.* Accordingly, all moments in time are held for our eternal exploration of them. Therefore, even though the damned are deeply committed to only the most unreal exploration of those moments, the real moments themselves are always there in Christ, and it is at least possible for any or all of the inhabitants of the nail wound in Christ's left hand to take a fresh, and refreshing, look at them. On their nine-millionth unreal revisit to a day that Jesus holds for them — to the day a red-winged black-bird flew across the gray sky, or to the time the beloved's eyes shone purple in the sun — the way is open for them suddenly to catch on to what it was really all about and come staggering out of nowhere with one huge laugh at all their fuss over nothing.

Set it up any way you like, then. Better yet, decide which answer you like best and rig the question so you get it. As long as you don't throw out any images, there's no reason why your theology shouldn't be fun.

32

Heaven in a Nutshell

About heaven, I think, the less said the better. Nowhere in theology is it more important — or more safe — for the mind to take off its dialectical dark glasses when it looks at the images of the Mystery. Our inveterate habit of trying to grasp the inexplicable by explanation, of wanting to write restaurant reviews of the Supper of the Lamb before we've tasted the meal itself — in other words, our infatuation with theologizing — is less helpful here than anywhere. For the subject of heaven is the point at which the eschatological imagery goes into an elation of itself, where we come face-to-face with the largest exhibit yet of pictures of the undepictable — where we see the final vision of the risen, reconciled creation that the Word and the Spirit offer to the Father in love.

And so it is the one place in theology where we ought to be willing, in complete simplicity, just to look. Since no image can ever be fancy enough to do justice to the reality of the heaven it is meant to figure, even the plainest, crassest images — even, perhaps, a literalism about such images — will always do more good here than harm. So I simply commend them to you: the New Heavens and the New Earth; the Holy City, the New Jeru-

279

salem, coming down from God out of heaven prepared as a bride adorned for her husband; the Wiping away of Tears; the Twelve Gates and the Twelve Foundations; the Pearls, the Precious Stones, the Pure Gold like Transparent Glass, the River, and the Tree of Life — and the utter triumph of it all: "There shall be no night there; and they need no candle, neither light of sun; for the Lord God giveth them light: and they shall reign for ever and ever."

With all of that to nourish you, you need nothing of substance from me — which is a good thing, since I have nothing for you, and neither does anyone else. Let me give you just two warnings, then, and let it go at that.

Whatever you think about heaven, remember that it has to be *real* and it has to be *now:* if you theologize at all about this last of all the last things, do it only with your mind fixed irrevocably on the actual color of your beloved's eyes and with your forefinger held firmly on the tip of your very present nose. And do it that way to remind yourself that if heaven is about anything, it is about *those* eyes and *that* nose — and that it is about both of them held risen and glorified *right now.* It is not something other than this world; it is this world as it is perfectly offered now in the land of the Trinity. It is all the moments of time and all the conjunctions of space as Christ holds them reconciled for the praise of the glory of the Father's grace. And it is all of them held for our endless exploration of their depths — depths which we, even at our best, even at the moment of seeing the beloved's eyes, have only just begun to suspect.

But it is precisely the expansion of our astonishment at that suspicion, the enlargement of our surprise at that glimpse into those depths, that heaven is really all about. It is not the shrinking of our love of earth — not a renunciation of the beloved flesh for some other, finer thing — but this gorgeous old familiar thing itself, this apple of God's eye, offered up in the resurrection as the Bride of the Lamb, the Holy City, the New Heavens and the New Earth.

And in every important sense but one, it is all of that *right now.* For "even when we were dead in sins, [he] hath quickened us together with Christ, (by grace ye are saved;) and hath raised us up together, and made us sit together in heavenly places in Christ Jesus" (Eph. 2:5-6).

If we are *now* in Christ, we are *now* in that new creation. Unless what we believe is a lie, it is just that simple, and the proof is as easy as the yoke of Christ. For if we are now dead with him, we are also now risen in him; and if we are now judged by him, we are also now reconciled in him. And therefore if heaven is the fullness of that reconciliation, it is that now, and we're in it already. The only important sense in which we are not in it is the least important sense of all; and the only catch to it turns out to be not a catch but the ultimate liberation: our apprehension of heaven face-to-face waits only for the easiest, most inevitable thing of all — our *literal, physical death.* That alone has yet to become true; everything else is true already. Therefore, we are as good as home *now.* Q.E.D.

•　　•

For the time being, of course, you can only *believe* that. All you can *know* now is the estrangement and bondage that come from your contradiction of the Word. But since it is such a lovely thing to believe — and since even in your bondage it will fill you with the freedom of your Father's house — I urge it upon you as your liberty and your life.

Even Angelo never made anybody an offer that was so hard to refuse.

33

Jesus, Jesus, Jesus

It is, I admit, all bizarre. And when it is not bizarre, outrageous — and if not outrageous, then vulgar. Not, mind you, what I have written; rather, what I have written about: the Gospel of the grace of God that reconciles all by the resurrection of the dead. Any outlandishness I contributed to the exposition was minor compared to the strangeness of the subject itself; any shock to your sensibilities, a mere nudge compared to the positively rude and bohemian assault launched upon them by God's word of free and unmerited salvation.

For (I hope you see the point at last) the Gospel of grace is the end of *religion,* the final posting of the CLOSED sign on the sweatshop of the human race's perpetual struggle to think well of itself. For that, at bottom, is what religion is: the human species' well-meant but dim-witted attempt to gain approval of its unapprovable condition by doing odd jobs it thinks some important Something will thank it for. If we can't offer God a nice Adam or Eve, we offer him a nice goat instead — an activity which, as God has frequently pointed out, is an exercise in futility, since it is not possible that the blood of bulls and goats should take away the entail of a fundamentally worm-eaten self-image.

Religion, therefore, is a loser, a strictly fallen activity. It has a failed past and a bankrupt future. There was no religion in Eden, and there won't be any in the New Jerusalem; and in the meantime, Jesus has died and risen to persuade us to knock it off right now. He has said that as far as God is concerned, we're all home free already, and there's not a single religious thing you or I have to do about it. We are, as I said a long while ago, simply invited to believe it, and to cry a little or giggle a lot (or vice versa) as seems appropriate.

"Ah, but," you say. "Doesn't that make it all dangerously . . ."

On second thought, I've decided you don't say anything. You, like Norman, have had your last "but." I suddenly find I'm tired. Tired of fussing over your perpetually offended sense of the proprieties. Tired, as Saint Paul was, of having to come to you hat in hand and explain for the thousandth time that the jailhouse door is really open. And tired above all of having to apologize for God because he doesn't run what you consider a respectable penitentiary. I shall not explode you out of the book as I did Norman; but I shall tell you what I think. I think you're a dummy — a great big ethico-religious klutz who really is dying to hear bad news after all, and whose one piece of luck is that only God is God. Anybody else, in his place, would have run you out of the store ages ago. You are one tough, sour-pussed, foot-dragging, door-slamming, tire-kicking, belly-aching customer balking at the best deal you're ever going to get. All I can say is . . .

But on third thought, there's no point in that, either. Theological billingsgate only adds to the pile of irrelevancies and resentments. Let me compose myself, therefore, and head for the barn.

●   ●

Three comments only: one about Religion, one about Ethics, and one about the Life of Grace.

First, about Religion:

I want you to set aside the notion of the Christian Religion, because it's a contradiction in terms. You won't learn anything positive about religion from Christianity; and if you look for Christianity in religion, you'll never find it. To be sure, Christianity uses the *forms* of religion — and, to be dismally honest, too many of its adherents act as if it were a religion. But it isn't one, and that's that. The church is not in the religion business; it's in the Gospel-proclaiming business. And the Gospel is the Good News that all our fuss and feathers over our relationship with God are unnecessary because God, in the Mystery of the Word who is Jesus, has gone and fixed it up himself. So let that pass.

Think instead of plain, ordinary, religion-type religion: burning incense at the evening sacrifice, pouring chicken blood on the sacred stone at sunrise, standing on your head and praying all night with your right thumb stuck in your left ear, trying with might, main, and promises of reform to expiate your irremovable guilt. What's that all about? Why do we all do it? Well, to be honest, we do it to fake out a repair job on the hopelessly messed-up inside of our heads, to kid ourselves into the impression that there is still *something we can do* — in short, to avoid facing the fact that we are dead and only grace can raise us.

And if any people say they don't make chicken sacrifices, they're lying to themselves. The only people who have even a chance of getting out of the sacred-stone business are believing Christians — and they spend most of their lives trying to resist their almost daily temptation to get back into it. Everybody since Adam is instinctively religious; there aren't any of us who, left to our own devices, won't burn incense to something. Until we can admit we are dead, we will, by the sheer necessity of pretending to be alive and well, invent a religion to protect us from what we cannot face. Let me show you.

Behold the mighty Swinger. Behold the man, the envy of henpecked husbands and the king of the singles scene, the suave lover liberated from the dark religiosities of the sect of his upbringing. Watch him spring for dinners without number at Lutéce and weekends ad lib in Acapulco with lovely, pliant creatures gathered like daisies into his arms.

Then listen to him as he lies in bed the next day and offers his morning sacrifice to the god of self-justification: "You're great, honey, and I really do love you; but I've got to be totally honest with you. This is all it can be." Was chicken blood on a stone ever more religious than this ritual oblation to his cockeyed sense of his own integrity?

Or hear him as he talks in the bar after work on the next Tuesday: "She was a great lay, but not much more. I couldn't have stood another hour of it." Was the pinch of incense ever more de rigueur than this evening sacrifice to his belief in his hard-nosed self-possession?

Do you see now why I told you the story of Paul and Laura? It was to help you see that until the day we can face the fact of our death, we will always try to live by our religion — and that for as long as we do, our religion will always kill us, because whatever it is, we will sooner or later fail it. Paul's religion, of course, was Romance, not Swinging or the Cult of Isis. But it worked the same way. For him, falling in love and being in love were the ultimate, all-justifying acts that enabled him to think well of himself. They redeemed him from the bondage of his otherwise disordered being. If he could be a true acolyte of Romance, he did not have to feel so bad about being Paul.

But acolytes must observe the ritual. Their fidelity must be proved by constant attendance at the altar. Suppose, however, they cannot do it? What happened when Paul found himself unable to boast of fidelity to his romance with Catharine because of his attendance on Janet et al.? Well, he wrote himself off as dead before his god.

On the other hand, acolytes must also worry about whether their god is faithful to them. It's not only that their self-esteem requires them to prove themselves to the deity; it's also that the deity must rend the skies and show a smiling face. There must be signs. But if there are not? If Catharine withdrew behind silent heavens? Well, once again, Paul died.

I gave you only five days of Paul's affair with Laura, and only the first five at that. And I promised you no contretemps. But it is no default on that promise to remind you that Paul will not shake his religion of Romance quite as easily as he received the fullness of Laura's grace. He will still — perhaps for years, perhaps for life — be tempted to go on seeing his inevitable failure to be a true acolyte of Romance as damning evidence of his unacceptability. And all that, even though their relationship came into being solely because of her willingness to bear his unacceptability herself — to accept, as she put it, a voluntary crucifixion for his sake.

And he will still, for just as long, be tempted to put her to the test — to torment himself, and her, by demanding signs of her divine approval. And when they are not forthcoming: when, for example, either because she just answered the phone out of a deep sleep and made no sense, or because there were children in the room and she couldn't say "I love you" (or, more profoundly perhaps, because she had gone well beyond his fussy creed of Romantic Exclusivity and was now more *in* love *with* him than she ever had been in love with him), he does not hear the word his need demands — in short, when she moves herself into the heaven of total disinterest in religion — he will go into an agony of fear at his rejection. And all that, again, in the interest of an idiotic effort to find out if the lover whose grace saved him from the shipwreck of exclusivity is herself faithful to the religion she excused him from.

286

It is all foolishness. Religion begins after relationship has broken down. The minute anyone re-establishes relationship by grace, religion simply ends. It lives only in foul air. When grace cuts off its supply of bus fumes and sewer gas, it coughs itself to death. Paul's joy in love will be in direct proportion to the quickness and thoroughness with which he learns to breathe the fresh air of acceptance. And our joy in the love of God will be the same. Our best example will be that other Paul, the Apostle himself, who was the champion bus-fume inhaler of all time and still managed to kick the habit. He did successfully with the religion of the Law what my Paul was only beginning to do with the religion of Romance: Paul the ex-Pharisee stopped putting himself to the test, and he stopped putting the deity to the test. He finally saw that in the divine love affair, nobody needs to earn his or her way.

Admittedly, he had help. The Law he tried to keep was a manifest impossibility; and the God he tried to tempt just wasn't having any. The only sign he got was to be blinded by Jesus until he stopped asking for signs altogether and concentrated on grace. But when he did! . . .

The Epistle to the Romans has sat around in the church ever since like a bomb ticking away the death of religion; and every time it's been picked up, the ear-splitting freedom in it has gone off with a roar. The only sad thing is that the church as an institution has spent most of its time playing bomb squad and trying to defuse it. For your comfort, though, it can't be done. Your freedom remains as close to your life as Jesus and as available to your understanding as the nearest copy of Saint Paul. Like Augustine, therefore, *tolle, lege,* take and read: *tolle* the one, *lege* the other — and then hold on to your hat. Compared to that explosion, the clap of doom sounds like a cap pistol.

Second, about Ethics:

While we're setting things aside, let's get rid of "Christian" ethics as well as "Christian" religion. Not only because it too is a contradiction in terms but especially because it's nothing but puffery which, given any houseroom at all, elbows the meaning out of both Christianity and ethics.

Ethics is the subdivision of philosophy that deals with moral questions as distinct from, say, logical or ontological ones. As such, it is a strictly human activity. Unlike religion, however, it is not of itself a fallen one. It is a natural and proper response of the curious human mind to the astonishing intricacy of the creation that God has set before it. It's a *study,* an exploration of the wonder of human *behavior* just as logic is an exploration of the wonder of human *thought.* And, like all studies, when it addresses its chosen aspect of reality (in technical language, its *material object*), it does so in the confidence that everybody else who undertakes the same study is likewise addressing the same material object. Whether we investigate ethics, logic, music, gardening, tennis, or cookery, we assume that there's something "there" that is the same for all of us — we assume, in short, that dialogue is possible.

To be sure, we all come at that something from different angles (in technical language again, with different *formal objects* in mind). There is Italian cookery and Chinese cookery, there is French oboe-playing, and English oboe-playing, there is symbolic logic, and there is situation ethics. But note two things. First, when oboe players get together, it's oboe playing they're primarily about, not Frenchness or Englishness. Their material object governs the discussion; their formal objects are incidental. But second, there is a limitation as to the range of formal objects that can be admitted. German cookery and Swedish cookery are permissible topics, and so perhaps is something as exotic as Architectural cookery, if you happen to be a whiz at *pastillage* and pulled sugar. But Canine cookery? Musical cookery? Symbolic cookery? And what about Angelic cookery or Divine cookery? Doesn't it begin to look for all the world as if the materiality has been knocked out cold by the application of a totally alien formality? Or else that the formality has been rendered meaningless by its association with inappropriate matter?

That, you see, is the trouble with *Christian* ethics. Of course there will be Christians who study ethics, just as there will be Christians who study cookery, gardening, and tennis. And it is entirely possible that their Christianity may lead them to prefer certain ethical, culinary, horticultural, or athletic postures to others. But it is difficult to see how such preferences could ever lead them to conclude that they had invented something called Christian gardening or Christian tennis. And it is therefore impossible to see how they could imagine there was such a thing as Christian ethics.

Ethics tells you what you ought and ought not to do in order to be recognizably and acceptably human. Christianity tells you about a God who takes unrecognizable and unacceptable human beings and re-cognizes and accepts them in Jesus, whether or not they happen to have done what they ought to have done. Christian ethics is like Angelic cookery: nobody in her right mind wants a meal fit for an angel, or an angel whose hobby is whipping up omelets; therefore, nobody in her right mind bothers with the subject at all. Ditto Christian ethics. Christianity and ethics must never be jammed into a single category. Doing that simply destroys both of them. Your Christianity forces you to say that unethical people can go to heaven, and so tempts you to say that ethics is barking up an eschatologically non-existent tree. And your ethics forces you to say that unethical people are really not what the Creator of the Universe has in mind, thus leading you to question whether the God who so blithely takes them home hasn't in fact gone soft in the head.

That, obviously, has been our problem all through this book. And I have deliberately aggravated it so you would see it as a problem and not go on thinking of it in your old way as if it were a solution. By hook or by crook — by adulterous parables or by pornographic dream sequences — I simply had to get you off the bastard subject of Christian ethics. You may — indeed, if you are to be free, you must — take your Christianity neat: grace, straight up, no ice. And you may also — because your sanity and your love of God's creation require it — take your ethics with all the seriousness it deserves. But you may just as legitimately strive to improve your backhand, your French bread, or your annual to-mato crop — with precisely the same benefit, because those things are neither more nor less worthy than ethics of your time and attention as a human being — as a priestly creature in the image of a God who loves them all.

But you may not take the oranges of morality and the apples of the Gospel and mush them up into a marmelsauce called Christian ethics. Because if you do, you will lose your grip on the Mystery that alone can keep them unique and reconciled. You will, in short, get sick of your weird concoction and go back to imagining that you have to choose between them. And the saddest thing about such an unnecessary choice is that, given the way we are, we will usually decide to keep the ethics, which can no more save us than our backhand or our bread, and lose the Christianity, which is the only thing that promises us a God who can and does.

So don't mess with hybrids. Keep a spirited Christian horse and a useful ethical donkey. But don't try to breed a mule. Only a jackass does that.

Third and finally, about The Life of Grace:

Let's make a clean sweep of it: let's throw out the idea of "the Christian Life" as well. Admittedly, it's not strictly a contradiction in terms like the other two notions; but it's nearly so. The word *Christian* has, through a process of guilt by association, acquired such a freight of religious and ethical meaning that *grace,* which is the first thing it's about, is almost the last thing people think of when you use it.

I prefer, therefore, to end as I began, with nothing but grace — just as Paul and Laura and Vito did, and just as you and I and everybody else do, under God. The life of grace is not an effort on our part to achieve a goal we set ourselves. It is a continually renewed attempt simply to believe that someone else has done all the achieving that is needed and to live in relationship with that person, whether we achieve or not. If that doesn't seem like much to you, you're right: it isn't. And, as a matter of fact, the life of grace is even less than that. It's not even our life at all, but the life of that Someone Else rising like the tide in the ruins of our death. For us it is simply Jesus, Jesus, Jesus, as it was Laura, Laura, Laura for Paul. It is a love affair with an unlosable lover.

And that tells you all you really need to know about it. It tells you that there is only one sin you can commit against it — only one dangerous thing you can ever do — and that is to refuse to believe it. Because your trust in it is your only contribution to it. All the rest of its reality is simply a free gift from the other who loves you. Faith — not "fidelity" but simple trust, not "good faith" but plain belief — is all you need. The Gospel of grace is the announcement that all the incomprehensible Good News really is so: you *are* loved; you *are* vindicated; you *are* home. And you are all of that *now,* just because he says so. Trust him.

And when you have done that, you are living the life of grace. No matter what happens to you in the course of that trusting — no matter how many waverings you may have, no matter how many suspicions that you have bought a poke with no pig in it, no matter how much heaviness and sadness your lapses, vices, indispositions, and bratty whining may cause you

— you believe simply that Somebody Else, by his death and resurrection, has made it all right, and you just say thank you and shut up. The whole slop-closet full of mildewed performances (which is all you have to offer) is simply your death; it is Jesus who is your life. If he refused to condemn you because your works were rotten, he certainly isn't going to flunk you because your faith isn't so hot. You can fail utterly, therefore, and still live the life of grace. You can fold up spiritually, morally, or intellectually and still be safe. Because at the very worst, all you can be is dead — and for him who is the Resurrection and the Life, that just makes you his cup of tea.

That, then, is the first rule of the life of grace: it is lived out of death. It begins with a solemn proclamation of your death in Baptism, and it continues all your life long under that same banner: we believe in the resurrection of the dead. Death is the operative device that sets us free in Christ — that liberates us from the fear of loss that otherwise dogs our every step. What is it that you're afraid of losing? Your wits, your looks, your job, your grip? Your lover, your friends, your standards, your way? Don't be. Or do be, if you feel like it. It doesn't matter. Because you are dead, and your life is hid with Christ in God. The whole package — wits, career, looks, love life, and all the lucky or unlucky stars you may have in your chart — are out of your hands into his. You couldn't keep them if you tried; but in him you can't lose them except by unfaith. And if you ask me Norman's question now — if you want to know why God makes you sweat out this awful half-hour or half-lifetime without your beloved, your luck, or your health — I can finally give you the Christian answer: HE SAYS HE DOESN'T MAKE YOU WAIT. He says you have them all in him *now.* He says he is *now* your resurrection and your life, and he asks you to trust him that that is so. He asks you simply to believe that in your death you meet him, and that in him nothing is lost. All you do by unfaith is make yourself unavailable to the only Person who ever told you he had it all together.

And that will do for the second rule of the life of grace: your part in it is just to make yourself available. Not to make anything happen. Not to achieve any particular intensity of subjective glow. Certainly not to work yourself up to some objective standard of performance that will finally con God into being gracious. Only to be *there,* and to be open to your Lover who without so much as a by-your-leave started this whole affair. And your attendance upon him can include literally everything you do, because he has accepted it all in the Beloved: all good acts because they are vindicated in him; all rotten acts because they are reconciled in him; and even all religious acts because, in him, they have ceased to be transactions and become celebrations of something already accomplished.

Your life in grace is the life of a cripple on an escalator: as far as being able to walk upstairs is concerned, you are simply dead; there is nothing for *you* to do. But then you don't need to do anything, because the divine Floorwalker has kindly put you on the eternally moving staircase of Jesus — and up you go.

What you do and think about yourself as you ascend will be delightful, or sad, or terrifying — depending. Delightful, insofar as you celebrate your free ride. Sad, insofar as you fight the escalator. Terrifying, insofar as you forget you're on it and go back to dwelling on your own inability to walk. But while all of that will matter to you, none of it will count against you. You're on your way. All you have to do is believe it, and even the sadness and the terror become part of the ride up.

And therefore the last rule of the life of grace is that nothing can separate you from it. Not your faults, not your vices, not your being a brat about refusing the cross — not even your rubbing salt in the wounds of Christ or kicking God when he's down. Because he took you by a voluntary crucifixion for your sake, and he takes it all as the price of taking you. Eventually you will cry about that, and those tears will be your repentance. But there isn't even any rush about that. *He knows he loves you,* and that's all that counts. You catch up as you can.

And none of your terrors can separate you from that love, either, because they will all, late or soon, go down into your death. You can't hold them forever, and therefore they won't hold you. In the meantime, of course, they remain terrors, and the death out of which you live by grace remains no fun at all. There will always be worse deaths than you expected. But he says he raises you from them, and if you believe that, you're finally free.

• •

And there, I suppose, is as good an end as any. The only impediment to our freedom is our own unbelief; the only thing that jams out the joy that is set before us is the static of our unwillingness to take the leap into our own death in the faith that Jesus is there. All I can think of to add is that you mustn't fuss much over your faith, either. If only once in your life, for the space of one minute, you trusted him to be there, you would for that minute know the joy of your freedom. Even if you never managed to do it again — even if you never managed to do it even that once — it's still true that if he's there, he's there. And if he is, you're free.

In Jesus, we have never been anywhere but on the youngest, freshest day of the New Creation. We live in the grace that takes the world between noon and three — at that still point of the turning world, where the Word who is our end and our beginning speaks us reconciled in the Land of the Trinity:

That we too may come to the picnic
With nothing to hide, join the dance

Jesus, Jesus, Jesus

As it moves in perichoresis,
Turns about the abiding tree.

*There is therefore now no condemnation to
them which are in Christ Jesus.*